# IT H... MIND & OTHER STORIES

## Nick Roberts

Published by Crystal Lake Publishing—Tales from The Darkest Depths

Website: www.crystallakepub.com/

# WELCOME
## TO ANOTHER

## CRYSTAL LAKE PUBLISHING
### CREATION

Join today at www.crystallakepub.com & www.patreon.com/CLP

# Copyright Page

*For my father, Kit Douglas Roberts, Sr.*
*And my brother, Kit Douglas Roberts, Jr.*
*Eternally enjoying sunshine, saltwater, and Serenity.*

# Table of Contents

# SALLY UNDER THE BED

Tasha Brown had nothing, and she knew it. The pressure of contributing a monthly—sometimes weekly—article to her online publisher was as terrifying at times as it was a motivation. She normally thrived on deadlines. With years of experience cranking out quality work during crunch time, she learned how to trust her instincts and produce like the professional that she was.

Not this time, however. This time, the white page on her computer screen seemed determined to stay blank, taunting her with every wink of the cursor.

She specialized in darkness. Any "true" story of the supernatural was up for grabs, though she tended to stay away from legends that had been done to death: mainstreamers like Bigfoot, Area 51, Chupacabra, etc. Her investigative nose was drawn more toward the obscure. After her husband and daughter would go to sleep, she would put on a pot of coffee and scour the infinite recesses of the internet, reading one ghoulish tale after another, each more disturbing than the last.

The first story she sold nearly twenty years ago (back when physical publications' sales began their downward trajectory) was to a local quarterly magazine called *The West Virginia Review*. They were running a contest for new insights into known Appalachian cryptids. At first, she thought about researching the Mothman of Point Pleasant or the Braxton County Monster but figured everyone would try to cover one of those. She even briefly considered Bat Boy from the glory days of the *Weekly World News* tabloid, knowing full well that it was a completely fabricated story.

Ultimately, she landed on the "Hill People" of West Virginia—the supposed inspiration for the then-newly released film *Wrong Turn*, which depicted a group of stranded teens getting picked off by a family of inbred cannibals residing in the Appalachian hills. This portrayal of West Virginia hillbillies was not well received by the locals, so Tasha knew she was writing an uphill battle. It was her skillful approach of addressing the stereotype from the movie, as well as tracing the film's true inspiration back to the sixteenth-century account of the Sawney Bean clan of Scotland that won her the cash prize and publication, and her momentum never slowed.

All that meant dogshit right now. She had four days to produce a 2000-word profile of a relatively unknown "true" account of some spooky occurrence, and she had nothing. There was always the option of going on scary story websites and trying to track down anything that claimed to be based in reality, but that was the easy way out. She prided herself on discovering something new to bring to the world.

After sitting in her office/basement scrolling through decades' worth of old, digitized newspaper articles while her family slept peacefully upstairs, she was tempted to call it quits for the night. She let her eyes drift away from the screen and land on the 5" x 7" picture of her mother and father on the corner of her desk. They were in their early thirties, smiling, and had their arms wrapped around each other. Her mom had since passed from breast cancer at age 60, and her father had a fatal heart attack not more than a year after. Tasha realized that she was around the same age now that they were in that happy moment.

"Help me out here, guys," she said to the framed photo.

Her parents' fixed faces only smiled back.

"Got any paranormal encounters you want to tell me about?"

She let out a deep sigh and rubbed her temples. The clock on her computer read 2:32 AM. She looked at the empty coffee cup and was beginning to accept defeat when a long-forgotten memory surfaced. It was her mother, young, like she was in the picture, reading a newspaper while Tasha ate breakfast at the kitchen table at their old home in Mingo County.

Her father walked in, and her mom showed him something in the paper. His eyes widened, and he took the newspaper into the living room with her in tow. Tasha listened as they too loudly discussed the article about a local man shooting himself.

She remembered bits of what they said. Stuff about how the man's daughter had disappeared long ago, and he never got over it—how the mystery drove him insane. But the one thing they said that stood out was a chilling phrase.

"Sally under the bed," she muttered to the empty room.

Her heart beat faster. She grabbed the wireless mouse and clicked the search bar on the screen. She typed, "Sally under the bed," but nothing about any crime appeared. Page after page she clicked. The links varied from furniture stores to makeup shops to song lyrics with the name Sally in them.

There was nothing about a missing girl or a suicide.

She exited out of the search and went to an online newspaper database. If the man in the article shot himself approximately thirty years ago because his daughter vanished about twenty years before that, then that should place the girl's disappearance in the late 1960s or early 1970s. And the disappearance must have occurred in Mingo County if not in Williamson itself, the city where they used to live. She typed, "Girl disappears, Mingo County, West Virginia, 1968 – 1971, Sally under the bed" and clicked the search button.

Three articles resulted from the search, all from *The Williamson Daily News*. The first one was dated October 17, 1968, with the title, "Local girl missing from her home." Tasha clicked it and read about how ten-year-old Margaret Means was having a sleepover with her cousin and another friend at her parents' home in Williamson. The father, Amos Means, heard screaming from the girl's bedroom and ran inside to discover that Margaret was missing. There was no sign of foul play.

The second article written a few months later (January 18, 1969) was titled, "Case of missing girl remains unsolved." It detailed how the authorities had made no progress on Margaret's mysterious disappearance, and that the incident was ruled a missing persons case. There was one additional fact printed in the last paragraph of the story. Tasha's heart pounded again when she read, "The only lead investigators had to work with was that of ten-year-old, Suzanne Davies, who, when prompted about the case, could only say, 'Sally under the bed.'"

"Sally under the bed," Tasha echoed with glee.

The final article must have been the one her parents read that morning in the kitchen. This one was written twenty years after Margaret's disappearance and was titled, "Father of long-lost missing girl takes own life." It summed up the original case from a twenty-year perspective and mentioned that the two other girls involved in the infamous sleepover—both of whom were now in their thirties—had each had traumatic lives since the event, stating that they had several run-ins with the law, resulting in Margaret's cousin, Wendy Means, moving out of town and Suzanne Davies, the speaker of the "Sally under the bed" clue, becoming something of a town recluse.

Tasha pounced on that lead, opening her people-finding software and typing, "Suzanne Davies, Williamson, West Virginia." The name and address popped up, and she fell back into her rolling chair extending both fists up in triumph. She knew that Williamson was only an hour and a half from where she lived in Charleston and planned to be there by tomorrow afternoon.

---

Tasha caught a quick glimpse of the faded Williamson city limit sign as she pulled into town. She drove past one historic building after another, remembering times she would stroll the downtown sidewalks holding her father's hand.

A gaunt, bearded man in a sleeveless shirt smiled at her from an alley, his mouth fitting for an anti-meth poster. Like many Appalachian regions, Williamson was fighting a growing addiction problem. *That's the real monster,* she thought and continued forward.

So much had changed since she had last been here, yet there lingered enough of the past to give her that swirl of nostalgia in her belly. She passed the Coal House and the new Hatfield and McCoy museum and briefly saw some obvious out-of-towners walking in for some local history. Almost as quickly as she entered the main drag, she was off it, driving parallel to the Tug Fork River, which separated her state from South Williamson, Kentucky.

A few miles later her phone's GPS told her to turn right onto a gravel road that disappeared into the woods. She obeyed the directions and steered her Honda Civic onto the crunchy new path. Again, she looked at her phone screen. The robotic voice said, "Your destination is in two miles on the right."

The road dead-ended into a small clearing on a dirt-covered hillside. Tasha came to a stop and stared at a double-wide trailer sitting off-kilter on an uneven terrain. A rusty, green Chevy was parked out front. Two windows, blacked out by heavy curtains, were on either side of the front door. One of them slightly moved.

Tasha shut her car off and stepped outside. The cool, mountain breeze blew her hair across her face as she folded her arms and quickened her pace. She kept her eyes on both windows, which now appeared motionless. Three wooden steps led to the bottom of the front door, but there was a six-inch gap between the two. The flimsy staircase creaked and wobbled as soon as she put her weight on it. She balled up her fist and extended her arm to knock when the door jerked open before her knuckles made contact.

A skeleton of a woman, middle-aged but looking well beyond her years, stood wide-eyed inside the dark trailer.

"Yeah?" she asked with bulging eyes.

"Hi, my name is Tasha Brown…"

"What'dya want?"

Tasha couldn't help but notice the needle marks on her arms and meth scars on her face. She glanced at the mess behind the woman: dirty plates and cups were strewn about, empty vodka bottles were piled near one side of the stained couch, a full ashtray and what looked like a syringe sat openly on the coffee table. She averted her eyes.

"I'm trying to locate Suzanne Davies."

"What for?"

"I'm a writer…"

"Ain't interested," she said, taking a step back and closing the door.

"I'll pay!"

It opened back up.

"Pay for what?"

"If you're Suzanne Davies, I'll pay you to answer some questions about what happened the night Margaret Means went missing. And I'd really like to know about Sally under the bed."

A look of fear swept over the woman's already paranoid gaze. She took a quick step forward and shoved her finger in Tasha's face.

"Don't you dare say that fuckin' name!"

"I'm sorry," Tasha stammered and took a step back.

The two women stood in a silent showdown.

"I'm not here to cause harm. I just want to hear your story. *Your* story. The truth."

Suzanne lowered her finger.

"How much you gonna pay?"

Tasha fumbled in her jacket pocket and withdrew two fifties.

"A hundred now and two hundred more after you give me a story worth writing."

"What kind of news are you?"

"I write for a website about supernatural stuff. It's not like this will air on the evening news."

Suzanne hadn't taken her eyes off the cash since Tasha had pulled it out. She scratched the back of her neck, thinking about the dope she could buy. She snatched the bills out of her hand, took a step back, and pulled the door wide open. "Come on in, I reckon."

"Thank you."

Tasha walked inside and tried not to gag at the putrid smell of body odor, booze, and rotten food.

"Have a seat over there."

She sidestepped all the debris on the carpet as she made her way to a broken recliner in the corner of the room and sat with as little of herself on the chair as possible. The two rooms down the hall were empty from what she could tell: no bed, no other furniture. The kitchen was just as barren except for the gnats hovering over a sink full of crusty dishes.

She watched Suzanne sit on the couch, which had a pillow and a blanket on it. It also sat flat on the floor because the legs had been unscrewed, which she thought was odd. The woman glared at the stranger in her living room.

"What'dya wanna know?"

Tasha pulled her cellphone out.

"Do you mind if I record this conversation?"

"Hang on before you do that," Suzanne said as she hopped back up and walked to the kitchen on the other side of the room. "I was gonna save this for tomorrow, but now that I got a little bitta cash, I guess I don't need to."

Tasha watched her grab a small plate with some white powder from the top of the refrigerator and place it on the cluttered counter. She picked up a piece of a straw and looked over at Tasha.

"Do whatever you need to do," Tasha said, averting her eyes as the sickly woman snorted a line of methamphetamine.

She walked back to the couch clearing her nose. After she sat down, she reached for the ashtray and grabbed a cigarette butt with a little bit left to smoke on it. She lit it, fell back into the couch, and looked at Tasha.

"You can start recording now."

"Perfect."

She pressed record and leaned forward.

"Suzanne Davies, take me back to October 16, 1968—the night Margaret Means disappeared from her home here in Williamson, West Virginia."

Suzanne took a long drag, which brought the cherry down to the filter. She jammed it back into the porcupine of butts in the ashtray.

"I was ten back then. All three of us was. Wendy was my best friend. We did all kindsa shit together. She got invited to her cousin's house for a birthday sleepover—Margaret was her cousin. I never met Margaret before that night. Wendy told me that she didn't really like her, but her mom was makin' her go to her sleepover 'cause they was cousins. I guess Wendy told her mom the only way she was goin' was if she could bring me with her. I wish I woulda said, 'No.'"

Tasha forced an understanding look, making sure Suzanne knew that she had her undivided attention.

"Anyways, we get to Margaret's house, and it was awkward right from the get-go. Me and Wendy was just playin' with each other mostly. Wendy didn't want nothin' to do with Margaret because she was chubby and talked too much. I didn't think she was too annoyin', but I didn't know her like Wendy. I know that she musta asked us to play Twister at least a dozen times—ya know that fuckin' game where you bend 'round each other and shit?"

Tasha nodded with a smile. She could tell the meth was beginning to fuel her storytelling abilities. She no longer seemed as scared.

"Well, we never did play it, but she kept on askin'. She was dead set on playin' somethin'. She asked so many times that Wendy finally snapped. Wendy said, 'Fine, Margaret! If you wanna play a game, I got one for ya!' That's what got her to break out the rhyme game. I guess it's more of a *challenge* really..."

"What rhyme?"

"Sally Under the Bed," Suzanne said with confusion. "Ain't that what you're here for?"

"Yeah, but how is that a game though?"

Suzanne raised her eyebrows and took a deep breath.

"You really don't know, do ya?"

"I just know about what I read in the paper: your quote about 'Sally Under the Bed.'"

"That game fucked me up for good. I used to wonder about where that rhyme come from, but there's no use. Ain't gonna change nothin'.

"I guess I should start by sayin' that Wendy's mama's maiden name was Hatfield."

"The good old Hatfields and McCoys," Tasha began. "I can't tell you how many Hatfields I went to school with here. I actually grew up in Williamson."

Suzanne, completely uninterested in the reporter's upbringing, reached for something beside the couch. She yanked up a fifth of vodka that was some brand Tasha had never heard of. She poured some in one of the dirty glasses on the table.

"Want some?"

"No, thank you," Tasha replied feeling sorry for the woman. "I have to drive home."

Suzanne smiled at her guest's concern for following the law and brought the glass to her lips.

"Where was I?"

"The game and where it came from."

"Oh yeah. So, the rhyme supposedly come from a Hatfield a couple branches down her family tree. I'll tell ya how I heard it from Wendy that night. See, right after she said she had a game for Margaret to play, she started tellin' us the history of it. She made us shut off the lights and sit in a circle, and we was all three sittin' in Margaret's livin' room like Wendy wanted. We was supposed to be goin' to bed, but ya know how those sleepovers go."

Tasha nodded her head and glanced down at her phone to make sure it was still recording.

"Wendy told us that her daddy's daddy's daddy's cousin or some shit was a Hatfield. Huck was his name. I ain't never found no record of a Huck Hatfield, but that's what she said. Supposedly, ol' Huck had a crush on a girl named Sally, but Sally wasn't interested in him. He got drunk on 'shine one night and asked her to marry him in front of his friends. She shot him down...embarrassed the shit out of him. Huck went blind with rage. He waited until Sally was all alone and then he took her. Dragged her screamin' through the woods to his cabin on the hill. He threw her on the floor, lit his lantern, and beat the tar out of her. When Wendy told us this part, she made sure to do these slow, dramatic punches...ya know how kids tellin' ghost stories is."

Tasha forced a smile and continued to listen, already making a mental note to fact-check all of this when she got home.

"Anyways, Huck beat her to death plain and simple. Wendy made sure we knew that the girl's head looked like a smashed watermelon...said her eyes was busted in so bad they was nothin' but black holes. She was really layin' it on us.

"You'd think most people would feel bad when they realize they just killed the woman they love, but not Huck. Huck ripped off her clothes and did God knows what with her. And then he shoved her naked body under his bed and went to sleep! Didn't even bother to clean up the mess. I don't know why he done that other than maybe if he couldn't sleep with her, then nobody could.

"Now, when Wendy got to this part in tellin' the story— we was hooked already—but when she got to this part her voice got real low. She said somehow the lantern in that cabin mysteriously fell over. Everything went up in flames, includin' both of them bodies. People around town started spreadin' rumors 'bout what happened, and it became this little ghost story: somethin' the kids would tell to scare each other.

"Somewhere down the line, somebody came up with a game involvin' this rhyme. The game was that you say this rhyme about Sally, and she would appear under your bed at night, all bloodied and busted like she was just freshly killed.

"Needless to say, we was scared shitless by this point, but Wendy wasn't done. Just to make sure we *really* believed her, she told us about how she found the rhyme. *The actual rhyme!* That evil little bitch said she was noseyin' around her attic one day just lookin' through boxes of shit, and she come upon a trunk that had been passed down from her mama's side—the Hatfield side. She opened it and found this old journal with some Hatfield's name that was too smudged to read, but she flipped through the pages and found this rhyme…poem…song…whatever the fuck it is. She read it in her head over and over. The page opposite the rhyme told the game: say the rhyme if you dare but just know that you are disturbin' the rest of a vengeful spirit, and she probably ain't gonna be too happy about it.

"Wendy said she knew the rhyme by heart but never said it. She got up and walked over to Margaret's daddy's office supplies in the corner and scribbled somethin' down on paper for a minute. She came back with it and put it in the middle of our little circle. The top of the paper said, 'Sally Under the Bed,' and the rest was the rhyme."

"What was the rhyme?" Tasha interrupted.

"Hell no," Suzanne said as she downed the rest of her vodka. "Ain't you been listenin'? You can't say it."

"Are you saying that you believe in this?"

Suzanne looked at her with disbelief.

"I saw it. I saw what happened. You wasn't there, and the rest of you fuckers wasn't there neither! Everybody thinks I'm crazy, but I saw what I fuckin' saw!"

"OK, OK, Suzanne. I'm sorry. I didn't mean to offend you. Please, tell me the rest of the story."

The agitated woman went from rage to utter sadness in seconds.

"What Wendy wrote on that paper was twelve lines long…three sections with four lines each."

"Stanzas."

"Yeah, stanzas, whatever. Three of 'em. Well, I read the poem first in my head and then handed it to Margaret. It was one of the creepiest things I'd ever read. While Margaret was readin' the poem, Wendy whispered to me, 'Don't say the last line.' I thought that was weird at first but then realized that she was wantin' us to trick Margaret into sayin' the full thing by herself. Margaret finished the poem and put it back in the middle of our circle. Wendy said, 'We're all gonna say it, and whoever doesn't is a chicken,' but she gave me a little wink that Margaret didn't see.

"I agreed without really thinkin' about it. We both looked at Margaret, and it was obvious she didn't wanna say it. Wendy had to ask her if she was a chicken a few times and make those BAWK BAWK sounds to finally get her to do it, but she did.

"We all sat there starin' at that paper on the floor. Wendy said, 'Well, let's get on with it,' and we did. We said it line-by-line in that sing-songy way it was written. When we got to the last line, Wendy and I looked at each other, and we both stopped. Margaret said the last line by herself just like Wendy wanted. Margaret freaked right out. I remember Wendy sayin', 'Looks like Sally is just comin' for you tonight, Margaret!' Man, it was so fucked up. Kids are fucked up, ya know?"

Tasha gave a slight nod. Suzanne poured herself another drink. She took a big gulp and sat there staring at the table in front of her for a moment before continuing.

"After Margaret yelled at us a good bit for trickin' her, we all settled down and went to bed. We was in Margaret's room. She was on her bed, and me and Wendy were on the floor in sleepin' bags. Margaret was tryin' to go to sleep, but Wendy wasn't done with her yet. She whispered to me that we should crawl on the floor and make scratchy sounds and *really* scare Margaret. I agreed to it, but I felt rotten about it.

I never picked on no one before, but I didn't want Wendy to look at me like she looked at Margaret.

"So, Margaret was fallin' asleep, and she heard the scratchin' beside her bed. I heard her up there start to breathe a little faster like she was scared. I looked up and saw that she had the covers pulled over her head. Wendy held her hand up to me and used her fingers to count down from three. I knew what that meant: when she got to zero, we were gonna give Margaret the final scare, and we did. We both sprung up from the floor. I yanked the covers off her just as Wendy made a loud, growling sound and pounced on her. Margaret screamed, but Wendy covered her mouth real quick so she didn't wake her dad up.

"Once Margaret realized what was goin' on, Wendy let go of her and fell to the floor laughin'. She said, 'We got you good, Margaret.' I saw that she was cryin', and that made me feel real bad. Wendy kept laughin' though. The last thing Margaret ever said was, 'I hate you guys.'"

Tears were welling up in Suzanne's eyes as she stared off into space like she was afraid to keep going.

"What happened next, Suzanne?"

After a long pause, she continued.

"Wendy and I got back in our sleepin' bags, and she was asleep in two minutes. I don't know how she did that. I was starin' at the ceiling feelin' like a real asshole. I musta stared up there for a half hour. Margaret fell asleep before me too. I could tell that because she stopped sobbin' and wimperin' and started to snore a little bit. It's always the worst when you're the last one to fall asleep at a sleepover, but when ya add the guilt I was feelin', it took me extra-long.

"I guess it was a just little after that when I finally started to doze off. I was in that place when you're not quite sure if you're awake or dreamin' when I heard the sounds comin' from Margaret's side of the room."

"What sounds?"

Suzanne closed her eyes and a tear rolled down one cheek.

"I looked over there, and there was a dark figure layin' flat on her back under her bed. She was the size of a grownup and had no clothes on. I was frozen. I've never been so scared in my life. The dark woman's head slowly turned her face toward me until she was starin' straight at me. My stomach got all knotted, but I couldn't look away. Her left arm shot out first, and then she kinda pulled herself toward me real slow. I pissed myself when she got completely out from under there and gave me a good look at her.

"She was pale like a corpse that's been long dead. She had this dark hair that hung down around her face. Her face...the middle of her face was caved in and bloody. Her jaw hung sideways too. It almost looked like she was smilin'. Once she stood up, the moonlight gave me an even better view: there were two blackened sockets where her eyes shoulda been. One eyeball dangled by a nerve. She was facing me for a moment, but then she turned back to Margaret. I wish I had the guts to scream right then, but ya know what? I was just glad she wasn't interested in me anymore. Ain't that horrible?

"She climbed her naked body on top of Margaret. I heard her wake up and try to scream, but I guess that thing was coverin' her mouth. I closed my eyes and put my hands on my ears. I just couldn't take it anymore. I felt the thud of something hittin' the floor and peeked through one eyelid just enough to see Margaret on the floor starin' at me with those terrified eyes and that thing's hand around her mouth. The rest of it was back under the bed. It squeezed the bottom of Margaret's face and snapped her head completely around and then sucked her under the bed. They was both gone after that.

"I finally found it in me to scream. Wendy woke up, and Margaret's daddy came runnin' in to see what was goin' on. He obviously didn't find Margaret. He looked everywhere. He grabbed me by the shoulders and shook me, wantin' to know where she went. All I could do was point to the place she last was and say, 'Sally under the bed'."

Tasha was speechless. She felt for the woman. She felt how tortured and traumatized she was because she actually believed that that was what had happened.

Suzanne started to whimper and then stood up and wobbled a bit.

"I ain't slept in a bed since. I even took the legs off that couch. I ain't takin' any chances, and I'll definitely never talk about this shit again. I can't do it," she said as she stumbled back into the kitchen and took a snort of whatever was left on that plate.

Tasha hit the pause button on her phone.

"Thank you for sharing that with me, Suzanne. I know that wasn't easy."

"You don't know shit about it."

"You're right. I don't." Tasha got up and walked over to

Suzanne.

She pulled out two one-hundred-dollar bills as promised and placed them on the counter.

"But I feel like I know so much more thanks to you."

She put her hand back in her pocket and withdrew two more hundreds.

"And this is yours too…"

Suzanne looked at her in confusion.

"*If* you can remember that poem."

The stoned woman was shocked.

"Are you fuckin' nuts? Did you not listen to anything I just said?"

"I did. *Of course, I did.* But if I'm really going to tell this story, I have to know what it is."

Suzanne didn't know what to think.

"Fine," Tasha said as she pulled out the last of her cash and dropped it all on the counter. "There you go. All you have to do is write it down. I promise I won't print it. If you say that's off the record, then it's off the record."

Suzanne scooped up the cash and walked to one of the back rooms. She came back with a pen and a torn piece of paper. Tasha watched as she struggled to write one word after another, her hands shaking uncontrollably. When she finished, she held out the paper.

"Here. Take it and go."

Tasha looked down and saw three stanzas of scribbled lines.

"Don't you dare say it," Suzanne warned. "Don't show it to no one neither. Just read it and burn it. Promise me that."

Tasha smiled at her and said, "I promise."

---

It was nearly dinner time when Tasha walked through her front door. Mike was in the kitchen cooking. Their five-year-old daughter was playing on the iPad in the living room.

"Hi, Mommy," Leah said without looking up from the screen.

"Hey, honey," Tasha replied.

She patted the little girl's head as she walked by. Mike turned around from the vat of boiling pasta.

"Hey, babe. Was it productive?"

"You have no idea," Tasha beamed with excitement. "Wait until I tell you. No, never mind. I want you to read it when I'm finished."

"OK..."

"I'm so excited, Mike. This is going to be the best story I've ever published. If I do this right, it could blow up." She took off her coat and sat her purse on the counter. Her phone was still in her pocket. "I've got to get started right now."

"Now? Don't you at least want to eat first?"

"I have to do it while it's still fresh in my mind," she said as she kissed him on the cheek and hurried back through the living room toward the basement stairs. "You know how these things go!"

"Mommy, where are you going?"

"Down to my office, honey. I'll be back up in a little bit."

As usual, Tasha lost all track of time while she was writing. She had spent the first two hours looking into the three girls' lives but not finding much that would enhance the story. Mike brought a plate of spaghetti down to her and sat it on her desk, but she never touched it. She went down several rabbit holes of any record she could find on different members of the Hatfield clan. There was no mention of a Huck Hatfield anywhere. After coming up short on that front, she decided to continue that research tomorrow. Worst case scenario: she'd issue a disclaimer before that part of the piece noting it as unsubstantiated backstory.

Once she started to play the recording, she never stopped transcribing. She got everything down in just ninety minutes. She spent the next few hours building a narrative. Rather than just report Suzanne's testimony as fact, she inserted herself into the story, which is something that she'd never done. Writing in the first person just opened the article up in a way that she knew would engage the reader. She would end on an ambiguous note—the way all good unsolved mysteries should. The one thing she didn't put in the article was the poem itself. Even though it would up the creep factor to include it, she knew that once someone tried the game and it didn't work, the story would lose its punch.

Satisfied with what she had produced, she saved her document and checked the time. It was just a little after 11 PM. She knew Mike had probably just put Leah down, so she booked it upstairs to tell her goodnight before her daughter fell asleep. She reached the top of the stairs and saw that her bedroom door was already shut. Mike was in their bed, shirtless, reading a book. Tasha entered their room.

"How long ago did you put her down?"

"About thirty minutes. I tried to keep her up, but she conked out on me. Sorry, babe."

"It's OK. I'm the one who worked…"

She stopped when she saw the paper that Suzanne had given her on the nightstand.

"Why is this here?"

"Oh, that, yeah. Leah pulled that creepy ass thing out of your purse and wanted me to read it to her."

"Did you?"

"Yeah. I said it, and then she wanted me to sing it like a song, so I did that until she knew the words and started singing along with me. What is it anyway?"

Before Tasha could answer, a faint scream came from their daughter's bedroom, but it was quickly silenced.

"What the hell was that?" Mike said, setting his book aside.

Tasha sprinted down the hall and burst into the room.

"Leah! Leah!" she screamed as she scanned the empty room.

She dropped to the floor and looked under the bed but saw nothing.

"Leah!"

She heard her husband getting up, now realizing that something was seriously wrong. Tasha pushed herself off the ground and ran to meet Mike in the hallway.

"What is it?" he asked.

Tasha's eyes widened with abject terror when she saw the woman crawling across the floor behind her husband. Mike whipped around just as Sally grabbed him by both ankles and pulled his legs out from under him. His body hit the ground causing the back of his head to crack the tile floor.

"No!"

Tasha desperately ran to her husband as he was being dragged under the bed. She dove for his hand and missed by inches. They both screamed as he disappeared into the darkness below. She wailed until her throat hurt. She kicked the nightstand and slammed her fist repeatedly against the floor. She didn't even notice that she had knocked Suzanne's note off until it drifted down and landed in front of her.

The cursed words taunted her bloodshot eyes, but she now knew what she had to do. She grabbed the paper and rolled onto her side, letting her cheek rest in the puddle of Mike's blood. There was no other way for her to be with her family. She spoke the title: "Sally Under the Bed," and then, in a hoarse whisper, she read what was in front of her.

They said, they said
Keep it in your head.
If you say it out loud
Then you'll be dead.

I said it, I said it
And now I regret it.
I sang this song and

I wish I could forget it.

They said, they said
Keep it in your head.
But it's too late 'cause
Sally's under the bed.

# THE DEAL

There are few things more exhilarating in this world than sitting across a table from a man you know kills for a living. That's where I found myself exactly five years ago. I remember it with the vivid recall of every other significant event from my life.

*Hitman.*

The term seemed too dignified—too professional—for the murderous lunk that sat before me. Hunched over with his elbows planted on the thick, wooden table coated with streaks of sticky beer.

He wore glasses…well, the glasses wore him; they magnified his eyeballs to cartoonish proportions. The heavy, Army-green jacket he wore kept his build a secret. He was a tall man—I could see that much—with dark black skin and a military-style faded haircut. If I were to guess, I'd say he was mid-twenties—about the same age I was at the time.

I was told to call him Ronald. No last name. Just Ronald. I'd like to think that if I had the opportunity to create my own alias and operate within the criminal underbelly of society, I would come up with something cooler than *Ronald*. It just didn't elicit much fear, and if you're going to make a name for yourself as a gun-for-hire, it sure as shit shouldn't be Ronald.

Listen to how judgmental I sound…

How I remember Ronald from that night only shows you how craftily I avoided looking at my own shortcomings—

deflection, I think they call it.

Sitting across from Ronald was me, Rufus. I know, I know. A guy named Rufus poking fun at someone called Ronald. I get it. I was, however, not entirely in my right mind. Besides, on the street, most people knew me as Fuss. You see, at this point in my life, I was strung out on prescription painkillers.

*Hillbilly heroin.* West Virginia's contribution to the drug game...

I don't remember what I was wearing on that cold, December night in that Appalachian dive bar; I only remember that I was wasted. Give me a break, I was still in mourning. My mom's funeral was earlier that month, and I couldn't shake the image of her casket being lowered into the frozen earth, never to be seen again. It was her dying wish that I clean my act up.

I may have exaggerated there.

The last thing she said to me before she died was how she wished I would get my life together. She didn't know she was going to die. No one did. She was driving to work and a drunk in a pick-up truck coming home from a long night drifted across the middle of the road and hit her head-on. They both died on impact.

My mom had a small life insurance policy through her employer that I received a couple weeks after she died. Her lawyer called me up, and I immediately drove to get the check.

Fifty-thousand dollars.

So how did I end up at that run-down little shack of a bar

in St. Albans, West Virginia that night five years ago? Well, after blowing through about ten-thousand dollars-worth of drugs and booze in a week and only overdosing once, I had what I can only assume was a revelation. Before my mom died and I inherited her house and car, I was basically homeless. I would pray for enough money to sustain my drug addiction to the point where I would never have to worry about being sick from coming off the drugs.

Dopesick.

Withdrawals.

As my habit progressed, so did the severity and frequency of those cold sweats, aching body contortions, and the early-morning spats of diarrhea.

Now that I was financially secure for the moment and as high as I ever wanted to be, I realized that life still sucked. I had made it to the end of the rainbow only to find the pot of gold filled with shit. I would drift in and out of consciousness amid fever dreams that would shock me into opening my eyes. I would see my mom's severed head set free from the shattered windshield fly in slow motion across the early-morning sunrise.

Not sure if I was awake or not, I would pace her empty house at night only to stumble upon her headless body standing there in the kitchen trying desperately to drink her morning cup of coffee to no avail. Her work clothes covered in hot coffee, gravel, and blood stains.

I got what I thought would make me happy and found that it was only misery gift-wrapped in a green bow. After a long day of drinking, snorting, shooting whatever I could, I stuffed the remaining forty-thousand dollars in a black gym bag and jumped in my car. I drove straight to Rich's house, my dealer. I gave him a wad of cash in exchange for the phone number of his dealer. He was reluctant at first, but I assured him that I didn't have the wherewithal to cut him out of the drug game, and he would continue to have my business.

Ten minutes later and I'm speeding down the highway toward Huntington—the drug port of West Virginia. Flooded by young, entrepreneurial dealers from Detroit, this is the city to meet someone on the next level of the drug game. For me, it was a suave, stout man that goes by the name J. I met him at a gas station and hopped in his car. I immediately told him I wasn't interested in buying any drugs, and he gave me a look of such offense you'd think that I just farted in his Denali. Before he could kick me out, I told him I needed someone "taken care of." The way I delivered that euphemism would've made any mobster proud.

J looked at me—a twenty-five-year-old white boy junkie from West Virginia—like I was playing a practical joke on him. I quickly told him that this money was for him; it was his finder's fee. All I needed was for him to have a qualified individual call me to set up a meeting to discuss further details. J smiled like he just made the easiest five-grand off the dumbest hillbilly and took down my phone number. Before I got out of his car, he told me he needed to know a rough idea of the person who needed to "get gone" so he could call the right guy for the job. I told him it was a nobody—a piece of shit junkie who no one would miss.

This brings us all the way back to Ronald.

Ronald, sitting there across from me as the cigarette smoke inside the bar began to burn my eyes, was completely unfazed by it. He just stared at me with those massive, bulging bug eyes wanting me to get to the point of why the hell he just drove 350 miles from Detroit to meet up with some strung-out dopefiend.

I grabbed my bottle of beer and asked him if he wanted to go out for a smoke in my car so we could talk. Still not blinking, the big, serious bastard pushed himself out of the booth and headed for the exit as I clumsily followed. I pointed out which car was mine, and we both climbed into our respective seats. I started the car to get the heat going while Ronald just stared through the windshield.

"So, what's the job?" Ronald asked with a voice so deep it was hard to differentiate syllables.

"Yeah, see that's the thing," I began. "It's not your average gig."

Ronald turned his gaze in my direction.

"Not that I would know what your 'average gig' is," I nervously clarified.

"What's the job?" he repeated, losing patience. I cracked the window and let the chilly winter air creep in as I lit up my smoke and thought of how to word what I wanted to say. It seemed like I had it so perfectly planned out earlier, but that was a few pills and many drinks ago.

"I'm the target," I blurted.

I could feel the warmth of Ronald's intense gaze on the right side of my face. He didn't say anything, so I turned to look into those big eyes of his, face-to-face.

"I want you to take me out," I said, hoping this rephrasing of the same sentiment clarified his confusion.

"You want me to kill...*you?*" he asked.

I nodded my head and turned back to looking out the windshield and took a long drag of my cigarette.

"What? Are you suicidal or some shit?"

"Not at all," I responded. "I'm fucking miserable and hopeless and don't really care if I live or die, but I'm not trying to leap off a bridge or anything like that."

I looked over and still saw Ronald struggling to wrap his mind around this.

"Look, Ronald, it's like this—I have no purpose in life. I'm not living. I'm just...*existing.*"

Ronald was still looking at me like I was a crazy white boy about to reveal that I'm strapped with explosives around my chest.

"I'm a dopefiend, man" I said. "My mom would pray every day that I would get my shit together. That I would kick drugs, make friends—*real* friends—get a good job that I liked, and maybe settle down with a nice girl. Seriously. She would pray for those things to happen to me. She just wanted me to be *happy.* I see now that I'm not content with what I thought would make me happy."

"Maybe you should just go to rehab?" Ronald suggested with what sounded like genuine concern.

"I've tried, man," I said as I closed my eyes and took a deep breath. "I just lack the motivation...and that's where you come in."

I opened my eyes and looked over at him.

"Do you see that gym bag in the seat behind me?"

Ronald shifted his massive frame around to peek in the back seat.

"Yes."

"In that bag, is thirty thousand dollars. When you get out of this car, you're leaving with it."

Ronald started to look confused.

"Consider it a retainer for your services," I said.

"Like a lawyer?"

"Exactly like a lawyer."

"OK...?"

I pointed to the neon-green time display on the dashboard that read, "10:58 PM."

"Call it 11 PM," I began. "At 11 PM on December 6th five years from now, if I don't have a college degree, have a job, have friends, have a girlfriend, and have five years of continuous sobriety from drugs and alcohol—if I don't have these five things in five years—then I want you to track me down and put a fucking bullet in my brain."

Ronald slowly started to nod his head as the method to my madness began to click.

"You need me as motivation to get your life together."

"Yes," I said with relief.

I was worried that once I said the plan out loud it would sound crazier than it felt when I thought it, but it felt right. Ronald looked like he was deep in thought, and then a sly smile crept across his face.

"Why are you smiling?"

"This is the first time I've ever been asked to *save* a life," he said. "My momma would be proud...so please don't fuck it up and make me kill your ass in five years," he pleaded as he extended his hand for a handshake.

I grabbed his hand with my own.

"You've got a deal," he said with a grin.

He began to move like he was going to get out of the vehicle but then stopped.

"Wait a second...what's to stop me from taking this 30k and turning ghost?" he asked.

"Nothing. But, as long as I believe that you'll keep your word, then that's all I need."

Ronald opened the car door, and the overhead light glowed.

He stepped out into the cold night, shut the door, and walked around to my side of the car. Before the dome light could fully extinguish, he opened the back door behind me, grabbed the bag, shut the door, and then walked to my open window.

"Before I get out of here, go ahead and write down your full legal name, social security number, current address, former addresses, and your driver's license number," he instructed.

A sobering shiver of fear ran up my spine as the full reality of the situation set in. He saw it in my eyes. I pulled a napkin and a pen out of the glove compartment and wrote down the requested information and quickly handed it to him. He folded it neatly and placed it in his pocket.

"There's no going back now, brotha."

I watched him walk to his car and drive out of the lot. I

closed my eyes and took a deep breath to slow the furious beating of my heart. The ambient Appalachian sounds of crickets and tree frogs seemed to come from nowhere even though I knew they'd been there the whole time. I went to reach for the gear shift and noticed the nearly full bottle of beer in the cupholder. As if on autopilot, I grabbed the bottle and poured its contents onto the ground outside of my window and then chucked the empty carcass into an open dumpster before I drove home.

Like I said—that was five years ago.

Right now, I'm standing in the living room of my house, peering through the blinds at the driveway outside. I turn and look at the neon-green time display on the cable box, and it reads, "10:57 PM."

Any minute now.

I'm still getting used to calling it *my* house. It's been years since my mom passed, but it still feels like hers. Even after getting married and having a baby—a family of my own—I feel like we're just guests. Speaking of my family, I arranged for a mini vacation for them while I stayed home to "work." My wife and son went to spend a few days with her mother down south so I could have a quiet environment to focus. Needless to say, I had an ulterior motive.

"10:59 PM"

There they are, the headlights I've been looking for. I see a luxury sedan park beside my car. The headlights go off, but the engine continues to idle. Once my eyes adjust back to the dark, I see Ronald's massive silhouette sitting in the driver's seat. I reach down in my pants pocket and nervously rub the sobriety chip between my thumb and pointer finger. Ronald kills the engine and steps out of his car.

"Let's do this," I say to myself.

I exit the living room and walk through my study, catching glimpses of my reflection in the framed college degree on the wall. Have I aged that much in five years? I wonder how different Ronald looks. The doorbell rings just as I step into the entryway. I take a deep breath, say a little prayer, and open the door.

The cold, December wind that seems to follow Ronald wherever he goes hits me hard. Without getting too good a look at my old acquaintance, I motion for him to hurry up and step inside. He shuts the door behind him and then turns around to face me. Before I can even say anything, he grabs my arm with a forceful grip and leads me in the direction of the kitchen.

"C'mon," he begins. "This won't take long."

I suddenly feel sick to my stomach as this is not the warm reception I was expecting. What does he think? What does he know? More importantly, *what does he think he knows?* And, how the hell does he know his way around my house (I guess it's my house now)? We enter the kitchen, and he somehow manages to release my arm while simultaneously pushing me down into my chair at the kitchen table. I quickly realize that this is the Ronald I paid for.

He stands beside me, looming tall like a monolith and just as ominous. His head blocks the kitchen light, making it difficult to see his features.

"I knew you would come," I say, breaking the silence.

"You struck me as a man of your word in our meeting five years ago—a true soldier."

Ronald says nothing. He slowly reaches into his heavy jacket pocket and pulls out a purple velvet bag. He unties the knot and carefully removes one item at a time from the bag, placing them in a neat row in front of me. From left to right, I see a spoon, a clean syringe, a lighter, a piece of cotton, and a tiny bag of what can only be heroin. Ronald walks over to my refrigerator, grabs a bottle of water, and slides it across the table to me as my final ingredient.

"You're right. I am a soldier," Ronald finally says. "I've been keeping tabs on you over the years. I saw you go to rehab, saw you go to college, saw you get married and have kids, saw you get your dream job—I saw you check-off those four things…but you hired me for five things," Ronald says holding up five fingers.

"I did."

"Only you know if you're clean. 'To thine own self be true'—isn't that what they say in those meetings you go to?"

I nod my head.

"I told you to put a bullet in my head if I didn't live up to my end of the deal," I say.

"Well, I took you as being metaphorical in that moment. This shit will kill you just as same as a bullet. I promise," he replies. "Plus, no one is going to be looking for the killer of someone that died from an overdose, are they?"

I look down at the collection of my old friends assembled on the table before me.

"So, this is my test?" I ask.

"More of an opportunity, really. If you're happy with your new life, then just bag all that shit up and hand it back to me. If you're not, then quit wasting both of our time and get to it."

I smile.

"Why are you smiling?" he asks curiously.

"The way you phrased that," I say. "You're testing me on being happy, not being sober. Most people don't understand the difference."

Ronald looks into my eyes and smiles like he did five years ago when I paid him to save a life.

"Ronald," I begin, "you are grossly underpaid."

# THE HALFWAY HOUSE

The knock on the door was soft, pathetic, and could barely be heard over the rain outside. Hayden Addams looked away from the TV screen toward the sound. He glanced across the living room at one of his roommates, Marcus, sitting in the recliner still engaged in the basketball game.

"Is someone at the door?" Hayden asked.

Marcus finally broke his gaze from the TV.

"Huh?" Marcus replied.

Hayden stood up from the couch.

"I think someone just knocked on the door. What time is it?" he asked as he looked at the digital clock display, answering his own question; "11:13 PM" lit up in green neon.

"Maybe it's Tim," Marcus said referring to their third roommate in the house.

"He doesn't get off until 1:30 in the morning," Hayden replied as he walked in the direction of the door.

"Make sure you know who it is before you open the door," Marcus warned. "Never know with this crazy neighborhood."

The three men lived in an addiction recovery house in a small Appalachian town plagued by the drug epidemic. The national opioid crisis had come to full fruition in their home state of West Virginia. Big Pharma had funneled prescription painkillers into rural towns with no discretion and limited regulation. When the government finally started to crack down on pill mills and reckless doctors, it was too late. The move to regulate legal opioids left a massive hole in the market just waiting to be filled. With its cheaper prices and easier availability, heroin gladly stepped in.

The illegal drug trade became even more deadly. Heroin was cut with whatever was available to meet the demand. It wasn't long before bodies started filling the streets. Ambulances couldn't keep up with the constant overdose calls. Soon, the small West Virginia town led the nation in overdoses. To combat the drug infestation, recovery houses and facilities sprouted up across the state. Led by state and federal funding, the ground-level effort started to gain some momentum.

Hayden had been clean for over seven months, and he felt truly indebted to the recovery house in which he currently lived. He approached the front door and looked through the peephole. He saw a scrawny kid in his twenties with a grey hoodie pulled over his head. He was shivering in the cold, wet night. Hayden stepped away from the door and looked back over to Marcus who was back into the game on the TV.

"I don't know who he is. Looks like he needs help though," Hayden said.

Marcus looked at Hayden, annoyed.

"Are we getting another damn intake? I swear, if Bob starts stacking beds in here like every other recovery house in town, I'm bouncing."

"I'm about to find out," Hayden said as he started to unlock the door.

The kid outside jumped at the sound of the opening door. He took a few intimidated steps backward, still remaining on the large front porch. Hayden noticed a black van parked in front of the house with its engine running. As soon as the driver spotted Hayden, he quickly drove away as the heavy rain poured on the dark street.

"Can I help you?" Hayden asked.

"My name is Cliff," the kid said with a raspy whisper, straining to speak.

He was drenched and stared meekly at the ground. His face was pale and clammy with tuffs of unkempt facial hair.

"I'm supposed to have a bed here."

"A *bed*?" Hayden responded with shock. "Who told you that?"

"Uhh, a guy named Bob. It should be all set up, man. I don't know."

The kid was shaking.

"I just need to lie down, man."

"Bob already approved it, huh?" Hayden said. "Just hang tight out here while I call him and figure this out. Just chill on the porch swing. I'll be right back."

Hayden backed into the house and shut the door behind him. He withdrew his phone from his pocket and called Bob immediately.

"Hey, bub. What's up?" Bob responded in his southern drawl.

"Oh, nothing," Hayden began with frustration. "I've just got a new guy at the door saying you told him that he could have a bed."

"Yeah, bub. I was just about to call you and warn you. The boy's dad called me today saying the kid needed some help. I told him we had a spot."

"We do. Space isn't the issue."

"What is it then?"

"He's still detoxing, Bob. He looks like he doesn't even have 24 hours clean. Our policy is that new clients must be referred here from a 28-day program, minimum."

"I know the policy, Hayden. I wrote the damn thing," Bob said with that assertion he reserved for boss-moments like this. "The thing is, we just aren't generating enough money with three guys in the house, and we aren't getting any new referrals. It's my job to keep the lights on and your job to run the house. His dad paid six months' worth of rent...*in advance*. I told him that if he was discharged, there would be no refund, and he said he understood."

Hayden shook his head with disappointment. It always came down to money in the end.

"Bob, he's a risk to myself and the other two guys in the house. I just think it's a terrible idea to have this guy *who may still be high* around other people in recovery trying to do the right thing."

"I understand, bub. I do," Bob said. "Just let him go lie down and sleep it off tonight. I'll come by in the morning and get a feel for him. He's here to stay, and we're going to help the boy."

Hayden knew that that was that.

"Fine. See you in the morning."

He hung up and opened the front door. Cliff was sitting on the porch swing hunched over and legs frantically bouncing up and down.

"Come on," Hayden said.

They walked inside and Marcus looked at them curiously.

"Marcus, this is Cliff. Cliff, Marcus," Hayden said with defeat.

"Hey, man," Marcus said without getting off the recliner.

Cliff nodded his head in acknowledgement without looking up from the carpet. In the light of the room, Hayden could see how bad Cliff truly looked.

"Can I go to my room now?" Cliff asked.

"Sure. It's this way," Hayden said leading him upstairs to the bedrooms.

They stood outside one of the four rooms' doors. Hayden turned the knob, pushed it open, and flicked on the light.

"This is you."

Cliff brushed past him and sat down on the bed. He rolled over on his side, facing the wall.

"Can you turn off the light, please?" he asked.

"Sure," Hayden said as he turned off the lights. "Let me know if you need anything. We'll do all your paperwork in the morning when Bob comes." After a moment of consideration, Hayden added, "And if you have anything on you that would put anyone else in this house in jeopardy, now would be the time to tell me about it."

"I don't, man," Cliff replied, speaking to the wall. "If I did, I wouldn't be here yet."

"Fair enough," Hayden said, shutting the door behind him.

---

Not a minute after hearing Hayden march down the stairs, Cliff sat up in bed and began fumbling through his jacket pockets. His hand finally felt what he was looking for. He withdrew a plastic sandwich bag containing a syringe that was already full of liquid. The needle was protected by an orange safety cap that he quickly removed. After rolling his sleeve up, he began poking around in his arm until he hit his vein. He withdrew a small amount of blood into the rig and depressed the plunger of what he thought was heroin into his system.

The warm rush didn't come. He sat there waiting for the heroin withdrawals to dissipate, but nothing happened. He shook his head because he knew the circumstances that got him this shot of dope were too good to be true.

Just an hour ago, he was walking down a rainy back alley in town feeling like death. He was desperate for a fix. He was broke, homeless, and completely out of ideas for scoring. Completely cut off from friends and family, he had resorted to sleeping wherever he could and stealing and pawning to maintain his dwindling habit. Just as he was working up the nerve to go steal some booze from the gas station, a parked van he didn't even see turned on its headlights. He shielded his eyes from the brightness.

"Hey, you," the driver called from behind the lights.

Cliff lowered his hand and peered into the light but couldn't see anyone.

"Yeah?"

"You trying to score?"

Cliff walked a little closer and out of the light's direct glare so he could see better. The silhouette of the driver came into view. He was a large, muscular man wearing a black hoodie.

"No thanks, officer," Cliff said as he started to walk off.

The sliding door of the van opened, and a second voice spoke from the darkness within.

"You can hear my proposition and feel right as rain within the hour, or you can keep walking down that road and be sick. It's your choice, young man. There are many junkies on these streets. You just happen to be the first one to hear my offer," the voice of an older man said. "And I am definitely *not* a police officer."

Cliff had nothing to lose. *Why not?* he thought as he turned and walked toward the van.

Back in the recovery house, Cliff sat on the bed still hoping that a delayed rush of dope would hit him at any minute. He thought about how dark it was inside that van. It had smelled clinical, like a hospital. The light in the van was dimmed so low that he never got a good look at the old man in the back who he spoke with nor the two bigger men in the front seats that remained quiet the entire time.

That lying old man had told him that he was going to give him a shot of high-grade heroin already loaded into a syringe. The only thing Cliff had to do was to go to a local recovery house and pretend to want help. The old man assured Cliff that he would arrange for him to have a bed, and that he would promptly be admitted. Once he was alone in the room of the house, Cliff was to inject the drugs, enjoy the rush, and then was free to leave. The old man told Cliff that it was his intention to expose the faulty practices of recovery houses, and this would aid in his cause.

Just as Cliff stood up from the bed to head back to the streets, he felt a strange tingling sensation at the injection site on his arm. It spread up his bicep and around his shoulder. His heart felt constricted, and he was finding it increasingly difficult to breathe.

He fell to his knees and grasped his throat. His skin burned. He felt like he was boiling from the inside out. All control of his muscles relaxed, and he rolled onto his side. Blackness filled the whites of his eyes like spilled ink. His esophagus burned just as he vomited a geyser of black bile across the carpet.

———•——

After Hayden shut Cliff's door, he walked downstairs to talk with Marcus. Marcus hadn't moved from the recliner. Hayden collapsed on the couch adjacent to him.

"New guy's weird," Marcus said.

"You said two words to him," Hayden replied.

"Just a vibe, I guess."

"Look, we have rules in place to protect the guys in the house that are doing good," Hayden started. "That kid should've been referred to an inpatient rehab, but Bob's greedy ass is only thinking about money. Be careful around him. Don't leave your wallet out and damn sure don't let him drag you down with him if he decides to use."

"Don't worry about me. I'm not fazed by that shit

anymore."

"Were you ever?" Hayden teased. "Even when you first got here, you never struggled with staying sober."

"It's not a problem for me. Just worry about your own recovery."

Hayden detected a degree of defensiveness in Marcus that irked him. Before he had the chance to respond, both men heard a groan and thud come from upstairs. They looked at each other with concern. Hayden quickly stood up to go check on the new guy. Marcus made no effort to abandon the recliner, but Hayden did notice that he at least thought about it briefly. As soon as he ascended the stairs, Hayden knocked on the door.

"Hey, man. You OK?" he asked.

He could hear movement inside the room, but Cliff didn't respond.

"Cliff?" Hayden said as he twisted the doorknob and stepped into the dark room.

There was a foul stench that he suspected was the result of the irritable bowels caused by detoxing. He saw that Cliff was under the covers in bed. There was a slow movement.

"You OK, man?"

Cliff just grunted with frustration as he shifted his body beneath the thin comforter.

"Just…need sleep," Cliff strained.

Hayden peeked over Cliff to get a good look at him. His eyes were shut, and he continued to face the wall.

"Sorry to bother you. We heard a sound, and I had to make sure you were OK."

"Mhmm."

Hayden backed out of the room and went downstairs.

"Is the weirdo still alive?" Marcus asked.

Hayden shot him an annoyed glance, but Marcus didn't divert his gaze from the TV.

"He's trying to sleep it off. His phone must've fallen off the bed or something," Hayden replied. "I'm going to head upstairs. I'm beat."

He walked into his room and shut the door behind him. He put his earbuds in, turned on some music, and collapsed onto his bed.

---

Two hours later, Tim was parking his car in front of the recovery house. Having just gotten off work at the pizza place down the street, he was exhausted and ready to relax. These inconsistent late shifts were messing with his sleep cycle. He was grateful to be employed but was tired of always being tired.

Tim hopped out of the car and quietly shut the door behind him. Just as he was walking up the sidewalk to the house, he noticed someone looking out of one of the second-floor windows. His two roommates were rarely awake when he got home, but what was even stranger was the fact that the figure was in the vacant room. He couldn't make out the features of the person, but he knew he was being watched. He gave a slight head nod, and the figure abruptly disappeared from the window.

"Please, not another intake," he muttered to himself.

He was just now getting used to sharing a house with two other guys. The reason he chose this recovery house was because of the low number of clients. If Bob started crowding the house with clients, he didn't know how much longer he would stay.

Tim locked the front door behind him after he stepped into the dark house. It was eerily quiet, especially since he knew that at least one person was awake. He looked around the living room but saw no one. The upstairs hall was a black hole until his eyes adjusted. After a moment, he could see that the vacant room's door was open, but no lights were on.

A dish rattled in the kitchen. Tim jerked his head toward the startling sound. He turned on a lamp in the living room and approached the kitchen. As soon as he rounded the corner into the room, he turned the lights on. Someone he didn't recognize was leaning over the sink with his back to Tim.

"Hey, are you a new guy?" he asked, fully ready to swing on this stranger if he wasn't supposed to be in their house.

The stranger didn't acknowledge him. He took a step forward, and the stranger's upper torso violently spasmed like a cat coughing up a hairball. He stopped in his tracks.

"Bro, are you OK?"

Cliff spun around so quickly that the black bile dribbling down his chin slung across Tim's face, completely blinding his vision. Tim stumbled backward and bumped into the wall. Before he could scream, he felt a clammy hand cover his mouth. He tried to reach up and defend himself, but Cliff had him pinned. The hairs on the back of his neck stood on end as he felt Cliff drag his nose from neck to ear, inhaling deep sniffs like a wild beast tracking a scent.

Tim managed to blink away some of the ooze in his eyes. He felt Cliff's face pull back from smelling his neck. His vision was badly blurred, but it was returning. Just as he got a clear look at the stranger with the black eyes, he felt a piercing pain in his abdomen.

He looked down to see Cliff plunge the scissors into his gut three more times. His screams were muffled and then abruptly silenced by the scissors piercing his throat. He tried to breathe but only inhaled steady gulps of warm blood. Cliff withdrew the scissors and let Tim's leaking body slide down the wall and fall to the floor.

Marcus had just fallen asleep when he heard the thud downstairs. His eyes shot open with rage. He had lost count of how many times he had told Tim to be quiet when got home from his late shifts. He knew it was hard on Tim to work nights, but the other two guys in the house had to be up early for their own jobs. He threw off the covers and jumped out of bed.

"Inconsiderate *prick*," he whispered as he opened his bedroom door and stormed into the hallway.

He looked at Hayden's door and knew that he probably sound asleep with his earbuds in. The only time he woke up was when you walked in there and shook him awake. Just as he turned to go down there, he jumped in shock at Cliff standing in the darkness at the top of the stairs. He tried to look at Cliff's face, but it was too dark to make out his features.

"What are you doing out here?" Marcus asked as he caught his breath.

Cliff took a few steps toward Marcus and stopped. He inhaled two deep breaths through his nose. Marcus watched with puzzlement as Cliff seemed to be pondering something after sniffing the air. Seemingly satisfied, Cliff turned into his own bedroom and shut the door.

"What the fuck was that?" Marcus said to himself.

He knew something wasn't right. He looked downstairs but no lights were on. Apparently, Tim wasn't home from work yet. He felt bad for immediately assuming he was the source of the noise.

Something was off about this new guy. The way he sniffed like that could easily mean that he had just snorted something. If he was the house manager and lived here rent-free, then he would go in there and confront Cliff; however, he wasn't, and that was Hayden's responsibility. He turned and walked into Hayden's room.

As suspected, Hayden was conked out, listening to music. Marcus walked over to his bed and shook his leg. Hayden jolted awake.

"What? What?" Hayden said as he sat up in bed.

"Shh," Marcus said as he quietly shut Hayden's door.

He walked back over to Hayden.

"Something is wrong with the new guy."

Hayden was slowly awakening as he tried to comprehend what Marcus was telling him.

"What do you mean?"

"I mean he is creeping around the house in the dark, sniffing like he just did some lines. I think you need to drug test him. He might need to go to the hospital or something."

Hayden rubbed his eyes and threw off his covers, clearly agitated.

"I'll take care of it," he said as he walked out of his room with Marcus following for backup.

As soon as they stepped into the hallway, they heard one of the metal trashcans in the backyard tip over onto the concrete.

"Somebody's out back," Marcus said.

They hurried to the opposite end of the hallway to peer out the window overlooking the backyard. Hayden raised the blinds and looked down. Two large men, both dressed in black, were carrying someone through their yard like furniture movers. There was a black van idling in the back alley that appeared to be their destination. Marcus recognized the pizza place uniform on the lifeless body being carried and knew it was his roommate.

"Holy shit. That's Tim!" Marcus exclaimed.

Hayden felt a chill come over him as he realized it to be true. He looked at Tim's dead eyes gazing up at the stars and the maroon stains covering his shirt.

"Let's call the cops," Hayden said.

Marcus turned around and led the way to their rooms, but both men came to an abrupt stop when they saw Cliff standing in the dark hallway in front of his room.

"Jesus!" Marcus shrieked. "Stop doing that!"

After the initial scare subsided with Hayden, he addressed Cliff, still standing behind Marcus.

"Cliff," he began, "we have a situation here. There are…"

Hayden cut himself off when Cliff started walking toward them. Something looked off about him, but it was too hard to see in the darkness.

"Dude, what's wrong with you?" Marcus asked, but Cliff ignored him entirely as he passed right by; he was zeroed in on Hayden. Cliff stopped right in front of Hayden and took a deep sniff right in front of his face. Hayden watched as the smell initiated some change in the new guy. His eyes filled with blackness, and an ink-like substance drooled out of his mouth. Just as Hayden began to recoil, Cliff lunged at him and bit down hard on the fleshy meat atop his collarbone.

"Oh my God!" Marcus screamed as he turned and ran into his bedroom.

Hayden dropped to the floor with Cliff's full weight on top of him. He tried to break free, but his assailant was too powerful. Hayden had scrapped with much bigger guys than Cliff in his day, but Cliff was displaying a strength beyond human capability. He wailed with pain as Cliff bit down with what felt like pointed fangs and thrashed his head like a dog with a chew toy. Blood quickly pooled on the floor. Hayden felt the sticky liquid on the side of his face, felt himself becoming woozy, and closed his eyes.

Just as he ceased to struggle, he heard a loud metallic THWACK. The pressure on top of him immediately subsided as Cliff fell to the floor beside him. Hayden opened his heavy eyelids and looked at Marcus standing over him holding his aluminum baseball bat. There was a strange growling on the floor beside him.

Hayden rolled his head over and saw Cliff lying face down on the floor with a badly broken jaw. Even with bone protruding from his cheek, Cliff was still snapping at Hayden as he inched his way closer. Cliff's black, lifeless eyes reminded Hayden of a shark: no conscience, no discernable motive other than pure instinct.

Marcus slammed the bat down on the side of Cliff's face, creating a sizeable dent below his orbital socket. After three more quick whacks, it was nothing but a mushy crater.

"Take that, you fucker," Marcus said as he dropped the bat, audibly out of breath.

Hayden relaxed on his back and stared at the ceiling as he struggled to stay awake. Just as he felt like closing his eyes again, he heard the back door below him slam shut.

"Someone just came in the house," he struggled to say.

Marcus quickly picked up his bat as the sound of footsteps ascended the stairs. He turned around.

"Who are ..." Marcus started to ask but was cut short by two quick chirps of a silenced pistol.

He dropped to his knees. Hayden was deliriously looking at the back of Marcus's head just as a third flash in the dark blew a hole through his cranium. Wet skull fragments hit Hayden in the face, and Marcus toppled over on his side, dead.

Two men dressed all in black emerged from the darkness

with their silenced pistols extended in front of them. Once they determined that the threat had been eliminated, they relaxed their postures. Hayden instantly recognized them as the men from the backyard that had carried Tim away. One of the men stepped forward, assessing the situation. He crouched near Cliff and examined him intensely. He looked back at the other guy.

"Dead," he said matter-of-factly.

The man standing back raised his wrist to his mouth and spoke into his smartwatch.

"The subject is dead sir. Two out of three targets are deceased. One is on his way out."

Hayden felt sobering panic at overhearing his diagnosis: "on his way out." For the second time that night, he heard the back door below him open and shut. Moments later, a third man walked up the stairs.

Hayden stared into the darkness until the figure emerged. He watched the silhouette fumble for the light switch on the wall until he found it. The overhead light temporarily blinded him. He closed his eyes, slowly opening them until they fully adjusted to the brightness.

A tall, gaunt man in his late sixties stood in front of him. In sharp contrast to his all-black counterparts, he wore a beige suit and was not the least bit physically intimidating. As his vision came into focus, he realized the man was staring right at him.

"You look confused, son," the man in the suit said.

Hayden tried to speak but choked on blood and saliva.

"Oh, no. Don't do that. Just relax. Save your strength.

You'll need it."

"Is he going to survive, boss?" one of the big men said. "He looks pretty fucked up."

The older man nodded his head in confirmation.

"Without immediate medical attention, he won't," he answered.

Hayden continued to feel woozy, but the boss's response gave him a reinvigorating feeling of hope. He fought to stay lucid.

"I want to fill you in on what actually occurred tonight, son," the boss said as he took a few steps toward Hayden. "My name is Dr. Allen Starcher, and I specialize in pharmaceuticals. My son, well, my son is no longer with us, God rest his soul. You see, my son suffered from the same sinister affliction that you and the other young men in this house were cursed with. My son never acquired the willingness to seek help, unfortunately. He overdosed and died a little over three years ago. This infestation—this *disease*—killed my only child. I knew then that I must kill the disease.

"After a few years of research and development, my company created the cure," the boss said as he reached into his jacket pocket and withdrew a capped syringe. "*This* is the cure."

Hayden stared blankly at who he assumed was a rambling lunatic with too many resources.

"When an addict is injected with this serum, they are instantly imbued with infinite strength and desire to do one thing: kill others with the disease. As you can see by our young subject, Cliff, over there, they won't stop until they are stopped."

One of the big men looked puzzled.

"But boss, why didn't the subject try to kill both of them? When we entered the house he was attacking that one and had ignored this one," the man in black said referring to Marcus on the ground.

"The only reason why he wouldn't attack him would be because he was not an addict," the old man explained.

*I knew it*, Hayden thought as he instantly felt validated in his suspicions that Marcus didn't really have a drug problem.

"Why the hell would someone who's not an addict live in a recovery house?" the other big man thought out loud.

"Oh," the old man speculated, "deceitfulness is not exclusive to the disease of addiction, my friend. Who knows his reasons? Perhaps, he just needed a temporary place to stay. There are all sorts of people looking to take advantage of available situations. Capitalism in all its insidious forms."

Hayden stared at the old man but felt his focus begin to dissolve. He tried to say that he needed help, but only broke out in a coughing fit.

"Better take this one out to the van and administer immediate medical attention," the boss instructed as the two big men approached Hayden. "Once we stop the hemorrhaging, we'll give him the cure."

This statement shocked Hayden enough to get him to open his eyes in terror. The two men lifted him off the ground. He winced as he felt a throbbing pain from the bite wounds. Just before they carried him down the stairs, he caught one last glimpse of the mysterious old man in pharmaceuticals.

"Don't worry, son," he began, "we'll get you fixed right up and take you to a much bigger recovery facility." His taut face stretched into a sly grin, and a devilish delight gleamed in his eyes as he said, "It's important that you give away what was so freely given to you."

# THANKS FOR SHARING

Jack stepped into the freezing December night and instantly regretted not wearing a heavier coat. After taking several steps away from his front door across the crunching snow, he abandoned the notion of turning back. His black Chevy truck emitted a cloud of exhaust as it grumbled in his driveway.

*At least it'll be warm in the truck,* Jack thought as he found gratitude in its remote auto-start feature.

He gripped the cold door handle and realized that he was not wearing gloves.

Jack's brother, Teddy, sat in the passenger seat ferociously rubbing his hands together to generate warmth. Teddy's frail, gaunt build was not conducive to the cold.

"I see you forgot your gloves too," Jack said as he climbed up into the truck.

"I don't think I own a pair of gloves anymore..."

"Really? Did you pawn those too?"

"Don't think you can pawn gloves," Teddy countered. "If you could, most of the hobos in town would be bare-handed."

The hot air erupted from the vents. For a moment, Jack didn't want to put the truck in gear. He let himself sit there as the heated seat thawed his core.

"Are we going to an actual AA meeting, or is this like another intervention?" Teddy prodded as Jack closed his eyes in relaxation, tuning out his younger brother. "Because I've already asked for help. There's no need for another intervention if that's the case."

"Shhhh," Jack said as he reached his arm across the console to cover Teddy's mouth.

Teddy jokingly slapped Jack's hand away before it made contact.

"Alright, I'm ready," Jack said, shaking off his fatigue.

He put the truck in reverse, and just as he was about to back out of the driveway, he noticed his wife staring at him from the living room window with a look of grave concern.

A few miles down the road, Teddy broke the silence.

"It's not your fault, you know?"

"Never said it was."

"You don't have to," Teddy began. "You do that big brother thing where you assume responsibility for my actions. You can stop now. I'm twenty-six years old."

Teddy lit a cigarette and cracked his window.

Jack just sighed and stared ahead into the night as they drove down the rural road. Three more long minutes passed with nothing else said. As they got closer to their destination, Jack's palms started to sweat. He wiped them on his jeans as Teddy noticed from the corner of his eye.

"Nervous?" Teddy asked.

"Why would *I* be nervous?" Jack said with a tone. "I'm not the one that relapsed."

"Almost ten years sober and still a self-righteous prick."

Jack wanted to reply but just exhaled deeply. This irked him more than anything Jack could've said.

"When your friends in recovery relapse, you're the first one there to offer them a hand up, man. Hell, I've personally seen you hold other people accountable for not doing more for newcomers," Teddy continued.

Jack could sense where this was going and squeezed the life out of the steering wheel.

"So why is it so different with me?" Teddy asked, getting to his point. "Why do you have so much patience and understanding for others but look at me with disgust?"

"I don't look at you with disgust," Jack began but was cut off by his phone buzzing.

He picked it up and unlocked the screen. His wife had sent him a message that said, "Are you OK?"

He sat his phone back down without replying.

"Watching you spiral out of control was the worst time of my life," Jack finally said. "All of my experience working with people in recovery went right out the window when it came to how to deal with my own family. I guess the real reason I didn't have any patience is that I had higher expectations for you."

"You thought I knew better or somethin'?"

Jack thought hard about that question.

"Yeah," he realized. "I guess I did."

"Jack, you know as well as I do...you can have all the knowledge in the world, but if your heart isn't in it, you're a timebomb."

The yellow porch light hummed atop the side entrance to the church. Jack coasted the truck to an open spot in the crowded parking lot. He liked this meeting. He knew everyone here, and newcomers from the local treatment facility came by as well. He enjoyed seeing old friends with multiple years of sobriety but also felt like he was being of service to the people just coming in off the streets. The truck's headlights landed on a group of older men standing in a circle drinking coffee and shooting the breeze under a cloud of cigarette smoke. Jack knew all of them well.

"They're going to be happy to see you," Jack said to Teddy before shutting off the ignition.

"I'm not worried about it. Really," Teddy replied. "Are you?"

Jack jerked the keys out and hopped down out of the truck, slamming the door behind him. As soon as he approached the group of old-timers, they gave warm greetings as they extinguished their smokes and headed inside.

It was about thirty minutes into the meeting, and Teddy had not shared. Jack figured that he wouldn't. Teddy had the ability to spout pearls of wisdom in a down-to-earth way that almost everyone related to; however, Jack was curious to see if his relapse had humbled his mouth shut.

Old Man Joe, a giant of a man in his sixties, sat beside Jack hunched over and rattling on about how he was grateful to be an alcoholic today. As soon as he finished talking, Jack realized that he hadn't listened to a word the man said; he was only concerned with his brother.

"I'm Teddy, and I'm an alcoholic," Teddy blurted out.

Jack looked up from the floor at Teddy who continued to speak before anyone had the chance to say the customary, "Hello," after his introduction.

"About a year ago," Teddy began, "I relapsed. It started

off with a simple fleeting thought: 'Is this all there is?'"

Jack noticed that the men sitting in the circle of metal folding chairs didn't seem fazed by what Teddy was talking about.

"That fleeting thought wasn't so fleeting after all, apparently. I started to fear that my life at *that* moment was as good as it was ever going to be, and that terrified me. I was almost five years sober, I was working full-time, and I was completely miserable. I know now that I lost gratitude for my recovery and everything that I had gotten back in my life. I stopped coming to meetings—you all know this. I started isolating myself and not returning phone calls. It's obvious now that I ceased growing spiritually, and, wouldn't you know it, I had the insane idea to get a little buzz on.

"I felt like I was outside of myself looking down at myself driving to the store to get some beer. I knew it was a horrible idea, but once I had made that decision, there was no going back. Before I knew it, I was home with empty beer cans on the floor and a head full of guilt," Teddy admitted.

Jack couldn't take his eyes off his brother. This is the honesty he had been wanting to hear for a year now.

"I think I made it a week on just the booze," Teddy continued. "After some successful nights of drinking, the idea to go get what I *really* wanted snowballed until it became reasonable. I think it may have been day eight of my relapse that I decided it was OK to bring heroin back into my life. From that point on, I just strapped myself in and went along for the ride."

Time seemed to be frozen as Jack listened intently to his

little brother's confession. Everyone else in the room might as well have been ghosts.

"It's true what they say though: this disease is progressive. Right after I picked back up, I was worse than ever. I blew through any money I had saved up. Started stealing things again...burning people and avoiding phone calls. It got ugly quick," Teddy said as he let his head drop to the floor in shame.

Jack looked around at the old-timers. *They've heard it all,* he thought as Teddy resumed sharing his story.

"My family knew something was up because of my disappearing act. They tried to reach out, but I wasn't ready. I hadn't had enough yet, I guess. My older brother here showed up at my house a few times trying to strong-arm me into treatment, but I wasn't having it. The last thing he said to me was that I was going to die," Teddy said as he made brief eye contact with Jack.

"The last time I got high was a little over two weeks ago. I told one of my running buddies that I found a good deal on some H. He gave me money and waited for me to come back. Needless to say, I did not come back. I ended up getting some strong shit—stronger than usual, anyway—and pulled over in a McDonald's parking lot to cook up a nice, big shot to wash away the withdrawals. The pinch of that needle is the last thing I remember. I died right there in my car," Teddy said as he looked across the room at Jack who was tearing up. "I died alone and cold in a McDonald's parking lot. There was no one there to revive me. No Narcan. Just oblivion as I left this world, and it's no one's fault but my own. It's not your fault, Jack."

As soon as Teddy finished talking, Jack felt Old Man Joe lightly elbow his ribs. Jack looked over at the big man beside him and the curious expression on his face.

"What?" Jack said.

"You gonna share or pass?" Old Man Joe asked.

Jack looked over to where he imagined his brother had been sitting, but the chair was as empty as it had been since the meeting began.

*He's gone. Let him go. You did everything you could.*

"I...uh," Jack stammered. "I...pass."

"Thanks, Jack," the group said in unison, and then the man on the other side of Jack introduced himself and began to share.

Jack stared at the empty seat and felt brief bewilderment; it took him a moment to realize that he had gotten lost in his head again. A tear rolled down his cheek. He quickly looked to the floor and discreetly wiped his face. He felt a massive hand pat his back, and he looked over at Old Man Joe.

"It'll be alright, son," he whispered. "Time takes time."

The group knew what Jack had been going through the past year, these last two weeks especially. Jack did his best to stay focused for the rest of the meeting. The longer the meeting went, the more he latched on to what was being shared. For a few hopeful moments, he even forgot about his own troubles as he listened to others share theirs.

As the meeting was winding down, Jack let his eyes drift back over to the empty chair. He looked up at the door leading to the outside smoking area and stared at the frosted windows beside it. A familiar silhouette stood on the other side, impatiently smoking a cigarette in the cold.

Jack quietly shoved his hand in his pocket and pressed the auto-start button on his truck keys. He looked up at the clock. In a few minutes, the meeting would end, and he would have to go back into the cold. *At least my truck will be warm,* he thought, *and maybe Teddy will be there waiting.*

# The Paperboy

I've never told anyone what I'm about to tell you. I made a pact to do just that. However, enough time has passed, enough key characters have died, for me to feel comfortable confessing it, if only to a blank computer screen.

I grew up in a small neighborhood called River's Circle in southeastern West Virginia. A wonderful thing about living in my home state is the distinction of the seasons. Winter was cold, summer was hot, and we had everything in between.

River's Circle was aptly named. The main road, River's Circle Boulevard, was a circle nearly a mile in circumference. The Muddy River wrapped around three-quarters of the neighborhood, creating some nice riverfront properties. There was a second road cutting through the middle of the circle called Muddy Drive. If one of the many birds passing overhead would've looked down on us, they would've seen a shape resembling one of those "NO SMOKING" signs.

If you're wondering why I'm focused on the street design of my neighborhood, it's because I was the paperboy out there for eight years. I got the job a little after my eighth birthday in 1992, and my parents helped to train me on the responsibilities of a paper route. Being my first paying job outside of doing chores for my parents, I took great pride in it. I may have even told a few of the younger boys that I was a "Newspaper Distribution Engineer."

My job duties were as follows:

Step 1: Newspapers get dropped off by a delivery truck at

the intersection of River's Circle Blvd. and Muddy Drive at 4 PM daily.

Step 2: Pick up the bundles and carry them home.

Step 3: Roll the papers with rubber bands or fold and put them in plastic bags as dictated by the weather.

Step 4: Load all papers into a massive, officially licensed newspaper bag.

Step 5: Secure bag to front of bicycle handlebars.

*An alternate Step 5 is to wear the bag across the shoulder but be wary of a strained back.

Step 6: Using the list of subscribers, deliver newspapers to appropriate addresses.

Step 7: Once a month, collect bill from each customer.

On average, I would make about $200 cash with tips included, and, for a few days out of the month, I was rich.

After a few months, I knew every customer, and they knew me. I couldn't ride my bike anywhere in the neighborhood without someone shouting, "Hey, Jimmy!"

Even the dogs liked me, with the exception of one rogue ankle biter that lived halfway down Muddy Drive. I dreaded delivering to his house ever since that time he breached the screen door and chased me down the road nipping at my ankles as I desperately pedaled.

The only other anomaly on my route was Finister Shell's house at 417 River's Circle Blvd. The old man never came out of his house. His lawn was always overgrown with grass and weeds. The two massive sycamore trees on the front of his property twisted and contorted as if they were purposefully shielding his small stone dwelling from view like a hobbit hole. His porch was concealed by a row of neglected bushes. His elusive existence intrigued my inquisitive mind.

I was terrified the first time I had to collect Mr. Shell's bill for the month. This was back when my parents were still training me, so my mom drove me around to each house in the beginning. She came to a stop in front of 417. I looked at the grotesque trees and the dark porch behind them and then back at my mom. She motioned with her face to go on. I opened the door and stepped out.

The cement sidewalk leading up to his porch was cracked in several places with skeletal vegetation protruding through the openings. I felt like I was walking the plank of a pirate ship. I looked back at my mom watching me with impatience. I decided there that I was a professional and would not be deterred from the task at hand.

After a deep, calming breath, I marched up his porch steps and headed straight for the door. The wooden planks beneath me squeaked with pain as if they weren't used to bearing the load of people. Before I could raise my hand to knock, Mr. Shell jerked the door open and stared down at me. He peered around the edge of the doorframe, caught sight of my mother waiting in the car, and looked back down at me.

"What d'ya want?" he grumbled.

He was a small, frail man in his seventies or eighties. If he ever had any color to him, it left long ago. Everything about Mr. Shell was grey, with the exception of the yellowish jaundice flaking of his eyes. There were tuffs of scraggly grey hairs adorning his scalp that connected to an unkempt beard. He wore faded overalls with no shirt underneath. When he spoke, years of booze and decay caked his breath. The only sounds coming from inside the open door were cats meowing and roaming about, but their smell alone alerted me of their presence.

I introduced myself and informed Mr. Shell that I was to be his new paperboy. He became more at ease once he figured out my purpose for being there. I told him how much he owed for the month, and he quickly produced a check with the worst handwriting I'd ever seen an adult have. He told me from now on he'd put the check in an envelope and tape it to the front door on the last day of every month to make it easier on everyone. I thanked him and was about to head back to my mom's car when he said one more thing: "Don't forget my paper, son."

"I won't, Mr. Shell."

"If ya find that they shorted ya papers, get on the phone with yer boss right quick and get mine delivered to me. Ya hear?"

"Sure thing, Mr. Shell," I said with feigned confidence. "You can count on me."

I'll never forget the desperation in that man's eyes as he pleaded with me not to forget his newspaper. There was a sadness as if his very life depended on me bringing him that rolled-up periodical.

My parents always told me to try and see the world from other people's eyes, but I just couldn't do it with Mr. Shell. I couldn't comprehend how important that daily delivery was to him. I finally settled on the supposition that the newspaper was his only connection to the outside world. He was a sad, lonely old man with nothing but his cats and his newspaper.

It was at that moment that the fear I had of Mr. Shell turned into sympathy, and once a month, I crossed that creaking porch and removed the taped envelope from the front door.

———·+·———

In the summer of 1994, I was ten years old and a veteran paperboy with over two years' of service. One hot June day, I was nearing the end of my route, and I heard some commotion coming from behind some of the houses along the river. I abruptly squeezed the brakes on my bike and dropped my shoes to the street, coming to a complete stop. Listening.

Kids. Splashing. Laughter.

Without hesitation, I directed my bike toward the sounds and pedaled with excitement. I still needed to finish my route, but up until then, it had been one of those boring summer days where I had all the time in the world but no one to enjoy it with. I had gone by three of my friends' houses earlier that morning, but nobody was home for one reason or another. It's funny now how much I longed for school to end only to complain about being bored during the summer.

There were kids, and it sounded like they were having the time of their lives. The worst time to discover your crew of friends is mid-delivery. I raced my bike between two houses— 401 and 403 River's Circle Blvd. if I'm not mistaken—and emerged into their shared backyard. I pedaled across the clearing to the trees lining the riverbank about twenty yards away.

There were three bikes propped against trees, and I recognized them all. I stepped off my bike and let it drop as I looked down the steep hill toward the river. There were three kids splashing each other. I squinted and recognized them as Charlie, Andrew, and his younger sister, Stacy.

Charlie was my best friend. He was a few months older than me but still in my grade. We had known each other since preschool and hung out almost every day. He was short and chubby ("husky," his mom had once said), but he was strong for his age. His brown hair was in a perpetual bowl cut at his mother's insistence.

Capitalizing on his size and shape, he was the goalie on our soccer team and averaged at least one yellow card penalty per game for temper-induced vulgarities. As much as I disliked seeing him get in trouble, it tickled me pink to see the parents of opposing teams be subjected to a child calling the referee a "blind cocksucker" or screaming "shit!" at the top of his lungs when he had a shin guard malfunction.

Andrew was the opposite of Charlie. He was a tall, skinny blonde boy with the coordination of a baby giraffe learning to walk. What he lacked in physical agility, he made up for with intelligence. Anytime our squad needed a brain of the operation, he was the guy.

One time when we were trying to convince Charlie's mom to let us all stay the night at his house, it was Andrew who concocted the idea of telling her we needed to "study for a group project," which wasn't necessarily a lie since we were all in the same class and had the same assignments. Telling an outright lie wouldn't sit well with him.

Aside from being the smartest of our bunch, Andrew was also the most religious. This combination of high intellect and deep faith naturally produced fits of anxiety in my friend. His parents made sure that he never missed a Sunday or Wednesday church service. One week out of every summer, he went to church camp, and we had to make do without him. He and Charlie used to butt heads over their wildly differing world beliefs, but they always made up. Charlie used to be able to rile Andrew up just by dropping a few F bombs, but Andrew quickly developed a thick skin and selective hearing.

Stacy, Andrew's seven-year-old sister, was surprisingly cool for a little girl. She was tall and skinny too, but not lanky like Andrew. If she ever wore anything other than blue overalls and her blonde hair in pigtails, I never saw it. Coming from the same religious upbringing, she was very similar to Andrew in temperament and social cues. The key difference between the two was how much more joyful and serene she was than her perpetually neurotic older brother. She never whined like other younger siblings, and she had a natural sense for knowing when she was overstaying her welcome with us older kids. Because of her uncanny ability to make us forget that she was even there, we let her tag along by default.

"Hey, guys!" I shouted at the trio who were about halfway into the shallow river.

Stacy was struggling to hold a pink plastic bucket in both of her hands, and the two boys were intensely searching for something in the river. They turned to face me with big smiles.

"Hey, paperboy!" Charlie shouted over the other two, abandoning his search. "Come get in."

"I can't," I began. "I'm not finished with my route yet."

I pointed with my thumb to the few remaining papers in my bag hanging off my bike behind me.

"Piss on that!" Charlie said, waving off my professional duties.

"You really should come right now, Jimmy," Andrew insisted.

He pointed at the bucket his sister was barely holding.

"We've found the motherload!"

I squinted at the bucket from the riverbank. Stacy intuited my efforts and gingerly angled the bucket so I could see its contents without it spilling.

*GOLF BALLS.*

Pristine, white, shiny, golf balls. I could see each of the precious little pearls so clearly now. Calloway. Nike. Titleist. Bridgestone. TaylorMade. All neatly polished by the river current and ready to be plucked for the harvest.

You see, on the opposite side of the river was Muddy River Golf Course. It was an 18-hole course known throughout the state for its scenic beauty and seclusion. At age ten, I was by no means a golfer, but I did go with my dad to the driving range a few times. I remember overhearing my dad and uncles talking about how it was a hidden gem in our little town. They also said they would meet golfers from all over the country on the course. I thought that was interesting, but I had no intention of mastering the game of golf. My interest in the course lay only with their policy to purchase back golf balls out of the river for their driving range.

When Stacy gave me a glimpse of the white gold glowing in the bucket, I lit up. Golf balls meant money, and I liked money. I looked back at my bike and the responsibilities attached to it. Andrew must have sensed my dilemma from where he was.

"Just come in for twenty minutes and help us collect. You can finish your route after. Who knows how many you'll miss out on if you wait?"

Hearing this suggestion from Andrew somehow assured me that it was the right thing to do. He was our moral compass, after all.

I settled on my decision and yanked off my shirt and shoes. My friends cheered me on as I waded into the chilly, brown water; it was appropriately named the Muddy River. The squishy river bottom sucked my feet down with each step. After a slow trudge through the strong current, I made it to my friends.

"How long have you all been out here?" I asked as I eyeballed their loot.

"About a half hour," Charlie said. "There are balls *everywhere.*"

"Let's spread out and cover more territory," Andrew suggested, and we followed suit. "Stacy, you stay close to me. This current could sweep you up."

"OK," she said without hesitation.

The four of us stayed near the middle of the river but in a

straight line. About fifteen feet separated us with the exception of Stacy and Andrew who were side-by-side.

"Everyone feel with your feet and bring what you find to Stacy's bucket," Andrew said.

I knew the drill already. I had already pocketed five balls just in the time it took us to form a line. We plundered the river like that for a good fifteen minutes as we moved slowly toward the golf course side of the river. The plan was to grab every ball in our section of the river and then walk up the bank and through the golf course to sell them back. I would have to trust my friends to give me an appropriate cut of the earnings, since I had to return to my route when we were finished.

The water was knee-deep as I scoured the surrounding area for any last stragglers. I noticed a glowing whiteness poking out from the wet sand and immediately snatched the ball. I looked up at the steep riverbank and the thick vegetation protruding from it.

There were numerous weather-beaten trees growing out at a slant over the water. Rogue sticks and fallen branches poked from the sandy hill at all angles. Shards of brown, broken beer bottles lay in random pools from littering golfers. It was a daunting climb, especially with armfuls of golf balls, but well worth it in the end. I was grateful I didn't have to make that journey today. Just as I was emerging from the water with my score, I overheard a snippet of a conversation that has haunted me all my life.

"…and then she just grabbed my dick, Phil. Strangest thing!"

It was a golfer just above me on the green atop the riverbank. I couldn't see him through the thick plants. He didn't sound as old as my dad, but he was definitely not a kid near my age. I then remembered hearing about how college kids would often frequent the course during the summer. I looked back at my friends who were a little further down-river from me. They had already made it to the sandy bank and were preoccupied with tallying their balls. I paused and continued to eavesdrop on the intriguing conversation.

Another young man laughed.

"You're full of shit," a third voice said.

"No, for real," the first voice began. "I know you think I'm joking right now, but we hooked up."

The speaker was talking slowly and obnoxiously loud. He slurred his words, and I knew he had been drinking alcohol. Every time I visited the golf course, I ran into people who were drunk. As far as I could tell, consuming booze while you played was part of the game.

"Keep talking shit, Phil," voice three said.

"Guys, no one fucked anybody's girlfriend, OK?" voice two interjected. "Now, let's just finish the hole and move on. You guys are just drunk."

"Shut up, Wade," Phil warned. "Mitch is just in denial right now. Look at him. He knows it's true. He knows Jessica has been acting differently toward him ever since I pounded her while he was passed out on the floor of our dorm."

Phil howled with laughter at his own admission.

I knew I was hearing things I wasn't supposed to, but I had to keep up; I was fascinated. I felt like I was listening to real grown-ups talk the way they do when there aren't any kids around. My trio of friends were still counting balls in the sand, but this trio above me who I still couldn't see were not getting along so well.

"I'm going to say this as simply as possible so that even a retard like you can comprehend it, OK?" Mitch started. "If you say one more fucking word about…(he let out a boozy hiccup)…about my girlfriend, then I'm going to break your stupid fucking face."

I started feeling butterflies in my stomach as I listened. I'd never seen a real fight before, but it sounded like one was about to happen. I carefully placed my balls in the sand and began to ascend the hill to get a closer view. I crawled on all fours, avoiding the pitfalls and pokey debris.

"Guys, seriously, calm down!" Wade begged again, trying to defuse the drunken escalation.

My eyes finally peeked over the hill where the muddy riverbank met the clean grass. There were three young college-aged guys standing beside a parked golf cart loaded with coolers and golf bags. I couldn't tell who was who at first, but I knew they were all drunk.

"Ok, you're right, Wade," Phil said as he walked over to his ball on the green.

He stopped less than ten feet from where I was but didn't notice me. He stood in position like he was going to putt but was swaying a bit in his intoxicated state. It appeared like the altercation was over before it began.

"Just one more thing, though," Phil said as he pulled back his putter to hit his ball. "Were you able to get it up the last time, or was Jessica lying about that?"

Phil putted his ball in the hole. He chuckled to himself and didn't even notice Mitch grab a chipping wedge out of one of the golf bags and stride toward him. Phil reached down to retrieve his ball just as Mitch reared back the club.

"Mitch, no!" Wade screamed from the cart.

The golf club came crashing down on Phil's jaw just as he was standing back up. There was a sickening crack, and his eyes went blank as he stumbled back. He grabbed his jaw as it dangled unnaturally from his face. When I saw the wound, I felt my lunch fighting to come up. Phil tried to speak, but only blood and drool dribbled out.

In a quiet hurry, I shimmied backward down the riverbank to regroup with my friends. I didn't know what I was going to do, but I didn't want to have to do it alone. I heard the men getting closer to the riverbank and looked back up at them.

Mitch followed the stumbling Phil screaming, "It's hard to talk shit with a broken jaw, isn't it?"

My eyes widened as I watched Phil trip over a root near the green and fall down the steep hill toward me. His limp body gained momentum the more he tumbled, and I braced myself for collision. I crawled backward on all fours in one last attempt to avoid being crushed.

Just a few feet before he was going to hit me, his rolling body was stopped by a jagged branch jutting up from the ground. There was a wet piercing sound, and a warm mist sprayed my face. I wiped my eyes and looked down at the dark blood that covered my hands. I looked up at Phil hanging lifelessly from the sharp branch piercing his neck. Blood shot out in rhythmic spurts from his exterior jugular vein.

I screamed like I had never screamed before. My friends came running up the sandy bank. Stacy was the first one to see, and she let out a shrill yelp that felt like a needle in my eardrum.

"Oh my God," Andrew said, terrified.

"What the hell did you do to that guy?" Charlie asked with disbelief.

Before I could tell him that it wasn't me, we heard the golfers run up to the edge of the course above us.

"Mitch, you fucking killed him," Wade panicked.

"It was an accident. I wasn't trying to kill him," Mitch said, sobering up by the second.

His gaze quickly went to the four of us standing near the body.

"Hey, there's fucking kids down there!"

I felt like I was going to lose control of my bowels.

"Hey, you! Stay there!" Mitch shouted as he started sliding down the hill toward us holding his golf club.

Wade didn't seem to know what to do, so he blindly followed Mitch.

"Shit, we gotta get out of here," Charlie said.

We collectively snapped out of our shock and realized the validity of his claim.

"Come on!" he said as he started running down the riverbank, and we followed.

"Kids, come back!" Wade yelled. "It's not what you

think."

We ignored him as we sprinted full speed. They were sluggish compared to us. In addition to being familiar with the dangerous terrain, none of us were intoxicated. I looked back at the two men who finally made it down the hill to the sandy beach.

"We just need you all to talk to the police with us!" Mitch yelled.

I turned back around and continued to run with my friends. I had no idea where we were going and was desperately hoping Andrew had some secret plan up his sleeve, but he appeared to be running as blindly as the rest of us.

"Fuck off!" Charlie shouted back mid-sprint.

For a husky kid, Charlie could move when he wanted to.

We hurdled slippery rocks and curved roots as we fled our pursuers. I realized that we were soon coming up to the end of our beach. The riverbank was about to turn into nothing but a steep wall of mud and rock.

Charlie came to a dead stop when he ran out of sand. The three of us nearly ran into him. I looked back at Mitch and Wade, who were rapidly closing the gap between us.

"We have to get in the water. We can't climb on that," Andrew said as we all realized that he was correct.

"Kids, stop!" Wade screamed.

Charlie was the first one to trample into the water, and we jumped in right after him.

"Hurry!" Charlie said as the four of us maneuvered through the sinking murk in a diamond formation.

"We're not moving fast enough," Andrew said. "The mud is too thick."

I knew he was right. I looked back and saw Wade and Mitch reach the water and jump in without a second thought about it.

"Swim!" I screamed. "Lift up your feet and swim!"

We all dove forward and swam against the current as best we could. The rushing water pelted my face as I kicked and paddled like never before. I didn't bother looking back. I knew they were literally right on my heels. Stacy was struggling to keep up, so Andrew grabbed his little sister by the shirt and jerked her forward with adrenaline-fueled strength.

The sounds of the men splashing behind me were getting louder. They were catching up to us, and we were still less than halfway across the river. If we could only make it to our bikes, we'd be home free.

"Stop, you little shits!" Mitch screamed directly behind me.

I felt a strong hand grab my ankle, but I jerked and slid it free. My right hand touched the bottom of the river to keep my head from going under. I felt the round rock with my palm and immediately gripped it. I spun around to face my attackers and chucked the rock at Mitch's face. The heavy stone bounced off his forehead and dazed him to a stop.

"Fuck!" he screamed as he closed his eyes and cupped his throbbing skull in pain.

Wade ran into him from behind and knocked him face-first into the water. Mitch popped right back up soaking wet and screaming in a blind rage.

"Shit, Mitch. I'm sorry," Wade said as he helped Mitch get back to his feet in the rushing water.

I continued to swim to try and catch up with my friends, who were nearing the shore.

"They're getting away!" Mitch panicked as the two men resumed their chase.

I saw Andrew and Charlie step onto the sandy beach. Andrew grabbed Stacy's arm and helped her out. Charlie turned around and saw how far behind them I had fallen.

"Come on, Jimmy!" Charlie yelled. "Move your ass."

If I had any breath to scream I would've told that ungrateful dick that I just saved us all. Instead, I used my anger as fuel to swim faster than I ever had in my life.

Relief washed over me as I felt the sandy incline of the shore beneath my feet. I ran up to meet my friends.

"They're coming," Andrew said looking at the two men who were about fifteen feet away from land.

"Where are our bikes?" Stacy cried.

"Oh, shit. The current dragged us way down the river," Charlie realized.

I looked in the direction of where our bikes were parked, but there was about a quarter-mile of unscalable terrain between our new beach and the other friendly shore. I looked down the opposite direction and saw somewhat of an overgrown pathway running parallel to the river.

There was a row of houses somewhere above us, but climbing up to them would be too difficult from our current position.

"You can't go anywhere, kids," Mitch said from the river, almost to the shore.

"Let's go!" I yelled and took off running down the path.

If my friends were uncertain before, they didn't show it now. I heard them beating down the path behind me, and I did my best to keep at full speed. This was a path I had never explored, and it was becoming increasingly more narrow and slippery. Small rocks and exposed roots were just waiting for one misstep, and we'd be tumbling down the riverbank.

The two men were now out of the water and running behind us once again. They were too big to sprint along the path like we were. When tree branches hung too low or the path took a sharp turn, they had to slow down and carefully maneuver around the obstacles. One wrong move and they'd end up like their pal, Phil, back there.

After an eternity of running, we were all beginning to show signs of fatigue, especially Charlie. We were all panting and wheezing as our paces gradually slowed.

Luckily, the two men behind us were just as tired as we were, so they never closed the gap on us. I had lost track of where we were in relation to the houses above us. We could be anywhere. I wouldn't be surprised if I took a sharp left turn straight up the hill right now and ended up in the back of Charlie's house (he lived on the opposite side of the neighborhood from where we parked our bikes.)

It must've been over two hours since I had decided to abandon my newspaper delivery responsibilities and jumped into the water with my friends. I wondered how my day would have been different if I had told Charlie, Andrew, and

Stacy that I was going to finish my job and meet up with them later. Who knows if they would have even gotten mixed up in this had I not been there to overhear the conversation on the green?

The sun was setting just ahead of us behind the rolling hills. It may not have been terribly dark elsewhere in the neighborhood, but where we were, under a canopy of thick river trees, it was becoming difficult to even see your feet running against the weathered path.

I nearly ran straight off the edge of the hill onto jagged rocks beneath, but I stopped just shy of the sudden drop. Thankfully, my friends were paying attention and stopped before running into me.

"There's no more path," I said as I looked at the path that dead-ended into the riverbank.

I looked back at the men chasing us, and they came to a stop a few feet from where we were. They both put their hands on their knees, struggling to regain their breath.

"There's nowhere to go," Mitch said as he stood up and leaned against the trunk of a tree. "This shit ends now."

Andrew nudged my ribs with his elbow. I looked at him looking at the massive boulder just beyond our path and knew exactly what was on his mind. There was plenty of room on top of the stone, but it was about a five-foot jump from where we were. Anyone who didn't make it would fall about fifteen feet into a dark chasm of jagged rocks and puddling muck. I poked Charlie and tilted my head toward the boulder. Andrew did the same for Stacy, and we were all on the same page.

"Here's what we're gonna do..." Mitch began, but I turned my back on him and bolted before he could finish talking.

I leaped across the gap and landed hard. I was surprised at how easily I made it across.

"Move!" I heard Charlie yell, and I rolled quickly out of their landing area.

In three quick thuds, they all safely made it to the rock with me.

Mitch and Wade walked to the edge from where we just jumped and saw that there was nowhere for them to land. There was also nowhere for us to go.

"You kids are fucking nuts!" Wade chuckled.

Mitch looked back at him, unamused. Wade stopped smiling immediately.

"You guys are fucked!" Charlie shouted. "You killed that guy, and you're gonna go to jail."

"Yeah, just get out of here," Andrew said. "You can't kill us all and expect to get away with what you did. The cops probably already found your friend and are looking for you right now."

"And I guarantee our parents are looking for us, too!" I chimed in although I knew that wasn't true.

We were given free rein over our little neighborhood in these long summer days. My parents wouldn't get worried about my absence until late into the night.

"Nobody said anything about killing anyone," Mitch said. "We just need you to tell the cops that this whole thing was one big misunderstanding. That's all."

"How is it a misunderstanding?" Stacy asked from behind

Andrew's back.

Once again, I had completely forgotten she was even with us.

"I wasn't trying to kill Phil," Mitch replied. "Yeah, I hit him with my club, but he tripped and fell down the hill. Hell, I even did it in self-defense. He was about to hit me with his club, but I reacted first."

"That's bullshit!" I yelled. "I saw what happened. You were mad because he was teasing you. He bent down to get his golf ball, and you hit him."

Mitch looked over his shoulder at Wade for backup.

"He's telling the truth," Wade stammered unconvincingly. "You guys don't know Phil. He was about to attack Mitch. Probably would've come after me too if Mitch hadn't done what he did."

The sun had disappeared behind the mountains, and full darkness enveloped us all. The night sounds of the river were in full concert as we held our ground in this prolonged standoff. No one spoke as both parties just waited, unsure about the next plan of action on either side. I looked up the hill for one last unforeseen path to climb to freedom, but it was a steep incline of mud and rock.

"This is ridiculous," Mitch said, breaking the silence. "Either you kids get back over here or I'm jumping across there. You know that rock ain't big enough for all of us. At least two of you are gonna fall off."

We nervously looked at one another, fearing the truth in his threat. None of us responded; there was nothing left to say.

A twig snapped above us, but I was the only one to hear it.

"Alright, you little bastards," Mitch began. "Here we go. 3...2...1!"

Mitch leaped from the path at our rock, and we collectively closed our eyes bracing for impact. I took a deep breath and realized that nothing had happened. We should've been crushed by now. I opened my eyes and gasped at the sight before me.

Suspended in mid-air, Mitch was convulsing in pain. His eyes had rolled up into his head exposing only the whites. His mouth hung open and limp. I couldn't make sense of it. There was nothing under his dangling feet that he could possibly be standing on. His arms were hanging by his side, clearly not holding onto anything. I looked up at his head again, and that's when my blood ran cold.

I hadn't seen it before, but a massive spear had pierced through one side of Mitch's head and out through the other. His lifeless body hung like a rotisserie chicken from the sturdy weapon. When I looked at the protruding blade caked in blood and skull fragments, I realized that it wasn't pinned to anything. Whatever was keeping the weapon suspended in the air like that must be on the other end of the spear.

Stacy saw it first and screamed that ear-splitting scream again.

"Oh my God. What is that?" Charlie cried as he looked up at what held the spear in its hands.

Standing at the top of the hill was a massive beast of a man, twice as big as my father. He was hunched over, gripping the handle of the spear, effortlessly holding Mitch's deadweight.

I could see he was wearing faded blue overalls with heavy black work boots. He wore no shirt underneath, but his chest and arms were thick with body hair. As he gripped the spear, his bulging muscles constricted into tight knots. His long dark hair hung over his bearded face, concealing most of it. When I looked into his eyes, I fought the urge to soil myself.

There were glowing yellow lights where normal human eyes should've been. His large mouth was open, and his lips contorted into a fiendish grin across serrated fangs. The thing never blinked and seemed to be looking at us all at the same time.

Wade finally noticed the creature lurking on the hill above him.

"Fuck!"

The thing tilted the spear at an angle so that Mitch's corpse slowly slid down the pole, leaving a black trail of ooze behind it in the moonlight. Once his body was within reach, the thing grabbed Mitch and pulled him off the spear. He held Mitch by the neck with one hand and tossed his flailing body on the ground beside him.

Wade turned away from us and began to run. This made the creature on the hill hiss with laughter as it ran parallel to him looking down. Both Wade and the creature disappeared from our sight. We all stood there in silence, unable to move.

A sickening *THUNK* echoed across the river, and we heard the thing laugh in the distance. We knew it caught its prey.

"We have to get out of here," Charlie cried.

We snapped out of our shock and realized that he was right. It was now or never.

"Where do we go?" Andrew pondered. "If we jump back the way we came, we'll run into that thing. We can't go up because that thing's up there."

"Then we have to go down," I realized.

"How are we going to do that?" Andrew asked.

I looked at Charlie.

"Him," I said.

"Huh? How do you expect me to get down there?"

"You're the strongest," I explained. "You hang off the rock and let us shimmy down your back one at a time. It'll still be a steep drop, but we'll be a lot closer to the ground than just jumping off the rock."

Charlie thought about it.

"He's right," he said. "Our only option is to go down and cross the river."

Without giving it a second thought, he dropped down to his knees and maneuvered his body over the edge of the boulder.

"Be careful," Stacy whispered.

Once Charlie was hanging completely over the edge in position, I looked at Andrew.

"You go first," I said. "When you get down there, you can help Stacy."

Andrew was apprehensive.

"Hurry up you pussy. We don't have much time," Charlie said from the side of the rock.

"Alright," Andrew consented as he dropped down to his

knees.

He flung one leg over Charlie and gripped onto his back. Charlie winced but held firm. Andrew slowly shimmied down Charlie until he was hanging onto his heels. Andrew looked down and it was only about a six-foot drop to the rocks below. He did not like the way those slippery edges jutted up at him, but he was choosing those over the beast above him. He closed his eyes and let go.

I watched his feet hit the rocks first, taking most of the force, and then he rolled over to one side between two larger rocks.

"I'm OK," he said as he slowly got back up.

I helped Stacy get into position, and she carefully climbed down Charlie just like her big brother before her. She dangled from Charlie's legs.

"Let go," Andrew instructed from below. "I've got you."

Stacy let go and fell onto her brother.

"We're good," Andrew informed us.

Charlie moved his hands on the rock, and I could tell that he was losing energy.

"I'll be quick," I said.

Just as I was about to get into position, I felt a glob of slime slide down my face. I wiped it away and looked up. The creature was kneeling on the hill above me, smiling with its head cocked to the side and drool pouring out of its oversized grin.

I screamed and stumbled backward, stepping on Charlie's fingers. Charlie screamed and released his grip on the rock, falling onto Andrew and Stacy. I looked down and saw that all three friends were alive. I took a deep breath, and just as I jumped from the rock, something gripped the back of my shirt and lifted me up. My pile of friends grew smaller as I ascended to the hill above us.

The creature held me by the shirt like a suitcase as it walked. I screamed and writhed trying to break free. I looked to my right and saw that it was gripping a rope with its other hand. The opposite end of the rope bound Mitch and Wade's bodies by their feet, dragging them across the grass.

Out of sheer panic, I slammed my balled-up fist into the thing's shin. It recoiled in anger and jerked me up to its face. Its head was almost the size of my torso, and I wholeheartedly believe that it could've swallowed me whole if it wanted to; instead, it just stared at me with its glowing yellow eyes. Its breath was a warm mist that hit me like opening a dishwasher that hadn't yet cooled down. I closed my eyes and felt hot urine run down my legs.

Nothing happened.

When I finally peeked through one eye, I saw the creature looking at me with curiosity. No, that wasn't it...*recognition.* The smile disappeared from its face, and it looked like it was contemplating something.

"Paper...boy," it hissed.

Tears welled up in my eyes, but I fought the urge to cry.

I nodded my head, and its grin returned.

"Bring...me...my...*paper!*"

I hung there suspended in air in complete confusion, but then I smelled the cats. It was an unmistakable smell from one of my newspaper customers who I had seen only once.

The monster's overalls were now familiar to me as well.

It released me. I fell to the ground flat on my belly. The air exploded out of my diaphragm. I rolled over on my back and looked up at the monster. It gave me one final, sideways look, turned around, and continued walking toward the back of a house, dragging Mitch and Wade behind it. I stared at the horrific sight in bewilderment.

When my senses somewhat returned, I recognized the house from behind. This was a house on my paper route. The creature walked up to the back of the house toward an open cellar. He tossed the two corpses in like rag dolls and then descended into the dungeon, slamming the wooden doors behind him.

I sat in Finister Shell's backyard, wet with urine and in a state of shock. I heard faint splashing sounds in the distance behind me and realized that my friends were making a safe escape. I wondered how much time I had until that monstrous version of Mr. Shell decided it was still hungry and would come back for me. Its words echoed in my memory: "Bring me my paper."

In five seconds, I was up and sprinting down the road. Even though I was beyond the point of exhaustion, the image of those yellow eyes motivated me forward. I didn't stop running until I reached my bike.

My heart was noticeably beating through my torn shirt. I wanted to collapse and disappear into a slumber that would take me far away from my current nightmare. Instead, I heaved my bike upright and sat on the seat.

Within minutes, I was pedaling toward my destination. I

let my feet drop to the pavement when I made it to Mr. Shell's sidewalk. I carefully leaned my bike against one of the sycamore trees beside me and withdrew a rolled-up paper from my bag. I took a deep breath and stepped up onto his dark porch. Slowly, I walked toward his front door. It would've been easy just to have dropped the paper and run, but I had to know. I had to know why he let me go. I had to know why he needed this paper. I felt it was worth dying for. Gripping the paper in one hand, I raised my other hand to the screen door and gently knocked.

There was movement inside. Things were shuffled around and then footsteps started coming toward the door. Locks clicked and clanged, and the doorknob slowly turned. The wooden door inched open, revealing a sliver of darkness.

I could see the silhouette of a man standing there.

"You're late," Mr. Shell gruffed from behind the door.

"I'm sorry, Mr. Shell."

He didn't move or speak. Seconds crept by like years.

"I made a mistake," I continued. "I saw my friends having fun and decided to play with them before finishing my job. I thought it wouldn't take long, but we ran into trouble. I never meant to be so late with your paper, Mr. Shell."

Tears started pouring down my cheeks.

"I'm sorry. It'll never happen again."

The door slowly pulled all the way open, and Mr. Shell began to step out into the moonlight. I stumbled back, unsure of what I was about to see. The old, frail man stood there in his overalls with that unforgiving scowl on his face.

"I don't reckon you'll ever be late with my paper again,

will ya, boy?"

"No, sir."

"Then I don't guess there's no need to report ya."

"Thank you, Mr. Shell."

"There's no need to *report* anything is there, boy?" he asked with a hint of a grin. "Cuz you'll always git me my paper on time, and there'll be no issue, right?"

"Right, Mr. Shell."

He smiled and nodded his head. He turned around and disappeared back into the darkness of his doorway. I saw a faint flash of yellow eyes in the abyss, and then the door slammed shut.

---

Childhood memories have a way of fading as one ages. What seems so important at that point in your life can hardly be recollected given a proper passage of time. There were events that I experienced that I'm not entirely sure of the exact details anymore. However, the day I was late delivering Finister Shell's newspaper is as clear as what I ate for breakfast this morning.

After I left Mr. Shell's that night, I rode home and went to bed. I met up with Charlie, Andrew, and Stacy the next day. I will never forget their faces when they saw that I was alive. I will never forget being hugged by all three of them at once. I told them about the creature grabbing me and then being scared off by a passing car. I lied and said that before it fled into the mountains it hissed at me to never speak of its existence again, or it would come back for us all. We all agreed that forgetting about the whole ordeal would be the best course to take, even though it was easier said than done.

My friends and I heard peripheral details of the police investigation into the disappearance of those college boys. The only thing the cops had to go on was an abandoned golf cart on the fifteenth hole of Muddy River Golf Course. I never expected them to find Mitch and Wade, but the fact that Phil's body disappeared as well sends a chill down my spine whenever I think about it. By the end of the summer, the whole fiasco was a distant memory for the town.

We resumed our summer, as best we could. We played in the river, rode bikes around the neighborhood, and spent the night at each other's houses. We tried to be normal. It was difficult at first but became easier as time went on, as things do.

I continued my paper route for the next few years; I felt it was my obligation to do so. It wasn't until I turned fifteen and saw an ambulance wheel out Mr. Shell's body that I felt comfortable retiring from the newspaper profession.

The mailman reported that Mr. Shell's box hadn't been emptied in over a week, so the authorities showed up for a well-check and found him dead from an apparent heart attack. Had I been able to peer through the thick bushes onto his porch, I would've seen a small pile of bundled newspapers underneath his door with many years' worth of untouched checks taped to it. You see, since that night on the river, I never charged Mr. Shell for his newspapers. I figured I just owed him one.

# Hunting Season

Barren McNeil had always been good with a gun. Ever since he was eight years old and his father took him to shoot beer cans with BBs, he knew he was a natural. He could instinctively aim; immobile targets never stood a chance. The first time he fired his dad's rifle, the kick and BOOM of the gun created a rush of adrenaline that his body relished. Pretty soon he and his old man were targeting clay pigeons careening through the sky. Barren savored the rare grins of approval from his father as the targets exploded, raining debris across the open field. He didn't know which he enjoyed more: firing weapons or pleasing his dad.

After his tenth birthday, he and his father always went out together for hunting season. With each progressive season, Barren's skills sharpened. Throughout his early teenage years, Barren dominated the youth competitive shooting scene. Never once did he feel fear or intimidation stepping onto the range with his weapon. As soon as he stared down the sight of his rifle, everything but the target dissolved away. The noise of the crowd, the wind, and the birds all just evaporated from existence. The only thing he was aware of at that moment in time was the rhythmic THUMP of his heart as he focused on the solitary target.

After proving himself time and time again with kids his own age, he began entering adult competitions. No one could best him, regardless of age. His parents helped him secure a marksman scholarship, and that's how he made it through college. All through this time, as soon as hunting season rolled around, Barren and his dad would hit the woods. When his father passed a little after Barren's 25th birthday, he continued the tradition, until recently. He could swear that he felt the old man's spirit out there in the woods with him, and he liked that.

For roughly the next twenty years, Barren's life course was similar to many other Americans. He finished school and then toyed around at various entry-level business positions until he discovered that he was a natural at selling real estate. He obtained his license, made some profit, and began a successful real estate agency.

At his ten-year high school reunion, he ran into a former girlfriend named Kim, and the sparks reignited. Barren and Kim dated, fell in love, and got married. They quickly bought a beautiful house on a large farm. The many acres of private property was a necessity for Barren and his favorite pastime of target shooting.

---

The chilly autumn wind blew against Barren's taut face, pulling him away from his memories. He stood alone in the silent woods. He was miles away from his empty home. It had been a little under three years since he had last spoken to his now ex-wife, and his real estate business was in a downward spiral. He knew he had no one to blame but himself—he had neglected them both since the accident.

The frigid dawn temperature was perfect for hunting. He

could sense the animals moving about to stay warm. The sun was just beginning to peek above the Appalachian mountain range that surrounded the sprawling West Virginia valley.

Forty-four years old now, Barren leaned back against a tall sycamore tree and took a warm swig of amber whiskey. Drinking during hunting season was a time-honored tradition, but this year it was a necessity. He assessed the half-empty pint in his hand and then slid it back into a pouch in his tan vest; his mesh-camo ballcap kept the bright rays out of his eyes. A disturbed flock of birds flew over his head.

God, he missed this.

It had been three long years since he had been in the woods. Three years with no hunting and lots of drinking. A few shots of liquor helped to dull the pain at first, but then he noticed that he needed more to get the desired effect. After what he'd been through, though, anyone would drink; at least, that's how he justified it.

He pulled the bottle right back out and took another generous gulp. The sourness of the bourbon coated his throat as he exhaled a deep, boozy breath. Numbness began to take hold, and he welcomed it. He took a slow look around the woods desperately trying to stay focused on the majesty of the forest. The last time he was out during hunting season was three years ago in this exact location, and he had returned to it intentionally.

---

The Morris family had recently adopted a new tradition of

renting out the Rusty Mountain Lodge for their Thanksgiving festivities. Originally, the family had celebrated the holiday at a different Morris's house each year. As time went on, there became many factions of the original Morris clan that had grown exponentially; larger accommodations were naturally in order. All of the elder siblings agreed that the best course of action was to rent a large enough venue for everyone to get together without tripping over one another. Located just an hour away from most of the family, the historic and luxurious Rusty Mountain Lodge was an ideal place for a gathering.

Arnold and Debra Morris drove carefully up the winding gravel road. Their two children, Nathan and Sam, sat in the backseat glued to their phones with headphones on their ears. On either side of them were miles of trees atop rolling hills. Arnold loved this part of living in West Virginia. He had seen the beauty the world had to offer during his time in the military, but nothing came close to fall in the Mountain State. Debra loved it, too. She stared with awe at the bright orange and yellow leaves barely hanging on by a thread to their branches. A swift wind would easily create a shower of fall foliage. As she looked deeper into the forest, she could make out shades of light brown and pink as the sun's rays made everything glow.

Arnold accidentally hit a deep pothole in the road, and everyone was bumped out of their respective trances. Debra gasped, and the two teenage boys looked up from their electronics obviously annoyed.

"Oops," Arnold said as he slowed down a bit.

The crunching of the gravel was audible as the heavy SUV crept along the road. Debra looked back at the boys.

"Put down your phones and appreciate the scenery," she instructed her sons.

Neither one heard her through their headphones. She reached back and snapped her fingers in their line of sight. They both looked up, and she motioned for them to free their ears. They did.

"Put down your phones and appreciate the scenery," she repeated.

Sam, the oldest by two years, placed his phone on his lap and looked out the window. Nathan, fourteen, just waited for his mom to turn back around so that he could resume his game.

"It is pretty out here," Sam said earnestly.

"Mhmm," Nathan mumbled without looking up from his screen.

After a few more ascending miles, the family arrived at a clearing in the woods. The two-story cabin stood tall in the open area. The building was from the Civil War era, but the inside had been modernized. It was ideal for a remote getaway without sacrificing all of the present-day amenities. Smoke bellowed from the stone chimney as many members of the Morris extended family were already inside cooking and drinking. Almost twenty cars were haphazardly parked around the building. Arnold didn't like being the last to arrive, but Debra had a cooking mishap earlier in the day that had set them back an hour.

"Here we are," he announced as they pulled into an open

spot beside a white minivan. "Everyone grab something to carry."

The family entered into a bustling cabin. The senior aunts and uncles were hidden away in the kitchen preparing the turkey and side dishes. A multitude of cousins in their twenties and thirties carried drinks, desserts, and hors d'oeuvres. There were quick, frenzied greetings as everyone rushed by attempting to prepare the massive Thanksgiving feast. Depending on where one stood in the cabin, smells of pies, wine, or turkey permeated the warm atmosphere. The teenagers mostly congregated on the porch out back, while the little children ran through the field playing tag. The grandparents lounged around the blazing fireplace.

About twenty minutes after Arnold and Debra's arrival, one of the great aunts shouted from the kitchen, "Dinner time!"

Everyone, no matter the location, dropped what they were doing and assimilated in the massive dining hall. A senior member of the Morris family led everyone in prayer, and then they all dug in.

Arnold and Debra sat together with Arnold's brother, John. Soon after finishing his first helping, Arnold did a quick glance around the room, trying to find where his kids were sitting. He looked at the two kids' tables, but his two boys weren't there. He scanned the remaining tables where the adults were but could not find them.

"Did Nathan and Sam already eat?" he asked Debra.

"I don't know. I haven't seen them," she said as she surveyed the room. "Did they not hear us call for dinner?"

"I'll go find them. They're probably still out back with their damn headphones on."

Arnold got up and walked over to the kids' tables.

"Hey, do you guys know where Nathan and Sam are?" Arnold asked the group of kids.

Jill, Arnold's teenage niece, said, "They went on a walk through the woods, but they said they were coming right back."

About a mile away from the cabin where the Morris family was enjoying their Thanksgiving dinner, Barren McNeil was walking through the forest, back to where he parked his vehicle. After sitting out in the cold all morning, he had not even spotted a deer. This was his first time at this hunting location, and he was not glad that he had come. If it weren't Thanksgiving and Kim wasn't waiting on him for their small family dinner, he would stay out all day. It was a last-ditch effort, but Barren was walking as stealthily as possible, hoping a buck might stumble upon his path. He was just thinking about how ridiculous that was when he heard the snap of a branch.

Barren's ears perked up out of sheer reflex. He immediately crouched down to one knee, carefully lifting the sights on his rifle up to his eyes. Leaves rustled from the same direction as the previous sound. Barren looked but didn't see the deer. There was another small sound of a stick breaking. Something with brown fur poked out from behind a tree about thirty yards away from Barren. He aimed the gun, but the animal retreated back behind the tree. Barren sat, waiting for it to get curious again. He was breathing, but it was so shallow and controlled that it was barely audible. Time seemed frozen.

Finally, the animal emerged, and Barren fired at the movement. The animal fell to the ground with a thud, disappearing from Barren's line of sight. He quickly stood up with his gun, listening for the wounded animal. The sound of the teenage boy screaming made his blood run cold and would go on to haunt Barren for the next three years of his life. He froze as a hollow feeling sank to his stomach.

The boy screamed again.

This was not a scream from pain, but one of confusion— one seeking help. Barren snapped out of his paralysis and ran toward the wailing. He leaped over logs and dodged tree branches as he recklessly ran through the woods.

"I'm coming!" he shouted as he heard the boy begin to cry.

As he approached the scene, he saw a pair of red sneakers poking out from behind a tree.

"Oh, no, no, no," he said as he ran up to the boy on the ground.

Another boy stood screaming in shock. Barren knelt down to look at the unresponsive child and nearly vomited when he saw the dark crater in the side of the boy's head. Music was still playing from the headphones lying on the ground beside him.

Barren finally looked up at the screaming boy and saw the red mist covering his face. He wanted to say something to calm him down. He wanted to say that it was an accident. He wanted to say he was sorry. Instead, he just shook his head, mouth agape, with a frozen look of bewilderment. Barren thought he heard someone else scream from afar. He stood up and looked in the direction.

"Nathan!" Arnold Morris screamed from afar as he desperately searched for his boys. "Sam! Where are you?"

Barren stood up from beside Nathan's body. Sam walked backward into a tree and let himself slide to the ground, weeping into his knees.

"Over here!" Barren yelled to their father. "There's been an accident!"

---

The following months were an emotional whirlwind for all involved. Barren was arrested, while the Morris family grieved the loss of their child. Although Nathan's death was clearly an accident, Barren had broken the cardinal rule of hunting: always identify your target before firing. The lawyer Barren had on retainer was the best criminal defense attorney in the state. He struck a deal with the prosecution; Barren plead guilty to manslaughter and received ten years' probation and no jail time. The Morris family was satisfied with the guilty plea and never saw Barren again.

After the trial, Barren attempted to return to his life, but soon he realized that he was a pariah in his own town. He couldn't deal with the looks he'd get from people when they realized who he was and what he did. Conducting business became impossible, and he started delegating tasks to the point where he didn't even come to the office anymore. His empire crumbled.

His home life was no better. Kim tried to be there for her husband, at first. She knew what he had done was accidental, and she wanted him to move on with his life. Although it was intolerable at times to deal with the infamy, she was willing to weather the storm if he was. However, Barren sank deeper and deeper into self-pity and resentment. He began drinking more, and she bore witness to it all. Once his business disintegrated, she gave him an ultimatum: get it together or she was leaving. He was alone in the house the very next day.

It wasn't until the third anniversary of the hunting accident that he realized something had to give. He knew that how he was living was no way to live. Sitting alone in a house all day desperately trying to numb the pain with alcohol was not living—it was barely existing. He thought back to what brought him joy. He thought back to his childhood and shooting cans out in the backyard with his dad. He thought about his dad's grin when he'd nail a target. He thought about what his dad would think of him now. Without wasting any more time, he pulled his rifle out of the closet and headed back to the woods.

———•———

Barren stared at the rising sun, now fully emerged from the mountains in front of him. He took off his camo hat, shut his eyes, and let his face bask in the warm rays. Tears formed as he swayed a bit from intoxication. He opened his eyes and took a sniff of the cool autumn morning, savoring the smell of dry leaves and dirt. He picked up his rifle and continued his trek through the forest.

The tree looked different than he had remembered it three years ago. Of course, the last time he looked at it he was approaching it from a different direction. This time, he was walking from the Rusty Mountain Lodge, where he left his vehicle. He had intentionally walked the same path that Nathan and Sam had walked that fateful Thanksgiving afternoon. Now, having reached his destination, he eyed the massive tree.

The tall sycamore was older than he'd ever get and had no doubt witnessed many gunshots in its time. He doubted it had ever seen someone get killed until three years ago. Looking at it, it was no different than any of the hundreds of trees surrounding it. Only one with a knowledge of its past would find anything significant in it. He looked up at its branches high in the sky and let his vision move down the thick trunk until he was staring at a spot a little over six feet off the ground.

The bloodstains in the bark had browned and darkened, but they were still there. Even in the chaos of the shooting, Barren remembered the stain; it was forever etched in his memory.

He took a moment to appreciate the beauty in his surroundings. The birds were chirping, the sun was shining, and the leaves were doing their annual autumn dance just before being released by the inevitable wind. He slid his hand into his vest, withdrew the flask, unscrewed the top, finished off the bottle, and put it in his pocket—careful not to litter. The cool wind blew against his cheeks as he leaned back against the marked tree.

His hands were moving as if on autopilot, but he only listened to the birds. He listened to anything that distracted him from that song in Nathan's headphones that had been playing on a loop in his head for the last three years. His hands cocked the gun, and he felt the rifle's cold barrel press against the bottom of his chin. He exhaled and fired.

Barren McNeil had always been good with a gun.

# GRANDMA RUTH

Annie stood in her kitchen staring down in shock at the text message she had just received. The message was from a number that wasn't saved to her contacts, but the sender quickly identified himself. The text read: "Annie, this is your cousin, Sheldon. Long time, no see, I know. I'm afraid I have some bad news. Grandma Ruth was put into a nursing home last year, and she's not doing well. I'll just come out and say it…she's dying. Dementia. They don't expect her to live through the month. I know you all had your issues, but I thought you would at least want the opportunity to say your goodbyes. Call me if you want to know more. I'd love to catch up."

Just hearing Grandma Ruth's name brought back a whirlwind of suppressed memories. It had taken Annie a lifetime to learn how *not* to think about her. Just as she was settling down into the semblance of a normal life, she was hit with this. It just wasn't fair.

After that hollow feeling left her stomach and the initial sting dulled, Annie found it within herself to set her phone down without replying. She smelled burning eggs and realized that she had forgotten about her breakfast cooking on the stove behind her.

"Shit," she cursed as she quickly grabbed the skillet handle and dropped the steaming food in the sink.

She looked down at the scrambled eggs that were now stuck to the pan with a brown adherence. Had this been a normal morning, she might have been more frustrated; however, she had lost her appetite the moment she read that name.

She looked out the window to the driveway and front yard of her quaint little house. The sun was in the process of rising, highlighting a sheen of frost that had draped itself across the world overnight. Her eyes shifted focus, and she caught sight of her reflection in the glass. Her blue eyes and blonde hair were atypically sad and unkempt, even for morning. She was only 26 but looked like she had aged several years since reading that text message.

Footsteps suddenly bounded down the carpeted stairs behind her, and Sage appeared at the bottom. She was dressed in sweatpants and a hoodie, obviously preparing to go to the gym to train for kickboxing like she did every morning. She had long, black hair that was buzzed on one side. Her olive skin and striking features gave her an exotic look. Even having just rolled out of bed and dressed in sweats, Annie thought she looked sexy.

"Pee-yew!" Sage said entering the kitchen. "What the hell did you burn?"

Annie sidestepped the sink to let Sage have a look at the scorched eggs.

"Aww, no…and there was even enough for me in there. Double bummer," she said as she leaned toward her girlfriend to give her a good morning kiss.

She stopped when she saw the look of concern on Annie's face. She quickly forgot about the eggs.

"What's wrong?"

"My cousin, Sheldon, texted me," Annie began.

"You have a Cousin Sheldon?"

"Yes."

They had been dating for two years now, but Sage's selective memory never ceased to amaze her.

"On my mom's side. I've told you about him before."

"OK, and?"

"He told me that my Grandma Ruth is dying in a nursing home right now," she said.

Sage instinctively raised her eyebrows with sympathy and hugged Annie. It then dawned on her that Grandma Ruth was the mean old bitch that Annie said she didn't speak to. She rubbed Annie's back and tried to comfort her. After a moment, she pulled back and looked down at the petite girl.

"Isn't this the lady that disowned your mom?" Sage asked with caution.

Annie nodded her head.

"She was—*is*—a real piece of work," Annie said staring down at the floor in a daze.

Sage could see a barrage of memories fluttering through Annie's eyes like an antique film projector.

"Are you OK?"

"Yeah. I don't even know why I'm so upset over this. She's been dead to me for ten years anyway."

"I know. You've only talked to me about her once in the entire time we've been together."

"I guess it's just the finality of death, you know?" Annie said while Sage nodded her head, attempting to follow along. "When someone's alive there's always a possibility of reconciliation. When they're dead, the resentment lives on...forever."

"Well..."

"'Well,' what?"

"I mean, she's not dead yet," Sage said.

Annie's eyes widened slightly, and she began to shake her head.

"No. There's no way I'm going to see her," Annie blurted.

Sage took a step back from her girlfriend and walked over to the refrigerator to get her water bottle.

"No one is forcing you to," Sage said as she pushed herself up on the kitchen island and sat down. "I just think it would be an excellent chance to get some closure."

Annie knew she was right but stared at Sage with frustration for pushing her into doing what needed to be done. She turned back to the sink and twisted the faucet, letting the water drown her pathetic pan of eggs. She squirted some dish soap in the mix and shut it off.

"This is the last thing I want to deal with right now," she admitted as she leaned against the sink with her head down.

Sage felt bad for her but kept her distance on the island. In her experience with Annie, she had found that the less she fed into her self-pity, the quicker Annie bounced back, stronger than before.

Annie let out a deep sigh and raised her head back up to look out the window once again. The sun was shining a little brighter, and the frost looked nervous.

"I'll go," she said.

Sage hopped off the island and wrapped her arms around

her from behind. Annie rubbed her forearm.

"We'll go," Sage said and kissed her on the cheek.

———

The next day, Annie and Sage were on their way to the nursing home nearly two hours away. Sage insisted on driving, while Annie stared out the window watching the world pass by in a blurry stream. She had been in a weird funk since she received the text yesterday morning, and it was concerning Sage. Annie could tell and decided it was time to completely update Sage on her history with Grandma Ruth.

"I need to tell you something," she said, still staring out the window.

"Finally," Sage blurted out.

Annie looked over at her in surprise.

"What?" she began. "You didn't think I knew you were holding something back? I know you too well."

Annie didn't realize she was so transparent. Still, it comforted her to know that she had grown so close to her girlfriend in the last two years. She had never been this close to anyone, really.

"Anyway, continue," Sage said with a smile.

"Do you remember the reason I told you that I don't speak to Grandma Ruth?"

"Yeah. Your grandma didn't show up to your mom's funeral. Her own daughter. That's fucked up."

"Well, there's more to it than that. A lot more."

"OK, I'm ready."

"My grandpa, my mom's dad, died when my mom was only ten years old. She told me that she had overheard her parents downstairs arguing a few nights before he died. The next day, Grandma Ruth went out while grandpa stayed home from work. She said he was acting sick and was just sitting in his chair coughing and sobbing. Something else was obviously going on. She said he looked *scared*.

"Later that night, she heard them talking at first and then he started yelling. It sounded like someone fell to the ground. Then she said she just heard her mom laughing. She didn't stop. My mom couldn't take it anymore and put her head under her pillow until she fell asleep.

"The next morning, my mom went downstairs, and it was completely quiet. She walked from room to room looking for her parents, but no one was there. Finally, she headed to the kitchen to make herself some breakfast but stopped dead in her tracks at what she saw. Her dad hung by his neck from the ceiling fan above the knocked-over kitchen table. His face was purple and bloated, and his tongue dangled from his open mouth.

"My mom ran outside screaming for the neighbors. One of the ladies that lived next door heard her and went inside to see for herself. My mom waited in the front yard and heard her neighbor scream at the sight as well. They called the police, who ruled it an obvious suicide. There was no sign of struggle, and he left a note on the table below him that just said, 'I'm sorry.' Grandma Ruth came home from the grocery store to find the police in her home and her husband dead, but mom said she never saw her cry."

Sage was gripping the steering wheel and staring out the window. When she realized Annie had finished her story, she looked over at her and said, "Do you think your grandma killed your grandpa?"

"Who knows?" Annie replied. "But the one time my mom talked about that incident, I could tell she felt something wasn't right. I remember her telling me that until the night she heard them fighting, her mom was a loving mother. She told me one day she was just different. She was distant and had a blank look in her eyes. Later that night was the start of their fighting, and grandpa was dead two days later."

"That's twisted."

"That's nothing," Annie chuckled.

Sage looked over at her with concern.

"There's a lot more than just that."

Sage kept her eyes on the busy highway as Annie told her tale.

"You know I've never met my dad. I've told you I'm the product of a one-night stand. The fact that it was just my mom and I in a small house was probably the reason why we never hosted family holiday gatherings. But, when I was eleven, we had a big Thanksgiving dinner at our house. Normally, we went to my cousin Sheldon's house—his mom was my mom's sister. I'm not sure why we had it at our tiny little house that year, but we did.

"The only time I saw Grandma Ruth was on Thanksgiving and sometimes Christmas. Talking to her always weirded me out, even as a child. She just had this dead look in her eyes that made me uncomfortable. It was like I was talking to a puppet."

"That's creepy."

"You have no idea," Annie continued. "Even in a room full of people, Ruth would find a way to sit in a chair off to the side away from everyone. That Thanksgiving, I had my friend Katy from next door over. She didn't have the greatest home life, and my mom didn't care to let her stay with us whenever she wanted. No one knew—not even Katy—that I was in love with her.

"We were alone in my room after dinner. Well, almost alone. My German shepherd puppy that I had gotten for my birthday a few months before was sleeping under my bed. He must've been around three or four months old. Scooter...that was his name. Anyway, I was alone with Katy, and I just went for it. I told her that I saw something on TV and wanted to try it with her."

"I like where this is going."

"Shut up," Annie said with an embarrassed smile.

"I'm sorry," Sage said. "Continue."

"I kissed Katy, and she kissed me back. I remember how excited I felt doing that for the first time and knowing that she liked it too. We lay on the bed kissing for God knows how long. Just as her hand started to touch me under my shirt, the door swung open. We split apart like repelling magnets and sat straight up. Grandma Ruth stood in the doorway with a vague grin on her face. We tried to play it off, but we knew we were caught. Grandma Ruth looked down both sides of the hallway and then stepped into the room with us, shutting the door behind her.

"'What are you two *girls* doing?' she said to us. She knew. It was obvious that she was just fucking with us and enjoyed doing it. I lied and said that we weren't doing anything. She walked right over to me, sat on the bed, and stared down at me, smiling. I remember hearing Scooter growl his little growl from under the bed, obviously sensing something was wrong. Grandma Ruth tilted her head as she looked down at the sound coming from below and then back at me. She looked at Katy, who was mortified. Grandma Ruth smiled wider.

"'There will be none of this in my family,' she said. 'Dykes burn in Hell. Do you two little girls want to go to Hell?'

Her dead eyes came to life with this kind of talk. She spoke like Hell was just a place the next town over.

"'No, Grandma Ruth,' I said to her. She looked at Katy.

"'How about you, little girl? Do you want to burn in Hell?' she asked.

"'No, ma'am,' Katy said.

"Grandma Ruth stuck her pinky finger out to Katy and said, 'Pinky promise?' Katy extended her pinky, and they shook on it.

"'Your turn,' she said to me with her pinky right in my face. As soon as I raised my pinky she grabbed my wrist and put my finger into her mouth. She covered my mouth with her other hand and bit down into my bone. She shook her head back and forth like a dog.

"Dear Jesus," Sage said in disgust.

"After a few muffled screams, she let go. My pinky was hanging on by a flap of skin. She spit my own blood all over my bedspread and then used it to wipe her face. Scooter shot out from under the bed snarling at her. She snatched him by the back of the neck and lifted him off the ground. Before he could nip at her hands, she snapped his neck and dropped him on the floor. Katy was curled up in the corner of the room sobbing the whole time.

"Oh my God," Sage said. "How did that bitch get away with that?"

"She told us that we were going to tell my mom that we were playing with Scooter, and he went mad. He clamped his jaws on my pinky and tried to rip it off. Grandma Ruth heard the commotion and came in and yanked Scooter off, breaking his neck in the struggle. If we didn't say that every bit of that was true, she would tell the whole world that we were gay. We would live a life of shame before an eternity in Hell."

Sage sat in the driver's seat heartbroken and in shock.

"We did exactly what she wanted us to do," Annie continued. "And after that night, I never saw Katy again."

Sage tried to be as comforting as she could while driving on a freeway. She put her hand on Annie's leg and rubbed her as she switched her gaze back and forth from Annie to the road.

"I'm so sorry. I didn't understand," Sage said.

Annie wiped the forming tears out of her eyes.

"I didn't see Grandma Ruth for a few years. She quit coming to family functions or just wasn't invited...I don't know. I do know that from that Thanksgiving on, my mom's drinking got worse and worse. She started off drinking every night after work, and then I would see her drinking during the day. It got to the point that she always smelled like wine. I remember not having a lot of food in the house and her violent mood swings. I learned to stay out of sight when she was at her worst. There were tons of random men that came by nightly. This was my life until the age of fifteen.

"One night, my mom was in a really bad headspace. She was even more drunk than usual and going off on this tangent about how men are scum."

"Sounds like a wise lady," Sage quipped.

Annie ignored her and continued talking.

"She started yelling at the TV for some reason. I forget. I just remember her throwing her wine glass at the screen but missing completely. The glass shattered on the wall, and she became even more enraged. I was in the middle of getting up to sneak away to my room when I heard her cuss and wince in pain. I looked over at her and saw that she had sliced open her palm while picking up the shards of glass. I quickly called my older cousin, Sheldon, to see if he and his mom would come over to help my mom. They agreed to come immediately, but I didn't know that Grandma Ruth was at their house that night. It just so happens that they were trying to talk her into moving into an assisted living facility after falling around her house a few times.

"Sheldon, his mom, and Grandma Ruth showed up about twenty minutes after I ran to my room. Sheldon immediately came upstairs and hugged me. I could hear my mom and his mom talking at first and then yelling. Sheldon's mom came marching up the stairs and into my room. She told me that I was going to stay the night with them and let my mom get better. Just as I stood up to pack a bag, we all heard the front door open, and my mom's car start in the driveway.

"We ran down the steps to find that my mom had fled. I didn't think I could get any more scared until I noticed Grandma Ruth sitting on a chair in the corner of the room looking down at the bloody glass on the floor, giggling to herself.

"Oh my God."

"My mom hadn't driven a few miles past our house when she ran a red light and was hit from the side. I was told she died on impact. The other driver was wearing a seatbelt and only had minor injuries, thank God.

"My mom's funeral was a few days later. Grandma Ruth wasn't there, but that's obviously not the real reason we don't speak. I preferred that she *wasn't* there actually. The night my mom died was the last time I saw her. I guess she agreed to go to assisted living, and I went to live with Sheldon and his mom until I left for college three years later."

Sage hit her blinker and drove the car onto the exit ramp. She pulled into the closest gas station and put it in park. She looked over at Annie and felt so bad for everything the poor girl had been through.

"I'm so sorry that happened to you," Sage said as she leaned across the console and hugged Annie. Annie started to weep into Sage's shoulder. "Let's turn around right now and go home. I'm so sorry that I even suggested this. I had no idea what really happened. I'm a dick for pushing you."

Annie broke the hug and pulled back, wiping the tears away.

"No. We're going."

"But why?"

"I'm not doing this for her," Annie explained. "I need to be free of this hate."

This made Sage tear up, and she couldn't remember the last time she cried. She forcefully grabbed Annie, gave her a hug, and then kissed her on the lips. She stopped and looked deep into Annie's eyes.

"I will never be as strong as you are," she said and then hugged her again.

———————

The nursing home was a puke-green eyesore hidden on a hill away from the city. No one would know it was there unless they were looking for it. It was as good as forgotten, just like most of its residents.

Sage pulled her car into the lot and put it in park. She turned off her GPS and looked over at Sage.

"It's not too late to go back," Sage said.

Annie nodded her head in acknowledgement. After a moment, she said, "I have to do this."

"Well then, what are we waiting for?" Sage asked as she opened her car door and stepped out into the cool evening air.

Annie followed suit, and the two ladies walked hand in hand toward the main entrance. That hollow feeling hit Annie's stomach with each step they took. She suddenly felt like she was going to have a panic attack. Sage could sense Annie's discomfort coming through her clammy palms, and she gave her hand a comforting squeeze. Annie remembered to breathe and kept trudging forward.

The automated sliding doors opened so slowly that Sage nearly walked into them. Everything seemed to be operating at a reduced pace. As soon as they crossed the threshold, they were greeted by a stale, humid air that hung thick throughout the building. Annie couldn't believe how run-down the place was. For a moment, she felt sorry for her grandmother.

Sage looked at the stained yellow vinyl floor, then the wooden-paneled walls, and the light green ceiling.

"Yuck," she said a bit too loudly as a barely conscious front desk worker looked up at them.

"Can I help you?" the overweight, middle-aged woman asked.

"No, we're good," Sage replied on Annie's behalf. "Just headed to room…" she said looking at Annie.

Annie quickly looked down at her last text message from Sheldon to see which room Grandma Ruth was in.

"Room 417," Annie said.

"Elevator's at the end of the hall," the woman mumbled and shifted her attention back to the antiquated computer screen on her desk.

The air inside the elevator made the air in the lobby seem crisp and fresh. The metal doors slid shut as the two women shuffled inside. Annie had to cover her nose to keep from becoming sick.

"Dear God," Sage began. "How many times do you think someone shit themselves in this thing?"

"Stop. I'm trying not to puke," Annie replied as she hit the button for the fourth floor.

She watched the little lights ding their way from the first floor to the second, to the third. She prayed for the elevator to malfunction. In her mind, the cable attached to their cart snapped, and the elevator dropped three stories. Even that was a less terrifying outcome than the prospect of being in the same room as Grandma Ruth. As the fourth-floor button lit up, she was abruptly aware that she was about to face her biggest fear.

The doors slowly slid open.

Annie and Sage stepped into the dimly lit hallway. A few staff members sat huddled around a TV at one end of the hall. Random shouts and moans echoed from various rooms. Annie realized that this was the floor where people go to die. She looked up at the arrow pointing toward room 417.

"It's this way," she said, turning right.

Sage walked beside her in defense mode.

After what felt like the fastest walk of Annie's life, she arrived at room 417. They stood there staring at the brown door with the white room number. Sage looked over at Annie. Annie took a deep breath and looked back at her. She nodded, and Sage opened the door.

The foul stench of mildew and excrement immediately wafted in their faces. Annie didn't let it faze her as she stepped into the room. The small bathroom was on their immediate right, and the bottom of the hospital bed protruded from around the corner ahead of them. She could see two feet under a fuzzy green hospital blanket on the bed. She stayed focused and planted one foot after another.

"Grandma Ruth?"

The feet did not move.

A machine was beeping, and the TV was playing a soundless black and white TV show, but other than that, there was no sign of life. She rounded the corner and felt her stomach knot up. Sage followed with a comforting hand on Annie's lower back.

Grandma Ruth lay on her back staring at the ceiling. Her small, frail body was motionless under the blanket. Occasionally, her chest would rise slightly and take a shallow breath. There were tubes and cords running from the bed to the machines beside her. Her mouth hung agape, and a blank expression was frozen on her face. All signs of life of the once imposing force were now gone.

Annie's nerves immediately settled when she saw how close to death the woman on the bed was. She even felt a sense of pity as she looked at her relative at the end of her life.

"Grandma Ruth."

There was no response.

She walked around the side of the bed and sat down beside the old woman. She placed her hand on Ruth's thigh, but there was still no response to stimuli.

"Grandma Ruth, it's Annie."

Annie looked hard and deep into her grandmother's unblinking eyes thinking maybe, just maybe, a bit of the force that was Grandma Ruth was still in there.

"Are you in there?"

Nothing happened.

She looked back at Sage, who stood against the wall at the

foot of the bed. She could tell Sage was uncomfortable by death. Suddenly, Annie had become the strong one in the room. She looked back at her grandmother.

"Grandma Ruth, I've come to tell you goodbye," she began.

A droplet of drool started to form at the corner of Ruth's mouth.

"I've come to tell you that I know we had our differences in life. I don't understand why certain things happened the way they did, but I've accepted that I can't change them."

Tears welled in Annie's eyes as she continued.

"When I think back on our relationship, I don't want to continue to feel this negativity anymore. I don't want to feel scared, and I don't want to hate. I just can't keep living with it," she said as a tear rolled down her cheek.

Sage took a few steps forward and put a trembling hand on Annie's shoulder.

"I've come to tell you that I don't know what happened in your life. I don't why you did what you did or why you acted the way you did. Maybe you were sick, or maybe someone mistreated you—I'll never know. But I want you to know that I forgive you. I forgive you, and I know Mom forgives you too."

Annie began sobbing, and Sage felt herself tear up as well. She leaned over close to Ruth's face.

"I pray that you find peace in the afterlife," she whispered and then kissed her grandma on her forehead.

She pulled back and began crying uncontrollably. Sage leaned over and gave her a firm hug. Annie wiped the tears from her face, preparing to get up.

She stopped when she felt a slight movement on the bed. She looked at Grandma Ruth who was somehow turning her head to face Annie, ever so slightly. The old woman's eyes found Annie's, and she just stared blankly.

"Grandma Ruth?"

The sound of Ruth emptying her bowels broke the silence in the room. Annie felt the vibration on the bed and was hit by the foul stench that followed.

"I'll get a nurse," Sage said as she walked out of the room to seek help.

Annie stood up from the bed and slowly pulled Ruth's covers down.

"We'll get you cleaned up, Grandma," she said.

She pulled the covers down past Ruth's waist and stared in shock as Ruth withdrew her hand from her diaper and smeared a wad of excrement across Annie's face.

She recoiled in horror and screamed as she fervently wiped the feces from her face, the blanket falling back down on top of Ruth. The brown mush was caked in her nostrils, and it started to run into the corners of her mouth. She bolted out of the room suppressing the urge to vomit, leaving Grandma Ruth cackling on the bed.

---

The two women drove home through the night in silence. Annie sat in the passenger seat, staring through the windshield into the black abyss. Even though Sage had helped her wash it off in the hospital restroom, she still smelled foul. Sage pretended not to be bothered by it.

"I just don't see how she could physically do...*that*," Sage said, breaking the silence.

Annie looked over at her in disbelief.

"You don't believe me?" Annie asked.

"I didn't say that. I just don't see how she could physically lift up her arms, let alone a pile of shit."

After a few moments of silence, Annie started to smile in the dark. Sage looked over at her and saw her smiling and smiled back. Annie immediately burst out laughing. She didn't know why and certainly had nothing to laugh about, but she welcomed the change in emotion. If anything, she was laughing only out of sheer relief at having made it through that situation. Sage started chuckling herself but was more concerned with the hysteric tone under Annie's guffawing.

"You know what we're going to do tonight? I mean, after we go home and take a shower," Sage said.

"What?"

"Go out and get fucked up."

"I'm in."

---

Three hours and one shower later, the two ladies were inside their favorite bar not too far from their house. Annie sat at a table in a dark corner sipping her beer as she watched Sage dance with one of their friends. She knew Sage was going to walk away from this dance with some type of drug. After she gulped the last few drinks of her fifth beer, she stood up and stumbled to the restroom.

Sage walked in just as Annie flushed the toilet.

"Stay in there, hussy," Sage said from behind the stall.

Annie sat on the cold seat in an intoxicated stupor until Sage entered the stall, shutting the door behind her.

"I have something for you," Sage said with a smile as she pulled out a neatly rolled joint.

She lit the end, inhaled deeply, and straddled Annie, whose pants were still down by her ankles. Sage motioned for Annie to open her mouth. Annie did as she was told just in time for Sage to blow a warm blast of smoke into her lungs. She leaned back against the toilet, holding in the smoke. Sage put the joint in Annie's hand and stood up.

"Let's get out of here," Sage said. "I need to get you in bed."

Annie bobbed in and out of consciousness during the car ride home. She briefly came to life during sex back at their house but nodded out immediately after she climaxed. She didn't know how long she had been out when something suddenly jarred her from her delirium.

She felt a persistent buzzing sensation against her face and realized that she had somehow fallen asleep with her phone on her pillow. She pulled the device away from her face and stared at the screen. The dim light was a supernova to her sensitive eyes. Her migraine pounded like a snare drum. She could barely make out the text on the screen through her blurred vision. After finding her bearings, the letters on the screen started to formulate words.

The text message was from Sheldon. "Grandma Ruth passed this evening," was all it said. She didn't know if she was asleep or awake anymore. She sat up and blinked the sleep out of her eyes. Again, she looked at the message in disbelief. *Just a few hours ago the old bitch was feisty enough to smear shit on my face, and now she's gone.* The longer she was awake, the more relief she felt.

She looked around at her surroundings and realized that she was in her bedroom. Moonlight shone through the sliding glass doors that led to their balcony. Even with the heavy blinds, the penetrating light was enough to illuminate the room. She looked over at Sage, snoring away on the bed beside her.

"Sage," she said with a gruff voice.

She shook her sleeping girlfriend, but she was out cold. Annie cleared her throat so she could speak a little louder.

"Sage," she said, raising her voice.

Sage just rolled to her side, unwilling to part from dreamland. Annie exhaled a defeated sigh and decided that this conversation would have to wait until morning. She turned her phone off and sat it on the nightstand. Just as she was about to fall back on her pillow, she heard a scratching sound from the sliding glass doors.

She looked at the doors obscured by the thick blinds. Not as much moonlight was shining through now, and it took Annie a few seconds to realize why: a dark silhouette stood outside the doors, peering in through the blinds. Annie felt her heart freeze as she struggled to breathe.

The figure lifted an arm and started scratching the glass in small circles.

"Annie," a hoarse voice whispered from outside. "I know you're in there, sweet little Annie."

It chuckled.

Annie closed her eyes and started to cry.

"I'm dreaming. I'm dreaming. I'm dreaming."

"You're not dreaming, little girl," the figure said in a voice that Annie knew but didn't want to acknowledge.

"*You* forgive *me?*" it continued. "Ha!"

"You're not here!" Annie screamed. "You're dead."

The handle on the door started to jiggle. Annie, realizing that she didn't lock the door, lunged out of bed. She grabbed the handle and held the door in place while she locked it from the inside. She was hyperventilating and barely had any energy in her weary body.

The door handle continued to shake, and Annie held on with everything in her.

"You're gone," Annie began. "You're not here. You're gone. I forgave you, and you're at peace."

The room was silent. Annie opened her eyes and looked out through the glass door for the first time. No one was there. She suddenly felt clearer than she had all night. Relief washed over her as she thought back on all the booze, marijuana, and stress that had taken her system hostage this evening.

"Fuck this. Sage, you're getting up," Annie said as she turned around to wake her sleeping girlfriend.

She froze when she saw Sage's nude body hovering in the darkness as if crucified on an invisible cross above their bed.

Her eyes were a glowing white, dead and fixed, just like Ruth's earlier that night.

Ruth's cackling voice was somehow coming from Sage's lips.

"You'll never be free, you little *freak*," Grandma Ruth taunted as Sage's body floated toward Annie.

Annie slowly backed into the corner unable to accept what she was seeing.

Sage's mouth dropped open and spewed vomit down her breasts. Annie screamed as she slid down the wall, sinking to the floor. Grandma Ruth chuckled as Sage's body began to rotate like she was on a gyroscope until she was completely upside down, her arms still extended outward.

"I'm taking this dyke to Hell where she belongs," she hissed.

"No!" Annie screamed, finally getting the strength to face her attacker. "Take me instead."

Sage's head slowly began to twist like her neck was going to snap.

"Take me, Ruth!" Annie screamed as she stood up. "Take *me*!"

Annie desperately lunged at Sage's body but was stopped short by an unseen force gripping her neck. She watched Sage get tossed across the room and onto the bed like she was weightless. She screamed in a primal rage as something tightened around her neck, and then her world went black.

The next morning, Sage awoke to a hangover she didn't know was possible. Two seconds after opening her eyes, she rolled to the right and vomited all over the floor. Her neck was sore, and she had the worst headache of her life. She looked down at her body and was shocked to discover that she had vomited on herself in her sleep. *At least I'm not dead,* she realized; *lots of people die by vomiting in their sleep.*

She looked at the empty spot in the bed where Annie was supposed to be. Before she could guess where her girlfriend was, she noticed something in the middle of the room near the sliding glass doors. Her jaw dropped with a high-pitched shriek as she stared at the horrific sight before her.

Annie's dead body hung from the ceiling fan. An orange extension cord was pulled so tightly around her neck that her eyes bulged out of her purple face. As she dangled limply from the unstable fan, Sage noticed something carved into Annie's forearms. On one arm was the word "APOLOGY", and on the other was "ACCEPTED."

# PERCEPTO!

Orry Verdune rested his elbows on the sticky bar, twirling the amber bourbon around in his glass, like so many sad sacks before him. But he was by no means a regular, by God. *Not me,* he thought, looking to his right at the other slump-overs. He was dressed nicely: clean-shaven with freshly trimmed grey hair. It was obvious that *he* was just having a bad day. Clint, the too-handsome-for-this-small-town bartender, had been keeping Orry company for the last hour, waiting, as a good barkeep does, for him to sell his woeful wares. Orry downed the rest of his third glass.

"Need another, Orry?" Clint asked as he wiped his way up the bar.

"Make it a double."

"You sure, buddy?"

Orry stared at him with cold, black eyes.

"Come over here, Clint," he said as he sluggishly waved his hand.

Clint closed in on him.

"What's up?"

Orry looked to his left and right as if he were about to vocalize some highly classified intel.

"Rosie's cheating on me."

A weight lifted off him as soon as he said it. He felt his eyes starting to water. Clint was the first person he had told, and he doubted he would tell anyone else. No, Clint was the only guy around here who seemed to give a damn. Even though Orry wasn't a bar regular, the theater he owned was across the street from Clint's establishment. The two men shot the breeze almost every day on the sidewalk out front.

"She forgot her phone at home this morning," Orry explained while staring at the glass in front of him. "I was getting ready for work, and I heard it vibrate." Orry made a vibrating "BFFFFF" sound with his lips. "BFFFFF. BFFFFF," he repeated. "I picked it up, and it said it was a message from her sister. I opened it, naturally. It said, 'Good morning, beautiful.' Now I thought that that was an odd thing for Charlene to text Rosie, so I scrolled up through the conversation. It was nothing but back-and-forth flirting and dirty talk and pictures. Oh, God, the pictures. She was standing in front of the mirror in this gorgeous white dress she bought for me the day I retired. She was pulling the front of it down and showing him her cleavage. *My dress*...the one she bought for *me*!"

Orry put his face in his hands. He hadn't made eye contact since he started his story, but he slowly dragged his gaze up to meet Clint's. Clint seemed unfazed by the information.

"Did you hear me?"

"Yeah. Yeah, Orry, I heard you."

Now Clint looked around before he spoke.

"It's just that, I sort of knew that was going on."

Orry contorted his boozy face.

"Elaborate," he said.

"Orry, the whole town knows for Christ's sake."

Orry was baffled.

"They didn't necessarily keep it quiet, pal. And this is a

small town after all. I'm sorry. I didn't want to be the one to tell you. Didn't figure it was my place," he said as he grabbed a full bottle of bourbon from the wall behind him.

He sat it in front of Orry.

"On the house...as long as you ain't driving home."

Orry gulped the entire glass and quickly refilled it.

"I'm just going back to the theater tonight," he said. "But tell me, who is it?"

At first, Clint didn't know what he was asking, but just as he figured it out, Orry cut him off.

"Nevermind, doesn't matter..." he trailed off as he took another drink.

Clint nodded his head and resumed wiping down the bar. Infidelity was a common theme amongst his patrons. It was partially why he never planned on getting married.

"It's fitting," Orry said after a moment of silence.

"What's that?" Clint asked.

"I've been a joke to this town my whole fuckin' life. Why stop now?"

"Come on, now, Orry. You've got a lot going for you."

Orry scoffed.

"I'm an old cripple with a cheating wife and a dying movie theater."

"Nah, you can't look at it like that. Number one: You're a veteran. Number two: You've got all that money from your injury settlement," Clint said referring to Orry's forced retirement from the electric company ten years ago.

Orry had been working on a breaker at the top of a powerline when it malfunctioned and zapped him twenty feet to the ground. He broke several bones in his back and legs and suffered nerve damage. It left him with a permanent limp and constant trouble gripping things with his left arm.

"Number three: You own your own movie theater. Number four: You've got all your hair, and you're in shape. All of this makes you a fine catch in my book."

Orry almost smiled. That was the kindest thing anyone had said to him in many years.

"Thank you, Clint," he said. "Truth is...Rosie has burnt through most of that settlement money. The theater hasn't been profitable in two years. If it wasn't my passion, I'd sell it today. There's no money there. Everyone can sit at home and stream their movies. Why would they want to go to my old theater? No, much like my marriage, my time in the theater business is coming to an end."

He finished off the rest of his bourbon.

Clint was at a loss for words. Another patron down the bar called for a refill.

"Be right back," he said, and Orry nodded.

He looked around the small bar at the fifteen or twenty people spread throughout the establishment. A young couple was playing pool. A few of his old work pals were sitting at a table in the corner with a pitcher of beer, laughing, enjoying having survived another shift, and pretending not to see him. Lots of familiar faces and a few strangers sat or stood here and there. In this moment, Orry hated them all.

He thought about when he was in fourth grade and had an accident in his pants at school. Those kids teased him for years. He'd be in conversation when someone would randomly say, "Hey, remember when Orry shit his pants in Ms. Gerkin's class?"

Not to mention the time in high school when he was at a party in the woods and walked up and saw Mitchell Legg naked, mounting *his* girlfriend behind some bushes. What a fool he was for thinking she was the one. He tried to turn around and pretend he didn't see anything, but one of the other guys witnessed it and shouted, "Hey, Mitch is banging Sarah!" A crowd of kids circled the scene and watched, all sipping their red cups of keg beer and cheering on the show.

It was easy for him to join the Army and skip town for a few years.

When he came back, he got a job working on the power lines and met Rosie. Things finally seemed to be turning around for him. There were regular post-shift gatherings, Rosie introduced him to her friends and family, and, for the first time, Orry started to feel connected to this town.

It all ended the moment he was zapped off that goddamn electric pole. People made jokes about him again. Kids would mimic his gimpy walk. He was sure that he overheard someone in the supermarket say that the shock had made him start shitting his pants like that time back in grade school. And then there was the nasty rumor that his injury had rendered him impotent. He never discovered the source of that one.

It was no surprise that he loved to get lost in movies. For two hours at a time, he could be anyone, go anywhere, just shut up his mind. Throughout his whole life, movies were his only reprieve. Once he got his massive settlement check from the power company, he bought the old theater on Main Street and made it his own. Rosie thought it was a foolish investment, of course, but Orry satisfied her by giving her more access to the money. That old theater was the closest thing to joy that he had in his life.

Clint patted Orry on the back. Orry shot up, blinking, and realized that he was about to pass out in his memories.

"You OK, pal?"

Orry wiped his face and waved him off.

"Been a joke my whole life," he muttered.

Clint leaned in.

"Why don't you just leave, then?" he asked. "I wouldn't waste my life in a town that made me miserable. Divorce the bitch, take what's left of your money, and go wherever you want."

Orry smiled at the thought.

"I wouldn't give them the satisfaction," he finally concluded. "If I leave, it won't be because I'm tucking in my tail and fleeing. I'd leave on my terms. Hell, they'd probably applaud me on my way out anyhow."

Clint nodded as Orry stood up from the barstool and grabbed the bottle of bourbon.

"I'm gonna go watch a movie," he said. "I get to pick from a new shipment of classic horror films that I ordered for Halloween."

"Sounds like a good plan. Be careful out there."

Orry pulled out several twenties and laid them on the bar. He headed for the door and swore that he could feel everyone staring and laughing as he left.

A gust of wind slammed the theater's front door behind him. Orry stumbled across the clean lobby, immune to the smell of buttery popcorn embedded in the walls. He approached a door between two pinball games, pulled it open, and walked upstairs to the projection room. The dank sweatbox lit up as the fluorescent lights flickered on. Orry stepped in and felt the joy of his happy place. Here, he was the director of the show. He looked down at the unopened box beside his rolling chair.

"Hello, gorgeous," he said as he bent down and pulled the tape off the cardboard, opening the folds and glancing inside.

There were several canisters in the box. He counted four different films and checked the titles: all early Vincent Price horror features. A smile crept across his face. Even though he doubted many people would attend his Halloween Vincent Price marathon, he was excited for it. He noticed that one of the canisters had a separate, smaller box beside it.

"Hmm," he grumbled as he withdrew the foot-long, rectangular box. "What's this?"

There was a note written down the side in black permanent marker: "GOES WITH THE TINGLER." *The Tingler* was one of the titles he had ordered. He looked at the reels in the box marked "TINGLER" and then back to the small box in his hand. Curiously, he pried it open.

Orry held out his palm and dumped the contents. Three identical metal devices and a rolled-up bundle of papers fell out. He dropped the box and picked up one of the little metal things with his other hand. The object was rusty and shaped like a hockey puck. There were two spots on the sides with small strips of Velcro.

"What the hell?" he said to himself as he carefully placed the odd things on the projection desk.

He unrolled the bundle of papers and realized they were stapled together. "INSTRUCTIONS FOR SHOWING THE TINGLER" was typed front and center on the first page. Something clicked in Orry's head: a vague recollection of how *The Tingler* was theatrically released in 1959.

He flipped to the next page and read the table of contents. There were four parts. He read, "PART 1: HOW TO INSTALL THE PERCEPTO! MOTORS."

"That's what it was!" Orry exclaimed as he now remembered what the devices were.

During his stint in the Army, he would read lots of film magazines in his downtime. He remembered the story of how horror director William Castle would use gimmicks to generate some buzz for his pictures in the 50s and 60s. During the finale of *House on Haunted Hill,* for example, a skeleton with glowing red eyes would suddenly fly across the theater on a wire. With *13 Ghosts,* movie-goers were given special "ghost viewers." At the climax of *Homicidal,* viewers were offered 45 seconds to flee the theater to demand a refund before seeing the really scary bits.

But it was the legend of *The Tingler* that was most appealing to Orry. The film was introduced by William Castle, who told the audience that some of them would feel a shocking sensation during the climax of the film. Some of the theaters in larger cities were given these tiny motors taken from airplanes, and they would be attached to the bottom of a few seats. In addition to vibrating seats, the film itself was interactive. At certain points the screen would cut to black and Vincent Price's voice would instruct the audience to scream for their lives to keep the tingler away. Castle dubbed this gimmick "Percepto!"

Orry glanced at the tiny motors. They were in rough shape. He doubted they would even work, but they were thrilling to own, nonetheless. He looked back down at the instruction manual meant for theater owners of 1959. He flipped through the short pamphlet looking over the step-by-step directions for the projectionist's role in the movie's presentation.

"What a find," he said.

Wasting no more time, Orry grabbed the film reels for *The Tingler* and loaded the first one into the projector, and turned it on. The screen lit up white, and the theater was glowing as the movie began. Orry grabbed his bottle of bourbon, settled into his seat in the projection booth, and took a drink. Just as expected, William Castle appeared on screen and warned the empty seats of the show ahead of them.

The movie played on as Orry watched and fought away drunken drowsiness. The plot of the film involved Vincent Price's character, Dr. Warren, discovering that every human being has a parasite latched onto their spines that would vibrate and grow as the host became scared. The only way to relieve the pressure from the bug and prevent it from snapping the spine in two was to scream. Dr. Warren dubbed this creature "The Tingler." Presently, Dr. Warren was watching his wife kiss another man outside of his own home. Orry's eyes opened wide, feeling the character's pain to his core, and his heart constricted.

"Cheating bitch," he muttered.

The film played on.

During the climax, a mute woman was scared to death, killed by the tingler that had grown up her spine because she was unable to scream and relieve the pressure. It was revealed that her husband orchestrated the whole affair after learning of Dr. Warren's parasitic discovery.

Orry didn't realize he was smiling. He wished *his* wife had a tingler. He would figure out a way to scare Rosie and make that bug break through her cheating heart. Just as he was getting lost in his fantasy, the screen cut to black. Vincent Price's voice began pleading for the theater audience to scream. Orry realized that this was when the motors would've begun zapping theater patrons in 1959. A sudden vibration against his leg startled him so much, he nearly dropped the whiskey bottle.

"My phone," he laughed as he reached for the vibrating device in his pocket.

He pulled it out and looked at the display. It was almost three in the morning, and he had a text message from Clint. Orry smiled at seeing his friend's name. *Thank God for Clint,* he thought, *He's probably checking to make sure I'm OK.* He opened it and shrank as he read the message that was obviously not meant for him: "Hey honey…sorry, running late again. The bar was full of sad sacks tonight. Tell you about it later. On my way soon."

"'Sad sack?'" he repeated.

He couldn't believe it. The one guy he thought was his friend referred to him as nothing more than one of the "sad sacks."

The movie came back from black. On screen, a theater full of frantic patrons were screaming and fleeing the scurrying tingler on the loose. Orry slid his phone back into his pocket without responding to Clint. His eyes drifted over to the three motors on the table.

"Percepto," he whispered with a grin.

———

Orry didn't sleep that night, despite the booze's best effort. When Rosie came downstairs the next morning, he was sitting at the kitchen table wearing the same clothes as the day before. She noticed the dark circles under his eyes and his overall disheveled appearance. Even so, when he looked at her, his eyes brightened with an enthusiasm she hadn't seen in years. He had no phone or newspaper out; it was like he had been waiting for her to get up.

"Hi, honey," he smiled.

He pulled the other chair out for her.

"Have a seat. I've got some news."

Rosie looked at him quizzically.

"Are you OK?" she asked.

Orry brushed her off.

"The best I've been in years, baby."

She took three steps toward him and sat down. The smell of the booze punched her in the face.

"Jesus, Orry, did you even sleep last night?"

"Not a peep, and let me tell you why."

She stared at him, waiting for clarification for this odd behavior. He reached out and took both of her hands in his.

"Rosie, I met with a land developer from out-of-town. His name is Mr. Castle."

"OK…"

"He wants to buy the theater. Said he *has* to have the lot."

"You want to sell the theater?"

"Baby, for this price, I'd be a fool not to!"

"What price?"

"It's seven figures," he said with raised eyebrows.

"What?" she exclaimed as she pulled her hands out of his and started laughing. "Orry, honey, he could buy the whole block with seven figures. He's pulling your leg."

Orry smiled and withdrew a folded piece of paper from his pocket. He slid it across the table to her.

"I signed the contract last night," he said.

Rosie looked down at the typed document that was a bill of sale for the land plot on which the theater was located as well as all the assets on it. The purchase amount was 1.2 million dollars, and there were two signatures at the bottom: Orry's and a Mr. W. Castle. Her eyes widened, and she covered her gaping mouth with her hand.

"We'll get the check in ten business days, but, honey, please keep this between us," he instructed.

Rosie was still in shock.

"This doesn't make sense," she said. "Why would anyone pay this much?"

Orry pulled the contract back before she could analyze it any further.

"Apparently, there's some tech company placing a warehouse right outside of town, and they're buying up all the land."

Reality finally settled in for her, and she looked at him like she did when they first fell in love. She ran around to his side of the table and hugged him, letting out a squeal of joy. Orry smiled, almost fooled by his own ruse, and patted her on the back.

"Remember, you have to keep this between us for now," he said.

"My lips are sealed. So, what's next?"

"This town's been good to me," he lied. "I want the theater to go out with a bang. I'm going to throw a farewell party and screen one final feature. Not charge a dime. First come, first serve."

"Do you think anyone will come?"

"If they won't come for the free movie, they'll definitely come for the free food and booze."

Rosie bristled at the thought but did her best to not ruffle her millionaire's feathers.

"You're going to give away all that?" she asked.

"Absolutely," he began. "We've been blessed, and it's the least I can do."

"OK."

"And I had another idea,"

Her heart sank in anticipation of whatever dumb proposition was about to come out of his mouth.

"You know how you've always wanted to see the world?"

"Yeah," she smiled.

"I want you to do that. I want you to travel wherever you want, do whatever you want, with whoever you want," he said with no hint of resentment.

"You mean *you* wouldn't go?"

"I'm too old and slow and crippled. I'd just slow you down," he smiled. "Besides, I saw the world when I was in the service."

"Orry, I don't know what to say," she said as she began to fantasize about her future plans.

"Would you like that?" he asked, doing his best to conceal his interrogatory intention. "Would you like to see the world by yourself? You out there living your life while I stay here?"

"Of course, I would, my love," she said without thinking twice.

His plan was finalized.

"Then, I only have one request."

"What's that?"

"At the farewell party, wear that white dress you wore when we went out for my retirement dinner. You still have that dress, right?"

She looked at her husband, unsure of whether or not she had picked up on something beneath the surface.

"Of course, I do," she replied. "And of course, I'll wear it for you."

"Then it's settled," he smiled.

———·—

The night of the party, Orry stood outside the theater entrance, greeting everyone as they came in and handing out free admission tickets. He smiled at each guest, especially the ones who had wronged him. He suppressed any negative feelings. He had to. Once the last person in line entered, he walked in behind them.

There was a massive buffet lining one of the walls and a fully stocked bar manned by Clint on the other. Orry stayed back, watching the townspeople mingle in his lobby. He noticed Rosie in the corner talking and laughing with the young veterinarian—Orry couldn't remember his name. The veterinarian discretely placed his hand on Rosie's lower back, and she quickly brushed it off.

The corner of Orry's mouth twitched slightly. He walked across the crowded lobby, smiling at the fair-weather crowd. Rosie took a step away from the vet when she saw her husband.

"I'm about to move everyone into the theater. Sit wherever you want. I'll be in the projection booth," he said.

"OK, honey."

He briefly looked at the vet, who was trying not to look at him. Orry winked and then headed toward the door leading upstairs. Before he went in, he addressed the crowd with his drink in hand.

"Attention, everyone!"

The crowd quieted and gradually looked toward the source of the sound.

"I want to thank you all for coming to the closing night of my beloved establishment. At this time, I ask that you take your seats in the theater," he said with all the showmanship of William Castle in his prime. "The film you will be seeing is the 1959 classic, *The Tingler,* starring Vincent Price. If you're not familiar with the history of this movie, the director made sure the audiences of the time had an interactive experience. I have arranged the same for you, but I'll let him explain that during the film's introduction. Now...the show is about to begin!"

Everyone clapped and then filed through the propped-open doors. Rosie thought about that name: William Castle. It rang a bell, but she decided not to dwell on it.

The theater was a throwback to the golden age of cinema. The green velvet walls were dramatically lit by house lights. The rows of connected metal seats with their foamy red cushions were all on the same level; there was no stadium seating here. Orry had no interest in digital movies. Only projected film graced this massive white screen. He knew the lack of new releases hurt his business, but he was never in it for the money.

Orry watched everyone from the booth above. As soon as most of them were seated, he dimmed the lights and started the projector. Sure enough, William Castle appeared on the screen and issued his preface to the show. The audience chuckled and slurped their drinks as the show continued. Orry watched Clint slip in the back door and take a seat. He smiled knowing that his old "buddy" would make it in time.

The movie played on, and a quick hour went by. Orry had been half watching the drunken crowd talk too much and half watching the film. He knew the climax was coming. On screen, Dr. Warren was hurriedly running around the fictional theater trying to find the tingler. The screen cut to black as the character was about to address the audience. This was the moment when the Percepto! motors would begin their buzzing, giving a few audience members a gentle jolt.

Orry looked at the three motors still sitting on the desk beside the projector, definitely *not* attached to the bottom of any seats. Those wouldn't provide a big enough shock for this modern audience. He looked out into the theater at the slight, unnoticed bulge under the carpeted red runners on either side of the audience. Only he knew of these hidden power lines that were attached to several new generators out back. Only he knew these lines, also siphoning power from the city's power lines, were connected to each side of the rows of metal chairs. And only he knew that this much power would generate an electric current that would pass through the audience at an average of 2500 volts.

Just as Dr. Warren instructed the audience to scream for their lives, Orry ignited the sprinkler system and simultaneously flipped the switch to power the electricity. There was an explosion of white light, and everyone in the theater began a collective spasm as sparks shot out from both ends of each row of seats.

Orry marveled at the jolting bodies below. He seemed to be viewing them in slow motion, savoring their shared suffering as if they had choreographed this death dance just for him. Their muscles were pulled taut as the current caused paralysis of their brains' respiratory centers. There were random, involuntary spasms throughout, each violent convulsion as unique as a snowflake. He knew that their hearts would soon stop, and the curtain would fall on this sweet show. The house lights suddenly flickered and popped during the surge.

Orry looked in his wife's direction, not wanting to miss her screen debut. She was beside her lover, of course, both of them contorting and smoking as their skin blackened. With a hiss, one eyeball popped from its socket like a grape in a microwave. The crispy flesh on the tops of her arms sizzled and charred atop the electrified metal armrests. She then lost control of her bowels, immediately ruining her prized white dress. The rest of the theater soon followed suit. Not one person in town could make fun of him for shitting his pants in Ms. Gerkin's class now.

A rising cloud of smoke, burnt flesh, and shit wafted up to the heavens of the projection booth. The atmosphere was now grey and burned his eyes. Orry Verdune knew that was his cue for the curtain call. He wrapped a noose around his neck, checked to make sure it was secured to the beam above him, and took a final bow. Tears of joy streamed down his cheeks into the corners of his smiling mouth. For a moment— just one moment—he saw his name on that silver screen and knew he had completed his magnum opus.

"Percepto!" he exclaimed and leaped into the cheering crowd.

# THE BITTER END

Gene Riley was still getting used to being homeless. He was reminded of this as he carelessly stepped into a pothole filled with brown water. His shoe became instantly saturated and cold, and he was suddenly aware that he had no other pair to change into. He carried two plastic bags full of aluminum cans, and if he hadn't spent most of the morning collecting them, he would've slung them across the road in a rage. He definitely wasn't living his "old life" anymore. He used to have several pairs of shoes and boots back when he was working at the plant, but that was before the booze took hold and his wife took off.

"Ahh, hell," he muttered as he shook his leg back and forth in a feeble attempt to air dry.

Comfortable footwear was a commodity that he no longer took for granted as he trotted down the alley behind several businesses in the small town. He had endured a rough West Virginia winter outdoors, staying at the shelter only on really bad nights. For the most part, he bundled up in his tent along the riverbank under the bridge. There were others there, too; most more experienced at survival than he. He doubted he would've made it through the cold without their advice. Spring was almost here, though, and for that he was grateful.

The warm sun was countered by the chilly wind. He threw his maroon hood atop his black toboggan. He was bald underneath and sported a stubbly, graying beard. He was in his mid-forties and had become skinny and gaunt with the exception of the alcohol reservoir that he called a belly.

Gene stopped when he reached his destination behind the All or Nothing Pawn Shop. The rear of the shop had a dumpster and plenty of room for loading and unloading deliveries. Train tracks ran parallel with the alley, with about twenty yards of unkempt vegetation separating them. It was in this mess of bushes that Gene stashed his loot.

About five paces through the waist-high shrubs, he bent down and opened his carefully hidden wooden box. He had found the box in the pawn shop's dumpster and initially thought it was a casket for a very small person or child. It was in fine condition, so he decided to use it for storage of recyclables—his main source of income. Keeping anything of value in the tent by the river was almost permission to give it away. He looked around to make sure no one was watching as he dumped the cans into a pile of various scrap metals. Once a week he made a run to the recycling center.

Just as quickly as he emptied his findings, he vacated the bushes and sat on a cinderblock near the pawn shop dumpster. He fumbled around in his coat pockets for one of his many half-smoked cigarettes that he accumulated throughout the week, mostly from emptying public ashtrays and picking up scavengers along the road. He withdrew a smoke and flicked on the flame of his small, plastic lighter. The yellow fire shook relentlessly, and this concerned him when he realized that the wind wasn't blowing.

*The shakes are getting worse,* he thought. He had initially noticed them over the winter. Early in the morning before the first beer, his hands would tremble. They were mild at first but have gotten progressively worse with his alcoholism. The only reasonable way for him to make them disappear was to drink more.

It wasn't until last week that he ever seriously entertained the idea of sobering up. A winter on the river coupled with his increasing dependency on booze took its toll on the middle-aged man. He decided that it was only going to get worse—the alcoholism, his destitute existence—everything was plummeting toward a bitter end. The first step for him to get back on track was to try to find some work. He had gone to Pizza Plus when they opened and put in an application. Since then, he had tried to drink as little as possible.

Yesterday he had made it until 10 AM without taking a drink. It was currently a little past noon, and he didn't feel as bad as he did the day before. *Progress,* he thought as he took another puff of his smoke. In those dumb twelve-step meetings that he went to a few times to appease his wife before the divorce, the attendees had talked about "progress, not perfection." At last, he felt like he related.

The train whistle blared at a crossing down the road. Gene looked to his right at the incoming locomotive in the distance. In less than a minute, it would be chugging along the track across the way from him.

He liked trains. He liked to watch them pass by as he fantasized about where they had been and where they were going. Back when he had a car, he hated the damn things. It seemed like every time he was running tight on time, he would get caught by one in the small town. Now that he was a pedestrian, he reveled in their majesty. He romanticized about being a hobo post-WWII, drifting from city to city on a railcar with only a knapsack and a few chums to keep him company. He imagined having nothing to tie him down and an entire American frontier to explore.

*True freedom,* he thought.

A white SUV stopped at the intersection to Gene's left. He looked over at the automobile idling in the alley. He couldn't even make out a driver through the tinted windows. The stationary vehicle had been traveling along the alley parallel to the tracks and didn't have its blinker on like it was waiting for the train to pass so that it could cross. It was simply motionless, and Gene felt like he was being watched. He flicked the butt of his cigarette across the road into the bushes, and the SUV drove forward, passing right in front of Gene.

Thirty minutes later, he had walked a few blocks across town for the daily free lunch that one of the local churches puts on. It was his only guaranteed meal of the day, so he made sure never to miss it. Most of the homeless population in town took advantage of the service. He ate the food, socialized with a few familiar faces, and left just as quickly as he had arrived.

Keeping with his decision to try and better himself, he decided to go check on that job application at the pizza place. It took him about twenty minutes to get to his destination. As he was walking across the large parking lot, he noticed a discarded, pint-sized bottle of vodka on the ground. Instinctively, he bent down and picked it up. The clear liquid inside rolled around in an enticing swirl as he saw that only about three-quarters of the bottle had been consumed. Something inside told him to drop it and keep walking, but his hand had already unscrewed the lid and brought the open container to his mouth.

The cold booze bore a glowing warmth to his stomach that radiated up through his esophagus. His lips tingled, and the shakes went away. He dropped the bottle where he found it and continued walking toward the pizza shop, doing his best to ignore the regret already forming in the back of his mind.

The bell attached to the door DINGED as Gene entered the warm lobby of Pizza Plus. The same friendly manager that Gene met earlier that week was working. He smiled and greeted him as the two men met at the counter.

"Welcome to Pizza Plus! What can I do for you, sir?"

Gene appreciated being treated like every other customer. A lot of employees at businesses that he frequented would roll their eyes or give outright looks of disgust whenever he entered the building, obviously homeless.

"Hey, bud. I'm just checking on the status of a job application I put in earlier this week," Gene explained. "Just wondering if you had a chance to look it over yet."

The manager nodded his head.

"I have."

Gene awaited further explanation in an increasingly awkward silence.

The manager's infectious smile slowly receded to a look of genuine concern.

"Look…" he began.

"Gene," Gene said, filling in the blank.

"Gene, I'm going to be honest with you. We need help. I got nothing but high school kids working for me right now, and I need another reliable adult with open availability."

"Great!"

The manager grew uncomfortable, and Gene knew that the other shoe was about to drop.

"I can't hire you, man."

Gene looked at him with confusion.

"You're wearing the same clothes that you wore when you dropped off the application. You could also use a shower and shave."

Gene's face reddened.

"All of that, I can work with," the manager explained. "The problem is your drinking. I can smell booze on you right now for God's sake."

Gene's defenses dropped. He understood. He simply nodded his head in agreement.

"Thanks for not being an asshole to me," Gene said.

The manager forced a smile, obviously feeling bad about the situation. He looked as if he had an idea and turned around to face the warming table for food. He grabbed a boxed pizza and looked back to Gene.

"Here, man," he said handing him the food.

Gene took the hot meal. The manager pulled a ten-dollar bill out of his wallet and offered it to Gene.

"Whatever you want to do with it is fine."

Without hesitation, Gene grabbed the money and headed to the door. The bell DINGED behind him as the manager watched him leave.

Gene walked past a gas station and stared at the beer advertisements. The money in his pocket was screaming at him, but he didn't listen. *No more*, he thought. He knew he screwed up, but he had decided to clean himself up and try to get a job somewhere else. As he walked across town to the rear of the pawn shop, he kept his eyes open for any "HELP WANTED" signs.

The pawn shop alley was just how he left it. He strolled back to his usual spot beside the dumpster and puffed on a half-smoked cigarette. Before he could finish the butt, the same SUV with the tinted windows pulled up to the stop sign again.

Now Gene was suspicious. The vehicle didn't idly sit and watch him this time. It pulled right up beside the dumpster and parked. He sat motionless as the dark window rolled down with an electric hum.

"Hey, don't I know you?" a familiar voice from inside the vehicle said.

Gene stood up from his perch and cautiously peered in. He studied the middle-aged driver. He definitely knew him, just couldn't place him.

"Sure, I do," the well-dressed driver said. "You're Gene Riley."

Gene remained silent and skeptical.

"Kurt Shamblin," the stranger said, and suddenly Gene remembered.

"From the plant," Gene said.

"Yeah, the plant," Kurt said with a grin. "Seems like a

lifetime ago."

"It was."

The two men stared at one another.

"Well, the reason I stopped was because I've seen you here before behind the shop. I actually own this pawn shop and a few others now," Kurt said.

"You want me to quit trespassing?"

"No, God no. Stay here all you want. I was saying that I recognized you the other day and hate seeing you out here on the street."

"Not anyone's fault but my own. Lots of guys got laid off from the plant and didn't end up homeless. I just used it as an excuse to stay boozed up. I'm trying to climb my way back up though."

"That's great, Gene. I think I might be able to help with that."

Gene stared but couldn't get a read on Kurt's plan.

"Hop in. Let's go get a cup of coffee or beer...whatever you want."

*What do I have to lose?* Gene thought as he opened the door and sat down, sinking into the cushiony car seat.

"Coffee would be nice."

After the two men picked up coffee from a drive-thru, they parked in a pull-off along the river outside of town. Kurt killed the engine and turned to Gene.

"OK, here it is," Kurt began. "Like I said earlier, I own that pawn shop. I'm in a situation now where I'm in way over my head. About a year ago, I started letting a guy named Frame Cook sort of *rent* my business after-hours."

"Frame Cook? I've heard of him," Gene said with a sip of hot coffee. "Fancies himself a drug dealer."

"He is. He's only a big fish in a small pond, though. I just happened to get to talking to him when he came in the shop one day. He was friendly enough and would regularly come in to buy electronics or guns. I guess once he was comfortable with me, he asked if I'd be willing to let him meet up with his regional connection at my shop after we closed. I had my initial reservations, but once he told me he'd pay me $10,000 to rent my shop out for one night, I consented."

"Can't necessarily blame you."

"It went well the first few months," Kurt continued. "Frame would show up at 10 PM on the dot, and about five minutes later his out-of-town connection would show up. I still don't know the guy's name, but you can tell he's higher up on the food chain. He always has two guys protecting him—all three of them dressed nicely. They'd check to make sure I killed the security cameras and then stay in my shop for about thirty minutes to do their business. Then, they would just go their separate ways. Each time, I would have ten grand in cash stashed in the store the next morning."

"So, what's the problem?"

Kurt let out a sigh.

"The problem is that I think the cops have gotten wind of it."

"What makes you think that?"

"Well, I got curious a few meetings in and decided to go watch what goes down. That's how I found out what they do and who shows up. The last few times they've met, the same two cars have shown up. They'll pass the shop a few times and then park over near the pizza joint down the road. I sit there in my car and watch the whole show."

"Sounds suspicious."

"It is, and I need out of it."

"How do you propose to do that? You've already entered their game. Getting out will be rough."

"That's where you come in, buddy."

If Gene had had coffee in his mouth at that time he would've spit it out all over the windshield on principle more than just disbelief.

"Me?"

"It's not as crazy as it may sound. All you would need to do is show up at the rear of the pawn shop at 8 PM this Saturday. The assistant manager, he's just a kid, he'll be closing up the store. When he goes to take the trash out to the back dumpster, you run over and catch the door before it closes. Barely prop it open with a rock or something.

"After you do that, hang out in the bushes until Frame and his connection show up at 10. Once they all enter the building, hurry over to a car that'll be parked behind the building. Inside the car will be some old-school cop car lights and a megaphone. Mount the lights on the roof of the car. Then, just drive the car around to the side of the shop with the display windows. It's crucial that you park there so that the lights on your car can be seen inside. Get out and use the megaphone to pretend like you're the cops. Tell them to exit the building with their hands up or some shit like that. The goal is to scare them so badly that they flee and never want to meet there again. What do you think?"

"I think it's fuckin' crazy."

Kurt chuckled.

"Yeah, the whole situation is crazy," he conceded. "But I think it's so crazy that it'd work."

"What about the cops supposedly scoping the place?"

"Worst case scenario is they are attracted by your antics, and they show up and apprehend you. Just act like a drunk, crazy, homeless guy and you'll be released the next day."

Now Gene laughed.

"I've got that act down."

"Look, you don't even have to enter the building. You'll never be in contact with the guys inside. Just pull the car up, turn on the bright lights, scream into the megaphone, and haul ass down the alley."

When Kurt put it that way, it seemed like a feasible task. It wasn't until Gene believed that the plan could realistically work that he realized there was nothing in it for him. Before he could voice his concern, Kurt jumped in.

"I'll give you $10,000 cash."

Gene thought about getting a place to stay, a car, his family...

"I'll do it."

The number may have well been ten million to him.

———

Three more nights on the river, and it was Saturday. Gene looked beyond the rear of the pawn shop at the bank across the street; specifically, the digital sign in the parking lot. The time was 7:59 PM. Gene stared at the back entrance with a focus he hadn't had in years.

It had been three days since his last sip of alcohol. Today was the first morning of his homelessness that he didn't experience the shakes. He had spent what would've been his morning beer money on a pack of bubble gum. He was currently chomping three pieces with all the subtlety of a cow chewing a piece of cud.

The back door of the pawn shop swung open and clanged against the brick to which it was attached. A kid in his early twenties stepped out with a small garbage bag. Gene hopped to attention as he watched the kid chuck the bag into the dumpster and turn around to head back into the shop.

Gene darted across the alley to catch the door before it shut. The kid disappeared back into the shop. The door was slowly closing. Gene nearly lost his footing in loose gravel and ruined the plan before it started but kept his balance. The door was two inches from shutting when he pulled the wad of gum from his mouth, extended his arm, and pressed it in the door latch. The door came to a squishy stop but was not locked.

*Perfect,* Gene thought as he quickly turned around to head back to the bushes. *Phase 1 of the plan is done.*

It had gotten darker and quieter in the last two hours. The bank sign now displayed 9:59 PM.

Gene watched two pairs of bright headlights pull into the front of the pawn shop: one, a black BMW; the other, a white Altima. He listened as doors opened and shut, and indistinguishable words were spoken in the darkness. The quiet greetings stopped, and Gene saw that they were now in the shop.

*Go time,* he thought as he once again scampered out of the bushes. He ran up to the old black sports car parked near the dumpster. This was to be his dummy police car that Kurt had supplied. It was no doubt a vehicle that was pawned at one of Kurt's shops and never picked up.

*It's definitely going to get some usage tonight.*

Gene went to the gas tank to retrieve the car keys. He popped open the metal door, but the only thing inside was a gas cap. He grabbed the handle and tried to open the car.

Locked.

He looked inside the window and saw that the prop lights weren't even in there. The entire plan hinged on this ruse. His heart started beating faster.

"Stay calm, motherfucker," a muffled voice instructed from behind him.

Startled, he whirled around to see someone wearing a black mask pointing an AK-47 machine gun at his face.

Gene felt his bowels loosen.

"Keep quiet or you're dead," the gunman whispered.

Gene, wide-eyed, nodded his head.

"We're going to walk in that door you gummed up," he instructed.

Gene felt terrified knowing that this person had been watching him all evening.

"Turn around and move…*quietly.*"

Gene did as he was told. He walked to the door and

carefully pulled it open to reveal a dark stock room. He felt the barrel of the weapon poke against his back, and he stepped inside. He heard the gunman slowly shut the door behind them, and they were both enveloped in complete blackness.

A bright white light beamed from behind Gene and lit up the stock room. He turned around to see that the gunman had lowered his weapon and was using the flashlight on his cellphone.

"Gene, it's Kurt," the masked man said in a now friendly tone.

He recognized the voice without the grovel and was now more confused than ever. The gunman shined the light on his masked face. Gene peered into the cut eyeholes of the mask and recognized the person looking back at him.

"Kurt?" he said with disbelief. "What the fuck is going on? I was just about to do my part."

Kurt waved him off.

"Listen carefully because we don't have much time," Kurt began. "I'm not the owner of this pawn shop. That drug dealing piece of shit, Frame, is the owner."

Gene's pulse quickened as a feeling of being stuck in quicksand took hold.

"My daughter overdosed last year, Gene. She overdosed on shit that that asshole brought into *our* community."

Gene was doing his best to follow along without getting lost in disbelief at this turn of events.

"After she died, I began investigating on my own because the cops didn't care who she bought it from. I followed the trail from the street dealer that sold to my little girl to a middleman and then to Frame. Once I started tailing Frame, I picked up on this little monthly meeting at the pawn shop. The out-of-towner in there—his name is Mace. He's the source."

"OK," was all Gene could say.

"Gene," Kurt began, "I'm going to end this little business arrangement before anyone else around here has to go through what I went through."

He held up the AK-47 for extra clarification.

"I'm out of here," Gene said.

Kurt stepped out of his way, making no effort to apprehend him.

"Wait," Kurt said as Gene grabbed the doorknob.

Gene paused.

"If you leave now, you'll miss out on the money. And, there's a lot more than ten-thousand in there."

Gene turned back toward Kurt.

"You can leave and take your chances as a homeless drunk, or you can help me do this job, take whatever money and drugs are in there—plus any valuables in the shop—and start your new life."

Gene thought about his options. He looked at the door leading to the alley. He knew what was at the end of that path: a riverbank. He looked back to Kurt, and Kurt could see in his eyes that he was willing to go through with this.

"Just so you know," Kurt clarified, "I'm not going in there to scare anyone."

Gene imagined walking out of the pawn shop in a matter

of minutes with potentially hundreds of thousands of dollars.

"I'm in," he asserted.

Kurt smiled underneath his mask. He pulled a black Glock 19 pistol that was tucked in the backside of his pants and another black toboggan and handed them to Gene. Gene stretched the mask over his face, straightening it until the eyeholes were lined up. He checked the clip in the gun to make sure it was loaded.

"Ready?" Kurt asked.

Gene gave him a nod.

The two men snuck through the back storeroom, careful not to bump into anything. They sidestepped rows of power tools, electronics, and musical instruments—all tagged with owner information.

They came to a stop behind the door leading into the lobby. A yellow light glowed from underneath. The men on the other side of the door were wrapping up their discussion of the deal. Their voices sounded distant, but Gene and Kurt heard them say, "one hundred thousand dollars." Kurt slowly raised his gloved hand to the doorknob, making sure Gene saw that he was about to breach. Gene gave him another nod. Kurt twisted the knob and pushed simultaneously.

A flood of light hit the two men as they stormed into the lobby. Gene immediately counted five men standing in front of them. The two men to his right standing beside the cash registers were the local guys: Frame and his chubby enforcer. The chubby one was in the middle of examining small packages of heroin. To Gene's left, leaning against the shop counter, were the out-of-towners: Mace and his two henchmen. An unzipped duffle bag full of cash sat on the counter in front of them. Mace could've passed for a suave lawyer, and his two hired guns looked like professional bodyguards. Gene knew they were outnumbered, but they had the element of surprise; plus, none of these men had their guns drawn.

For a microsecond, no one did anything. Kurt broke the silence.

"This is for my daughter," he said to Frame.

Multiple bursts of thunder exploded throughout the enclosed walls of the shop as the spray of gunfire unzipped the drug dealer's face. Crimson flecks covered the chubby bodyguard beside Frame.

Gene wasted no time as he aimed his pistol at the blood-covered man's throat and fired. It sounded like a water balloon popped as the bullet went in through his trachea and out the back. Frame was dead before his body thudded to the ground. His guard fell on top of him, spasming and gurgling his way to oblivion.

The trio to the left snapped into action. The taller henchman jumped in front of Mace as he withdrew his pistol, while the stocky one covered Mace from behind and pushed him down behind the counter.

Kurt swung the AK-47 toward Mace, but the tall man fired his pistol and hit Kurt in the shoulder. He winced, letting the machine gun drop to the ground. He looked up just in time to see the tall man shoot. The first bullet hit Kurt in the chest and dropped him on his ass against the wall. The next five cratered his sternum and slumped him over. He died with a smile on his face.

Gene jumped over the counter and landed on Mace and the stocky henchman. Both of them were in the process of drawing their weapons before Gene interrupted. He shoved the pistol in the stocky guy's mouth and pulled the trigger. His head exploded like a cherry bomb inside an apple. The lifeless body toppled onto the much smaller Mace, pinning him temporarily.

The tall man behind the counter near Kurt's body was reloading. Gene stood up and aimed at the man before he could finish. The tall man raised his arms to shield his head just as Gene fired. A chunk of the man's forearm peeled back as the bullet embedded into the muscle. The man dropped his weapon and slowly went to pick it back up. Gene tried to fire again, but he was out of ammunition.

Mace struggled underneath the heavy body pinning him to the ground but finally managed to get free. Gene watched Mace get to his feet with a gun in hand. In a split-second decision, he hopped over the counter and fled into the lobby, disappearing into the tall aisles composing the hardware section of the store. Just as he rounded the corner, he yanked a heavy power tool off the wall and flicked off the lights.

All three remaining men were now completely enshrined in darkness.

"You OK over there?" Mace asks his tall bodyguard who was just shot in the arm.

"Yeah," the tall man replied as he struggled to shove a new clip in his empty pistol. "Forearm is fucking useless, though."

His matter-of-factness about his injury assured Gene that

the man was experienced with violence.

Mace turned to look for Gene in the dark lobby. He hopped the counter and started stalking the aisles. Gene was crouched in a corner, watching from his hidden vantage point. He quietly picked up a hammer and chucked it across the lobby. It bouncèd off one of the metal shelves with a loud CLANG.

Mace pointed his weapon in the direction of the commotion. He fired several rounds without reservation. Gene snuck behind him and yanked the starter rope of the chainsaw he was holding. The machine roared to life.

Mace whirled around just as Gene turned the spinning blade sideways and buried it into the side of Mace's neck. The drug dealer immediately dropped his pistol and stood in a frozen spasm akin to an electrocution as the saw churned its way through flesh and bone. Gene released a primal scream until he had sawed the man's head completely off.

A headless Mace dropped to his knees as a geyser of blood erupted from the stump of his neck. His twitching body fell forward. Gene had to back up to avoid the pumping blood that was forming a small pond on the floor. He chucked the chainsaw across the lobby and picked up Mace's gun.

The tall man finally slid the loaded clip into his gun and pulled the barrel back. He was just about to stand when Gene held his gun over the top of the counter and unloaded the clip in the general direction of the bodyguard. Gene ducked back down behind the counter, listening for any sign of life. He heard the tall man cough and wince and slump over.

He peeked his head above the counter and looked down at

the man. The tall man was riddled with bullet holes but somehow was still pointing his pistol toward Gene. The man fired just as Gene ducked back down. The fluorescent light on the ceiling exploded above them as glass rained down.

In a last-ditch effort, Gene flung himself over the counter and landed on the bodyguard. He grabbed the tall man's arm and slammed it into the linoleum floor until he released the pistol, sending it sliding under a jewelry display case.

Gene painfully got to his feet and lifted the heavy cash register with both arms. His legs nearly buckled under the weight. He used his last energy reserves to heave the machine above his head. The tall man looked up from the floor at Gene, just in time to watch the cash register burrow into his face.

The shop was eerily quiet. Gene realized that he was hyperventilating. He took a moment to catch his breath before snatching up the separate bags of cash and drugs. He sat both bags on top of the jewelry case and then crouched down to retrieve the gun that had slid under. He used the butt of the weapon to break the display glass housing the jewelry. Just as he tossed the last bit of gold into one of the bags, he heard police sirens in the distance. Wasting no more time, he grabbed both bags and fled through the back door.

As soon as he ran into the night, he could hear sirens rapidly approaching from all directions. The only temporary reprieve from the wailing of the cop cars was the blasting horn from an oncoming train.

He ran across the alley and into the bushes struggling to carry both bags. He squatted to the ground to catch his breath. He felt like his heart was going to explode as the sirens got louder and closer. It wasn't until he felt the vibrations in the earth below him that he recognized that a train was bounding down the tracks behind him.

He saw the blue and red lights starting to bounce off buildings as the police cars sped down the main road. Gene turned to look at the train chugging along. He wrapped the straps of both bags across his shoulders and sprinted toward the locomotive.

Once he was only a few feet away from the train, he reached out and grabbed the rusty metal railing, and heaved himself onto the back of the car. He climbed the small ladder all the way to the top and peered into an empty coal car. With the last exertion he could muster, he rolled over the top and dropped down to the hard bottom below with a booming echo.

The fall knocked the wind out of him, but considering the circumstances, he was relatively unharmed. He untied the bags from his arms and rolled onto his back. He looked up at the stars shining brightly in the night sky. Tree branches and power lines occasionally interrupted the view. The blue and red glowing colors from the police lights were fading away along with the sirens.

He focused on the blazing white balls of gas burning above him, lightyears away. They looked like something, but he couldn't remember. He couldn't remember the glow-in-the-dark stars that he and his wife put on the ceiling of his child's room, back when the kid still talked to him.

The train car shook as it rounded a turn. Gene's body

wobbled, and he gripped the two bags on either side of him, squeezing them tightly. He couldn't remember why this position was familiar. He couldn't remember his wife and child, each nestled under one of his arms as the three of them fell asleep in the same bed.

It was just too long ago.

There was no more family. There was no return to his old life. He had been kidding himself all along. That's what the loot in the bags was telling him, at least.

A smile slowly crept across his lips as he realized that he had survived his war, earned his freedom, and was now heading across the country, barreling recklessly toward a bright, new American frontier.

# The Devil's Road

The smell of roadkill flooded the car through the open windows. Bailey Whitman scrunched her face and waved her hand back and forth.

"P U," she said as she looked at her boyfriend in the driver's seat.

Floyd had his cheeks puffed out, overexaggerating as he held his breath. She laughed and poked his face, causing him to inhale and gag.

"Good God," he chuckled. "That is the nastiest thing I've ever smelled."

"It's just some good ol'-fashioned West Virginia roadkill."

"No, thank you."

Bailey stuck her hand out of her window and let the passing strands of vegetation smack her palm. They were getting close to her parents' house. A warm feeling reassured her belly. She hadn't been home since she left for her freshman year of college last August. Her mom and dad went to their beach condo for Thanksgiving through Christmas, so she had just stayed in her dorm at West Virginia University. Now it was the beginning of spring break, and she was more than happy to spend it back home.

The laid-back break had actually been Floyd's idea. He was a senior nearing graduation, and they had been dating since December. They met in line at the bookstore and instantly hit it off. On Valentine's Day, he had asked her what her plans were for spring break. She rattled off some of the popular east coast beaches she had been considering. Floyd, having listened to Bailey talk about how badly she missed home, posed the notion of meeting her parents. The fact that he was willing—let alone interested—in meeting her parents solidified her love for him.

Floyd drove carefully along the narrow mountain road. Rays of sunlight beamed through the leaves of the surrounding trees, speckling his path. The car never breached 40 MPH, anticipating spots where the road would suddenly disappear around a sharp curve. He had never driven this type of West Virginia backroad. He tried his best to conceal his jittery nerves. Having grown up in the northern panhandle, which was practically Pennsylvania, he had never been south of his current college location in Morgantown.

Bailey brought her hand back inside the car and turned to her boyfriend, admiring his thin build under his white t-shirt and jeans. He was skinnier than her former high school boyfriend, Zack, a local football phenom whom her father adored. She had no fear that Floyd would not win over her parents with his charm and humor. He caught her looking out of the corner of his eye.

"What are you staring at?" he teased.

"Just taking you all in."

He smiled as his face reddened a bit.

"You're not so bad your..." he said just as a large truck came barreling around an unseen bend in the road.

Floyd jerked the wheel to the right to avoid being hit. The front of the car was inches away from going into the ditch due to his overcorrection. Bailey gasped and dug her nails into the interior leather, bracing for impact. He swerved back left as soon as the truck was out of the way, narrowly avoiding both obstacles. He slammed on the brakes as soon as he knew they were clear.

They were both breathing heavily.

"Are you OK?" he asked her, turning to get a good look at her.

"Yeah," she said wide-eyed. "I'm OK. Are you?"

"Fine," he replied but obviously still a bit in shock. "Sorry about that. I'm not used to driving out here."

He put the car in drive once he realized how dangerous it was to stay parked in the middle of the road.

"I'll try not to crash into the next tree I see," he muttered with a grin as Bailey's pulse settled.

After a few minutes of silence and decompression, Bailey spoke up.

"So, are you ready to tell me about your secret project yet?"

Floyd rolled his eyes and gave her a look.

"Come on," she prodded. "What's so secretive about a communication major's final project?"

Floyd didn't like the way she said the name of his field of study.

"An undeclared freshman wouldn't understand," he teased, and she mocked offense.

"I've told you why I'm not showing it to you yet," he quickly reminded her.

"Are you that much of a perfectionist?"

"I'll show you when it's finished. I promise."

"Is it still a podcast?"

He just gave her a quick look and nodded his head.

"And this is step one in your grand scheme of becoming the next big broadcaster?"

Floyd looked at her again to make sure there was no condescension in her tone. He couldn't stand when people doubted his dreams. She appeared earnest.

"Step one," he affirmed with a grin. Ready to change the subject, he said, "How much further to Bennettsville?"

Bennettsville was the name of Bailey's hometown and where her parents still lived.

"Probably like thirty minutes. Why? Are you nervous?"

"Why would I be nervous?"

"Meeting my parents."

"Should I be nervous to meet the great Mr. and Mrs. Don and Kathy Whitman?"

"Well," she began with a chuckle. "Mom will love you no matter what; that's just who she is. Dad, on the other hand, will have to experience some of your trademark charm."

"A bit reserved, is he?"

"No, not so much reserved. You don't get to be as successful around here as he is without some sort of personality. He's just...methodical."

"Methodical?"

"Calculated," she clarified. "Dad likes to plan everything. And control everything."

"I guess that's why he's great at running a travel agency."

"Yeah. I mean, even when we would go on vacations, I can't think of a time when he didn't have a detailed itinerary.

He's super smart like you. That's why he'll like you."

"I hope so."

They reached the top of the steep incline and turned slightly to go down the other side of the mountainous terrain. Just before they descended, Floyd caught sight of the open valley to his left and stopped the car. The rolling hills were covered in variously colored trees that all had a golden hue from the sun. He could see miles of West Virginia wilderness.

"Whoa."

"It's so pretty up here," Bailey confirmed.

"Such a pretty place to have such a dark secret," he unintentionally said aloud.

Bailey tried to make sense of that statement as Floyd realized that he had just vocalized a private thought. He knew he had to explain.

"I Googled Bennettsville before we left," he said. "One of the first things I saw was that there were a bunch of unsolved murders like thirty years ago."

"The Countdown Killer," Bailey stated matter-of-factly. "Our local boogeyman. Everyone my age who grew up here knows the story inside and out."

"What I read was pretty dark stuff. I think it was nine people who were killed?"

Bailey nodded her head and filled him in on the rest of the legend.

"So, there's this five-mile stretch of road called the Devil's Road—we actually have to drive it to get to my house. One day someone found a dead body on the side of the road, a teenage girl. She was naked...strangled to death. She had the number ten carved ten times on her body."

"Jesus."

"Yeah," Bailey continued. "About a month later, another body appeared. This one was an elderly man—also naked—but he had the number nine carved in him nine times. Sure enough, over the next year, more bodies with numbers counting down kept showing up on the Devil's Road. Locals nicknamed him the Countdown Killer."

"I don't see how more people don't know about this."

"If it had happened in a big city, they would've heard. No one's going to throw a fuss about a few dead hillbillies, no matter how sensational the story," she said. "The craziest part is that there was never a body with the number one found."

"Yeah, I noticed that in the article."

"It's like his grand plan was never finished. The Countdown Killer either died, left town, or just stopped. It was never solved. Pretty easy to see how he became our generation's boogeyman."

Floyd carefully navigated the car around several deep potholes in the road. He surmised that any of them were severe enough to pop a tire. The car bobbed up and down as it endured the unsteady road. The movement rocked Bailey's already full bladder.

"I've really got to pee," she said.

Not three seconds after her admission did a gas station come into view in a clearing up ahead. The woods dwindled the further down the mountain they descended.

"You're in luck," Floyd replied as he directed the vehicle

into the empty parking lot, save for one beat-up Ford truck.

He noticed a sign that said "BENNETTSVILLE" and had an arrow pointing straight ahead. They stopped at the pumps, and Bailey hopped out.

"I'm going to get some gas," he said to her back.

She gave a wave of acknowledgement as she hurried inside. As soon as she was out of sight, he withdrew a digital voice recorder from his jean pocket and turned it on.

"The road to Bennettsville has been long," he spoke into the device with a dramatic tone. "After an unforgiving trek through the rugged Appalachian wilderness, we are quickly approaching our destination. Bailey and I stopped on the outskirts of town at a rundown gas station to refuel and recharge before we head to...the Devil's Road."

He kept his eye out for Bailey to make sure that she didn't see him in the act of recording his secret podcast. She just wouldn't understand. This was beyond the scope of just a school project.

"Side note: Bailey has yet to connect the dots. I am nervous about what's going to happen. I'll check back in later," he said and then shoved the recorder back in his pocket as he saw Bailey appear inside.

Floyd grabbed the gas pump, slid the nozzle into the open tank, and started to fill the car. Bailey walked outside smiling at him.

"Do you need to go?" she asked.

He noticed an elderly salesclerk inside and got an idea for an impromptu interview.

"Yeah."

She walked around the car and grabbed the handle out of his hand.

"Go ahead. I'll finish."

"Thanks," he said and headed toward the store's entrance.

"Welcome," greeted the clerk.

His friendly eyebrows peeked over his bulky glasses, and a faded name tag read, "MELVIN".

Floyd said, "Howdy, Melvin," and walked to the restroom.

When he came back out, the clerk was busy shuffling around cartons of cigarettes. Floyd grabbed a Mountain Dew, pulled the tip of his recorder out of his pocket and turned it on, then walked up to the counter.

"This all for ya?" the old man said.

"Yeah, that's all," Floyd replied and dropped two dollars on the counter.

He glanced outside to see if Bailey was paying him any mind. She was scrolling through her phone, oblivious to the outside world. The old man handed him his change.

"Sir," Floyd began. "I'm a senior at WVU, and I'm doing a research project on the Countdown Killer. Would you care to answer just a few questions to help me out?"

The old man looked like he smelled something sour as his welcoming demeanor dried up.

"The Countdown Killer, eh?" he groaned.

Floyd gave a nod.

"I reckon I can help you out, son."

"Great. Did you live in this area when the murders occurred?"

"Born and raised."

"OK. Could you provide any insight on what it was like to live in a town with an active killer on the loose?"

"It was terrifying. No one knew who to trust. This is a small town. Everyone was lookin' at each other with suspicion. If you were just a little different or did somethin' just a little odd by society's standards, people began to whisper."

Floyd detected some underlying resentment in the man's tone.

"Did you experience any of this scrutiny, sir?"

The old man reflected on a lifetime of perpetual bachelorhood in a town that just wouldn't understand why. He was about to open up but decided against it.

"Not me," he lied.

"Did you ever think you knew who the killer was?"

The old man shook his head.

"I just can't picture anyone that I know in Bennettsville doin' a thing like that."

"Do you think it's possible that the Countdown Killer is still in Bennettsville? That he just stopped for whatever reason?"

The old man considered the proposal as if it had been something over which he'd lost many nights of sleep.

"Of course," he said. "But...I just do my best to block it out, unless I get some random customers who want to drudge up some darkness from the past."

Floyd felt how pained he was.

"If what I think is true, this project that I'm doing might

help you out with that."

The clerk looked at Floyd with puzzlement. Floyd looked out the window and saw Bailey motioning for him to hurry up.

"Thank you for talking to me," he said as he carefully clicked off the recorder and left the store.

"What were you two talking about?" Bailey asked as he walked back to the car.

"I asked him about the Devil's Road—if it was as scary as legend makes it out to be."

Bailey smiled.

"You're about to find out. It's up here on the right."

A few minutes later, they passed the Bennettsville city limits sign. Less than a mile after that, Floyd turned onto Maple Lane. He was initially confused by the sign, until Bailey reminded him that the Devil's Road was just a nickname for the real street.

Trees multiplied on both sides the further out they drove. There was a steady incline as the pavement wrapped up and around another mountainside. Imposing branches jutted out over the road that could easily damage a taller vehicle. A ditch ran parallel to the road on the right side, while the left was a vertigo-inducing drop to the rocky terrain below. Floyd drove like it was the first time he had ever been behind the wheel.

"This is it," Bailey said.

"I could see how this could be called the Devil's Road even if there weren't multiple murders here."

"Yeah, it's pretty dangerous. Quite a few wrecks have

happened here. Mostly drunk people or people just not paying attention. I remember in high school someone from out of town broke through the guardrail and rolled down the mountain. I was on my way home and had to wait because they had the road blocked off for hours."

Floyd listened as he carefully navigated the vehicle up the slope.

"I wonder where they found the bodies…" Floyd muttered to himself.

Again, he realized that he was thinking aloud, but Bailey didn't seem to hear him. If she did, she didn't acknowledge it. She was too busy texting her mom that they were almost there. After a long couple of miles, the road began to descend, and the town of Bennettsville came into view.

"Take the next right," Bailey said.

Floyd turned onto an unmarked gravel path that ran deep into the woods on the outskirts of town. A quarter of a mile later, the mass of trees disappeared as they abruptly entered a clearing. There was a sprawling yard that ran on for acres. In the center of the lot was a gorgeous three-story brick home. Expertly manicured shrubbery adorned the base of a wraparound porch. The gravel crunched under the wheels as the car came to a stop in front of a three-vehicle standalone garage.

"You grew up here?" Floyd asked.

"Yes, I know," Bailey replied, always a bit uncomfortable by her family's wealth, especially in this area.

Floyd noticed the backs of two figures sitting on the porch swing. One was a short, brown-haired female, and the other was a taller man with trimmed grey hair. He assumed them to be Don and Kathy. As soon as Floyd realized that he was looking at Bailey's father, everything got real for him. His heart felt like it skipped every other beat, and his hands were getting sweaty. Bailey looked at him and noticed his complexion seemed pale.

"Are you OK?"

Floyd snapped out of it and returned her gaze.

"Yeah," he said. "I guess I am a bit nervous after all."

"Don't be," she smiled and got out of the car.

Bailey didn't know that Floyd had been preparing for this moment for half of his life. Ever since he had heard the story of how his aunt, Bethany, was murdered thirty years ago and how her body was found on the Devil's Road, he was determined to find out who did it. Aunt Bethany had lived in Bennettsville but frequently came to visit his family up north. She had been the Countdown Killer's ninth victim, which meant she had the number two carved twice into her exposed flesh.

Floyd had night terrors throughout his teenage years. He'd wake up in other rooms, sometimes standing up, screaming, and attacking invisible intruders. His parents did everything they could think of to help him: therapy, medication, a full social life. None of it abated the obsession insidiously buried in his subconscious. It didn't help that he became fixated on true crime books, TV shows, and podcasts. He was always in the middle of someone else's murder investigation.

It wasn't until his sophomore year at WVU that he experienced a true sense of relief. Floyd had been home visiting his parents, and they told him that they were downsizing and moving south. His mother showed him the boxes of his personal belongings from childhood stacked in the attic. He spent a few hours going through a bunch of old schoolwork, youth sports trophies, and toys. When he was nearly finished, he noticed a large lavender suitcase in the corner. He probably wouldn't have even noticed it had it not been for the shiny brass handle reflecting the yellow lightbulb's glow.

"What is that?" he had said as he crouched under the low beams and made his way to the treasure, carefully stepping on planks so he didn't come crashing through the kitchen ceiling.

The suitcase was heavy and completely packed full. Floyd looked it over before he tried to open it. There was an airline luggage tag attached to one of the zippers. He pinched it and flipped it over to read it. "LITTLETON, BETHANY" was printed at the top. Nervousness fluttered in his gut as he realized this was Aunt Bethany's remaining belongings.

Floyd squatted and popped open the latches. Overstuffed clothes bulged through the new opening. There were silk blouses, some pajamas, and a few dresses—all women's clothes. Some jewelry and other expensive-looking knick-knacks rolled around once they were no longer confined by the clothes. A leatherbound book was hidden at the bottom. There were no words on the front, only the initials BML. Floyd picked it up and felt the warm leather in his hands. He thumbed through the thick pages and glanced over the handwritten entries. It was obviously Aunt Bethany's diary.

Curiously, he flipped to the last entry and noticed the date was the same year that she had died. He read the page and then went to the previous one. There were no daily contributions, but she had written in it at least once a week. Reading backwards, he learned much about his aunt's final month of life, but the one detail that stood out the most was her infatuation with a new man she was seeing: Donald. She first described him as being charming and flirtatious with her even though he was a married man. The next entry detailed their first affair and how Don seemed like two different people at once. Less than a week later, he told her that their affair had been a mistake. Bethany wrote in the diary's final entry that she thought she was being watched.

Floyd closed the diary and pondered what to do next. No one had obviously even bothered to open the diary before him. He was now the only person with this lead. He considered telling his parents or taking it to the police. Something inside him decided that this was his responsibility; he would be the one to expose the Countdown Killer, and he would document the entire process.

"Floyd," Bailey said to him from beside his window.

He blinked quickly and took a deep breath before getting out of the car.

"Are you sure you're OK?" she asked again.

She noticed something was off in his eyes.

"Bailycakes!" her father said as he walked down the porch steps.

Bailey turned around and smiled as her father strolled across the front yard with his hands in his slacks.

"Daddy!" she exclaimed and jumped on him.

Don caught her with ease and gave her a big hug. Kathy caught up to them and rubbed her daughter's back.

"Hi, Mom," Bailey said with tears in her eyes.

Floyd stood about ten yards away, awkwardly observing the family embrace. Kathy made eye contact with him and then nudged Bailey.

"Want to introduce us to your friend, honey?" she said.

Don released her, and she dropped back to the ground.

"Of course," Bailey began. "Mom, Dad, this is my boyfriend, Floyd Hooper."

Floyd stepped forward and extended his hand with a smile. Kathy grabbed it first.

"It's so nice to meet you, Floyd. Call me Kathy."

"Sorry," Bailey said. "Floyd, this is my father, Don."

Floyd looked at the man, who was well over six feet tall. Don held out his hand and, for a split second, Floyd hesitated. Don saw it, and Floyd saw that he saw it. Floyd grabbed Don's hand and gripped it forcefully.

"Strong grip, young man," he said and smiled with only the bottom half of his face.

Floyd stared into Don's dark eyes and nervously withdrew his hand.

"Nice to meet you, sir," he said.

"Please, call me Don," he said. "You two come on inside."

The house was even more impressive once they walked through the front door. Don carried their bags as they followed him into the open living room. A decorative chandelier hung from the ceiling two stories high, and a wooden staircase wrapped up the wall and spiraled to the second floor. Floyd glanced at the leather furniture huddled around a massive stone fireplace.

"Follow me upstairs, and I'll show you where you'll be sleeping," Don said.

"I know where my room is, Dad," Bailey laughed.

"Not you, honey," Don replied.

Before Bailey could piece it together, Don reached the top of the staircase and turned into the first room on the left.

"This is one of the guest bedrooms," he said as he placed Floyd's suitcase on the ground in front of the bed.

Bailey just nodded her head and smiled. She should've known this was coming. There was no way her father would allow her to share a bed with a boyfriend under his roof.

"Looks great," Floyd said. "Thank you, Don."

Don gave that half-face smile again as he walked past Floyd back to his wife. Kathy came to life as soon as her husband put his arm around her.

"Let's give you the rest of the tour," she said with a genuine smile.

———————

Just as the sun started to retreat behind the western hill beyond their property, Kathy emerged from the kitchen wearing a floral apron and carrying a steaming ham adorned with pineapples and glaze. Don sat at the head of the table with Bailey to his left and Floyd beside her. Kathy placed the main course in front of them and took her seat on the other side of Don.

The dining room was just as impressive as the living room. It was dimly lit by smaller chandeliers and two candles on the table. Floyd studied the oil paintings on the wall, looking for anything that would alert him of some sinister, underlying intent. He spotted the bar and the countless bottles of liquors he'd never encountered in college. Kathy walked beside each person and filled their plate with slices of ham.

"This looks fantastic, Kathy," Floyd said.

"Why thank you, Floyd," she smiled.

"Yeah, Mom. It looks great."

Don smiled and took a sip of wine.

"Indeed," he said.

Floyd grabbed his fork and knife and began cutting. He pierced a thick piece of meat, and just before he brought it to his mouth, he stopped, realizing no one else had started to eat. Don was staring at him.

"How about we say the blessing?" Don said.

Floyd felt his face redden and was grateful to be in a dark room.

"Sure," he said. "Sorry."

Don waved it off and reached out to his wife and daughter who took his hand in theirs. Bailey grabbed Floyd's hand and motioned for him to reach across the table and take Kathy's. He awkwardly leaned over the food and extended his hand for Kathy.

"Oh, OK," she said as she completed the circle.

"Heavenly Father," Don began. "We thank you for this food and for the blessings of family. We thank you for bringing Bailey home safely and for our new friend, Floyd."

Bailey squeezed Floyd's hand. Floyd peeked through one eye at the other three with their eyes closed and heads bowed. He'd never seen Bailey pray before. Don continued thanking God, but Floyd tuned him out. *Why would God let a monster like you take away Aunt Bethany?* he thought.

The three of them said, "Amen," and Floyd looked back down and said, "Amen."

Everyone released hands and picked up their silverware. For a minute, there were only clanks and cuts, chewing and sipping as they enjoyed their meals.

"So, Floyd," Don said between bites. "Bailey tells us you're a senior?"

"That's right."

"What's your area of study?" Kathy asked.

"Communications."

"Interesting," she replied.

"What do you plan to do with a degree in communications?" Don asked.

Floyd cringed at the tone, and Bailey didn't have to look at him to know he was bothered by it.

"He wants to go into broadcasting, Daddy."

Don nodded his head as he listened to her. He took a big drink of wine and looked at Floyd.

"What type of broadcasting, Floyd?"

"Well, right now I'm interested in true crime."

Floyd studied Don's reaction. He thought he detected a slight twitch in the corner of his mouth, almost like the beginnings of a smile, but he couldn't be sure in this low light.

"True crime, you say?" Don said. "Kathy eats that stuff up."

Kathy hurried to swallow her food.

"Oh, Don. You make me sound so morbid," she said as she took a drink of wine. "I do like those serial killer documentaries though."

*If she only knew*, Floyd thought and then realized, *Wait, does she know?* He decided to prod even further.

"Really?" he began. "I figured people from this town would be sensitive to that kind of subject matter."

"Why is that?" Don asked.

"Because of the Countdown Killer," Floyd said.

Bailey glared at him.

"Can we possibly not talk about this at dinner?" she said.

Don ignored her.

"So, you've heard of our bloody history here?" he asked.

"Yeah, it's pretty unbelievable how they never caught the guy," Floyd started. "Someone so sick, yet so clever."

Don nodded his head, but Floyd spoke before he could say anything.

"Did you all live here when the Countdown Killer was active?" he asked.

"I was in college," Kathy spoke up. "But Don lived here. We actually met at WVU, and he was two grades ahead of me. Very much like you two."

"I was getting my business off the ground when all that was going on," Don said.

"It was a scary time," Kathy said.

"No scarier than today's society," Don said, piercing his

meat. He looked at Floyd and took a bite and said with a full mouth, "There will always be monsters out there."

"Unless we catch them," Floyd said.

"That's right," Kathy agreed.

"Speaking of bad guys," Don began. "Bailey, are you still carrying that stun gun I gave you?"

"Yes, Dad," she said without enthusiasm.

Don smiled and looked at Floyd.

"I insisted that she pack a pistol, but she refused to carry it on campus. We compromised on the stun gun," Don explained. "You can still do a lot of damage with one of those."

"I agree with you, Don," Floyd said. "I think it's best to stay prepared for monsters."

Don smiled and finished his wine.

"God bless the Second Amendment," he said.

Kathy had a lightbulb go off in her head while she was chewing. She swallowed and said, "Bailey, you should take Floyd on a walk of the grounds. Show him the trail."

"That sounds nice," Floyd said.

"You'll like it," Bailey smiled.

She was apparently full or had lost her appetite during the dinner conversation because her plate was still a little less than halfway full. "I'm ready when you are."

"OK, then," Floyd said getting up.

"You two have fun," Don said.

"The food was delicious," Floyd said. "Thanks again, Kathy."

"My pleasure."

The two of them took their plates into the kitchen. Bailey grabbed a flashlight from one of the cabinets, and they headed toward the back door.

"He seems very nice," Kathy said at the dinner table.

"You think?" Don said. "Seems a bit off to me—like he's hiding something."

"Oh, stop it, Don. You're skeptical of all of Bailey's boyfriends in the beginning."

Don smiled in agreement.

---

The path began fifty yards from the back door. The woods lined the clearing and continued straight up the massive mound of a hill. A dirt path ran beneath two tall trees and snaked its way into the dark forest. Floyd and Bailey approached it with Bailey and her flashlight leading the way.

"Here it is," she said.

"Where does it go?"

"Come here, and I'll show you."

The two of them walked about ten yards into the woods, and the path forked in opposite directions.

"All roads lead back here," she said.

"It's a big circle?"

"Yeah," she answered. "Let's go left."

"How long is it?"

"About a mile. Maybe a little more."

Bailey stopped when her flashlight revealed a piece of a fallen tree branch laying across the path. She bent down and picked it up. It was around four feet long, straight, and sturdy. She handed it to Floyd.

"Here's your walking stick," she smiled as she handed it to him.

Floyd fumbled the stick, and the tip of it hit his thigh and the recorder in his pocket. A muffled recording of Floyd's last entry began to play. Bailey instantly recognized Floyd's voice and knew that it was his secret project. He scrambled to turn it off, but she heard him and the gas station attendant discussing the Countdown Killer before he could pause it. He finally hit stop and slowly made eye contact with his girlfriend.

"What was that?"

"My project."

"You're doing a podcast about the Countdown Killer?"

"Yeah. I didn't want to tell you because I didn't know how you would react."

She looked confused by the deception.

"I don't get it," she said. "Why…"

"Because my aunt was the Countdown Killer's ninth victim."

The silent woods seemed even more so as Bailey processed Floyd's admission.

"What?"

He knew he had to elaborate.

"Listen," he began and took a step closer to her. "My aunt, Bethany, was killed here. Her body was found on the Devil's Road with the number two carved in her."

Bailey shook her head.

"I heard stories about the Countdown Killer my whole life. I had to go to therapy for it. I grew up hours away from here, but I was still terrified. My therapist suggested facing my fear, so I started to research what really happened. I started listening to true crime podcasts; they made me feel like I wasn't the only person who'd gone through something like this. A couple of years ago, I decided to make my own podcast about the Countdown Killer. It was just a crazy, cosmic coincidence that I met *and fell in love with* someone actually from Bennettsville."

Bailey's mind was overloaded. After a moment, she settled on a question.

"Is this why you wanted to come here?"

"No," Floyd answered, shaking his head.

"Did you even care about meeting my parents?"

"Of course," he said and held her gently by the arms. "I love you. I'm sorry that I didn't tell you, and I'm glad that it's finally out."

Bailey's gut told her that she was being used, but she did her best to ignore it. She looked into Floyd's eyes and wanted to believe him. Floyd took the recorder out of his pocket.

"Look, I won't touch this thing the rest of the time we're here," he lied. "All I care about is having a good time with your family."

Saying that pained him, but he didn't let it show. If what he believed was true, he was going to completely upend her entire life. She would hate him, and he knew it, but it had to be done. Maybe she would understand, eventually.

"Please," he began. "Just show me the rest of the path.

Can we just forget about this?"

Bailey looked at his smile and kind eyes and chose to give him the benefit of the doubt.

"OK."

Floyd took her hand, and they started to walk. He knew that most of what he told her was true. He wished he could tell her that he only approached her because he already knew who she was. After doing research on the information he pulled from Aunt Bethany's diary, he identified his suspect as Don Whitman, the only travel agent named Don in the area. He discovered Don's family and was ecstatic when he learned that Don's daughter attended the same school that he did. He found her on social media and tracked her down at the bookstore one day. Even so, he was OK with his current relationship because he quickly developed real feelings for her. He squeezed her cool hand, content with his own justification.

———•———

An hour later, Don and Kathy were drinking their nightcaps in the living room while watching some game show on TV. The back door squeaked open, and Kathy's heavy eyelids were suddenly wide awake.

"They're back," Don said.

Bailey and Floyd walked into the living room, both smiling as if nothing out of the ordinary had happened.

"How was your hike?" Kathy asked.

"Good," Bailey replied.

"That's good," she said and started to stand up from the couch. "I'm getting a bit tired. I think I'm going to head to the bedroom."

"OK, Mom."

"I'm glad you all are here," she said as she hugged Bailey.

"Me too," she replied.

"Have a good night, Kathy," Floyd said.

"Thank you, Floyd. You as well."

Don took a sip of his whiskey.

"I'll be up shortly, honey," he said as Kathy disappeared upstairs.

Bailey was exhausted from the trip and the walk.

"I think I might follow her up there," she said. "I'm worn down."

"I'll walk you up," Floyd said.

"OK," she replied. "Goodnight, Daddy."

"Goodnight, sweetheart. I'll see you in the morning," he said.

Floyd followed Bailey up the staircase and down the hallway to her room.

"Are you going to sleep too?" she asked.

He hugged her and gave her a kiss on the forehead.

"In just a little bit," he said. "I'm going to go hang with your dad for a minute."

Bailey looked up at him.

"Really?"

"Yeah. I'll let him fully vet me."

Bailey smiled and kissed him goodnight. Floyd shut her door and walked to his room a few doors down. He picked up his bag and unzipped it. The pistol was at the bottom hidden in one of his hoodies. The metal weapon was heavy in his hand. He had only recently fired a gun. Once he bought this one, he went to the shooting range in Morgantown and got familiar with it. After that, he loaded it and hid it in his bag for this moment. He gave the gun one more look and then tucked it in the back of his pants.

Don was still watching TV when Floyd came back downstairs.

"There he is," Don said with a smile.

Floyd could tell he was inebriated and knew that that was to his advantage.

"Here I am."

"Not tired, are you?"

"Not really."

Don stood up from his recliner, and the cushion conformed back to its default shape.

"I was just about to head to my study for a cigar," he said as he walked over to Floyd. He put his hand on his shoulder. "I'd love for you to join me."

Floyd returned his gaze, unaffected.

"Sure, Don."

"Great. It's this way," Don said as he walked across the living room.

Floyd followed closely. He carefully slid his hand into his pocket and pulled out the recorder only enough to see the record button. He turned it on and let it drop back down. Don walked down a long hallway that ran the length of the side of the house. There was a large wooden door at the end of the corridor on the left.

"Here we are," Don said as he turned the knob and pushed it open.

He flicked on an overhead light that illuminated the room. Floyd looked around, impressed by his surroundings. The walls and ceiling were a dark wood that gave the room an earthy feel. The wall directly in front of him had another stone fireplace with two bookshelves on either side. Above it was a mounted buck's head, its antlers casting shadows that crept up the wall like snakes. There were two leather seats by the fireplace and a table with an ashtray between them.

Floyd looked to his right at Don's desk. There was a stack of papers, a container of writing utensils, a letter opener, and a coaster. Covering almost the entire wall behind the desk was a detailed world map.

"Come on in," Don said as he strolled over to a humidor that Floyd had assumed was a minifridge at first.

Don opened the device's door and withdrew a cedar box of cigars. He lifted the lid and smelled the Cuban delicacies inside. He moaned and selected the one he wanted to smoke this evening. He looked back at Floyd.

"Care to indulge?"

Floyd detested tobacco and let his revulsion briefly show.

"No, thanks."

"Good boy," Don replied and slid the box back into the humidor. "Would you mind stepping in here and shutting the door behind you?"

"Oh, yeah," Floyd said as he closed the door.

"Have a seat."

Floyd could feel his nerves starting to get the best of him. His heart thumped in his chest as he realized the moment of confrontation was drawing near. He took a deep breath and thought of his aunt.

"No, thanks," he said with firm defiance.

If his response alarmed Don, he didn't show it. Don didn't look up from prepping his cigar. He grabbed the guillotine cigar cutter from on top of the humidor and sliced off the end of his smoke. He put the chopped end in his mouth and pulled a torch lighter from his pocket. The powerful flame heated the tip of the cigar as he rotated it, puffing it to a workable burn. Once satisfied, he withdrew the stick from his mouth and finally looked up at Floyd, who was still standing by the door.

"No?" Don said.

"No, Don," Floyd began. "I think I better just keep my distance from here on out."

Don puffed the cigar and tilted his head slightly.

"Why is that?"

Floyd knew there was no going back now. In addition to the gun in his pants, he had one other secret item that he brought for this moment. Don watched the skinny kid pull some rolled-up book from his hoodie pocket. Floyd held it out so Don could clearly see the cover of the leather diary.

"Do you see those initials?" he asked. "It says BML. This diary belonged to Bethany Littleton."

Don remained expressionless.

"Does that name mean anything to you?" Floyd asked.

Don took a puff of his cigar and then rested it on the

frisbee-sized ashtray. He looked back up at Floyd, and Floyd watched him smile the first genuine smile of the evening. He had the same face, but there was more animation to it now.

"I haven't heard that name in years."

Floyd's heart sank.

"How did you come to acquire Bethany's diary, Floyd?"

"She...she was my aunt."

"Ahh," Don began as he leaned against the front of his desk and folded his arms. "She was murdered wasn't she, Floyd?"

"By the Countdown Killer," Floyd confirmed. "Your name is in this diary, Don. You were having an affair with her, and then she ended up *naked* and *carved* on the Devil's Road. What do you have to say to that?"

Don let his eyes drift up from his feet and connect with Floyd's. He smiled again.

"Wasn't it Nietzsche who said, 'Beware that, when fighting monsters, you yourself do not become a monster?'"

Floyd didn't know what to make of that. Don could see that he needed to clarify.

"You found your aunt's diary with my name in it, and you assume that I'm the Countdown Killer. Then, you apparently did some research on me and found my daughter at your school. It's obvious that you used Bailey to get close to me. Am I right, Floyd?"

"Yeah," Floyd said. "That's right."

"So, I'm asking...have you become a monster?"

Floyd felt real guilt for the first time as he honestly looked at himself and his actions. He had a terrifying feeling that maybe he had been wrong about Don after all.

"No," he finally said after shaking away the recently sowed doubt. "I'm not a monster, but you are. You are the Countdown Killer."

He withdrew his gun and pointed it at Don.

"Tell me it's not true," he said.

Don wasn't fazed by the weapon. He let out a deep sigh.

"I just realized that I'm not the only person in the world who knows that now," he mused.

Even though Floyd knew it in his gut all along, hearing the admission from the killer's mouth nearly made his legs give out from under him. His eyes started to water with grief and rage.

"Why?" he began. "Why did you kill those nine people? What were you trying to do?"

Don reached for his cigar, and Floyd stepped forward with the gun extended.

"Don't move."

"I'm just getting my cigar, Floyd. If you want to hear my admission, it'll come out a lot smoother this way."

Don didn't wait for Floyd's approval. He picked up the cigar from the ash tray and took a few puffs.

"If you think that I'm only responsible for nine deaths, then you're grossly uninformed."

Floyd listened carefully as he knew his recording device was doing the same.

"What happened on the Devil's Road isn't unique," Don began. "There are unsolved murders all over the world. Owning an international travel agency has its benefits, you know."

"Are you saying that you've killed more people than just the ones on the Devil's Road?"

"I'm a manufacturer of evil, son," he answered with a stare that burned deep into Floyd's soul. "The Countdown Killer, the West Coast Prowler, the Everglades Butcher, all the other sensationalized, catchy names they came up with…there have been so many over the years, and those are just in the states. You see, these are all boogeymen that will live on long after I'm gone. I learned early in life that it's far easier to leave a lasting legacy with evil than it is with good."

Floyd could hardly process what Don was explaining.

"Why didn't you finish?" he finally asked. "Why wasn't there a final body?"

Don smiled and took another puff. He placed the cigar back into the ashtray and stood up from the desk.

"Well, Floyd, that's where you come in."

Floyd gripped the gun and kept it pointed at Don's head.

"What do you mean?"

"The Countdown Killer was in my backyard. I did it to see if I could get away with it. But I always knew that the likelihood of being suspected of those crimes was exponentially increased due to living in this town. I had to leave one spot open in case anyone ever suspected me. It was a vacancy to tie up any loose ends."

Floyd could feel the moisture in his palm as he tried to keep his extended arm steady.

"I have to admit, though. I never imagined they'd be nice enough to bring the incriminating evidence to my house," he said, referring to the diary.

Don took two steps toward Floyd. Floyd had no intention of shooting anyone; he thought just having a gun would be enough to get a confession and keep Don in check until he called the police. He realized now that he had no choice. He aimed between Don's eyes and squeezed the trigger.

Nothing happened.

"Oops," Don said. "It looks like someone got in your bag while you were on a walk."

Floyd's eyes opened wide. He was about to scream, but Don hit him in the temple with Bailey's stun gun. Floyd's body spasmed as he lost all control of his motor functions and fell to the floor with a thud. Don knew they were far enough away from the women upstairs that the sound would go unnoticed. He grabbed the letter opener from his desk and puts his knee on Floyd's sternum.

Floyd felt a tightness around his scalp and saw that Don was holding his head by the hair. He watched Don pull his arm back and plunge the shiny blade into his throat so hard that the tip of the letter opener scraped his spine. Don withdrew the blade. Floyd tried to breathe but just gargled and coughed. Don stabbed two more times for good measure. Blood coated the blade and his knuckles and was beginning to pool on the hardwood floor. He watched as crimson bubbles formed atop the holes in Floyd's throat, and then the boy went slack.

He wiped the letter opener on Floyd's shirt and pushed himself off his chest. Something poked out of Floyd's pants pocket. He bent down and grabbed the small device and noticed a little red RECORD light. He hit the pause button and rewound one minute. The conversation that he and Floyd just had was playing through the tiny speaker. He skipped all the way back to the beginning of the recording and pressed play.

———·——

It was still dark by the time Melvin Gibbons was driving to work. He liked to get to the gas station no later than 5 AM, so he could get the coffee pot full and the cash register ready for the day. Melvin always enjoyed the drive through downtown Bennettsville. Mostly everyone in the town was still asleep or at home having breakfast before work. The one part of the commute that irked him on a subconscious level was traveling the Devil's Road.

He was not a superstitious man, nor did he scare easily, but he was alive when those bodies were being discovered on this road. He wasn't scared that someone was going to attack him in the dark just before the sun came up, and he definitely wasn't worried about wrecking his car; he could drive this road with his eyes closed. No, what bothered him was the possibility that he—being the first person to drive the road in the early morning—might encounter a new crime scene.

He turned onto the Devil's Road and drove while sipping his coffee. He navigated the twists and turns with ease, barely rocking the hot liquid in his thermos. Just as he rounded one of the last curves, two red brake lights appeared on the side of the road. He slowed down and angled the front of his car so that his headlights were shining on the idle vehicle. The car had obviously run off the road and slammed into an unforgiving tree. Smoke was rolling out from under the hood. Melvin crept a little closer and noticed the flickering amber lights inside the car. He realized that this wreck must've just recently happened, and there could be a person inside who needed help.

He stopped near the car and exited his vehicle. He hurried across the road and approached the smoldering vehicle from the rear. The driver's silhouette was slumped over to the right. He walked to the driver's window and peered inside. There were flames chewing their way up the interior of the car, smoke everywhere, and the stench of deployed airbags.

"Holy shit," he muttered, recognizing Floyd as the young man who had stopped in his store the day before.

Floyd's eyes were fixed and lifeless, his jaw hanging open. His forehead was badly cut, presumably from the wreck. Blood ran down his face and pooled at the neck. Melvin fought the urge to retch up his breakfast when he saw the hollowed-out throat and dangling strands of flesh. He looked at the broken windshield and figured that one of those shards must've serrated the poor boy's neck. Out of sheer instinct, Melvin reached through the open window and shook Floyd's shoulder.

"Hey!" he shouted, fully knowing that Floyd was beyond dead.

Floyd's head dropped face first into the airbag, and Melvin noticed an odd marking on the back of the boy's neck. Before he could examine any further, the smell of gasoline invaded his nostrils. He looked at the fire continuing to engulf the car and realized that he had to get out of there. As he backed away from the car, he stepped in a pool of fuel that he knew wasn't there just a few moments ago.

Melvin turned around and did his best attempt at running. He jerked open his car door and put it in reverse. The explosion lit up the night and echoed off the mountain, scaring Melvin so badly that he almost backed into the guardrail. The fireball floated up into the sky and disappeared into swirls of black smoke.

He sat in shock and watched the blazing inferno that used to be Floyd's car. He couldn't believe what was happening. His heart was beating furiously inside his chest. He knew what he had to do but was too paralyzed with fear.

Finally, he broke his stare from the carnage and reached into his pocket. He was going to call the sheriff and let them sort this out. What he was *not* going to do was tell them what he knew he didn't see. He knew his mind must've been playing tricks on him. It was still dark after all, and he was in shock. There could be no possible way that the number one had been carved into the back of that boy's neck. None at all.

---

Bailey woke up and walked down to Floyd's empty room. She stared at the bed that hadn't been slept in. She squinted in confusion when she noticed that his bag was gone too. She descended the stairs and entered the kitchen. Kathy sat at the kitchen table with a cup of coffee, reading the newspaper. She looked up at Bailey with concern.

"Where's Floyd?" Bailey asked.

Kathy let out a deep, sad sigh and said, "Your father needs to talk to you on the back porch, honey."

Her panic doubled in size as she breezed past her mom and through the back door. Don sat on a rocking chair on the back patio. He was smoking his morning cigar and drinking coffee. Floyd's voice recorder was on the table beside the ash tray.

"What's going on, Daddy? Where's Floyd?"

"Sit down, Bailey."

Bailey complied and eagerly awaited an explanation.

"Your boyfriend was working on some kind of project about the Countdown Killer. After you went to bed, I overheard him in his room speaking into this thing like he was some kind of radio host."

"Dad, I know all about his project. He told me last night."

"He did?"

"Yes. Now, where is he?"

"Did he tell you that he was using you, Bailey?"

"What are you talking about?"

Don hit the play button, and Floyd began to speak. Floyd described that he had just met Bailey at the bookstore and that she seemed like she could be easily manipulated. Bailey's jaw dropped in disbelief. Don paused the recording.

"He was a sick kid," Don said. "Earlier in that recording he says that he did a search on students at WVU to find out who was from Bennettsville. He got your information from social media and staged meeting you. He used you for his project. He just needed someone from our town."

Bailey felt a tear run down her cheek. Don leaned forward.

"Don't cry over that son of a bitch," he instructed. "I kicked his ass out of the house last night. His little project will never see the light of day either."

Don grabbed the voice recorder and chucked it into the pond beside the porch.

"Where did he go?" Bailey asked.

"I didn't ask. Do you really care?"

Bailey wiped the tears from her eyes.

"I guess not. I feel so stupid," she said as she shook her head.

Don stood up and walked behind his daughter. He placed his hands on her shoulders and gently squeezed.

"Don't feel stupid, sweetheart. There's nothing wrong with only seeing the good in people. That's a good thing. You just have to keep your guard up a little bit. There are lots of sickos in the world."

Bailey placed her hand on top of her father's and looked up at him.

"Thank you, Daddy."

# TWO DECADES DOWN AND I ONLY LOVE YOU AT NIGHT

*"Living in dreams of yesterday,
we find ourselves still dreaming of
impossible future conquests."*
—Charles Lindbergh

September 1971

Henry clutched his draft card. Ava sat beside him, weeping.

Vietnam might as well be on another planet. Henry, newly eighteen, had no worldly outlook. They'd begun dating earlier that summer.

"Just crumple it up," Ava said. "I'll go to Canada with you if you want."

Henry smiled.

"You could fake an injury or something, right? Hurt a foot or something?"

"I know you better than that," he grinned. "You'd have a hard time loving a man who ran from his problems."

Ava knew he was right. She put her head on his shoulder, and he wrapped his arm around her. He wouldn't be able to hold her like this for God knows how long. It made her cry even more.

"What if you don't come back?"

"I'll come back. I love you. And nothing on Earth is

stronger than love."

---

September 1991

The front of the aluminum jon boat went over a bulging river rock and came to an abrupt stop. The sudden jolt combined with the sharp scraping sound woke the shirtless young man awkwardly draped along the length of the vessel.

The brightness of a new day blinded him. A breeze blew his brown hair. The river's current rocked the back of the stuck boat. He looked down at his exposed body as if seeing it for the first time. He was tanned, thin but muscular, about six feet tall. Aside from a pair of tattered brown boat shorts, he was at the mercy of the elements.

*Who am I?* He looked around at the unfamiliar world. *Where am I?*

The river was between rolling hills, covered in green trees on both sides. Birds chirped and occasionally flew tree-to-tree. He felt the boat begin to budge. He slowly got to his feet, unsteady on sleepy limbs.

His shoeless foot sank an inch into the sandy riverbank. Twenty yards of beach segued into large rocks, then trees. Sparse sunlight shone through. A path began at the tree line.

The boat made a splash as the determined current finally wedged it off the rock and pulled it into the river. He spun around, trotted knee-deep into the rushing water on legs that weren't fully cooperating yet. Arms extended, he took three more steps and came to a stop. The boat drifted into some aggressive rapids downstream and disappeared. Somehow, he felt even more alone.

Unseen birds tweeted tauntingly from hidden branches. The man splashed angrily, sighed, and turned back to the shore.

Just as the riverbed was transitioning from stone to sand, the man stepped onto the jagged point of a rock, piercing the arch of his foot. He winced and gritted his teeth as he looked down. Blood twirled out of the wound in scarlet ribbons. He limped back to the beach and collapsed onto the warm, wet sand.

The deep gash continued to spew, and he looked around for something to use as a bandage. Rocks, sand, branches...nothing. He scooted across the sand to a fallen tree and propped his foot on it. The warm liquid flowed around his heel and began to dribble down his calf. He had to stop the bleeding. The steady red stream snaked under his knee to his inner thigh.

*It's going to bleed all over my...*

The man quickly pulled off his shorts. He rolled the tan pants into a noodle shape, wrapped his foot, and secured a knot. Satisfied, he set it on the fallen tree and fell back into the sand.

The wind across his body relaxed him and his flesh eagerly absorbed the sun's rays. He closed his eyes and felt the hum of the earth, the vibrations from the rushing river. His existence was a mystery; he was OK with that. Even the throbbing in his foot began to fade. Within moments, he was asleep.

A branch snapped in the distance. His eyes shot open; rustling came from the tree line. He sat up, grains of sand stuck to his back. He looked toward the path.

A young woman with curly black hair was standing at the edge of the clearing, staring at him in bewilderment. She was wearing tight black pants and a tank-top that had seen better days. Unsure what to do, the man instinctively crawled backward over the log until his lower half was shielded. The woman cocked her head, curious but cautious. She took a step forward in her brown sandals, hunting rifle in hand.

"Who are you?" she yelled.

The man was stuck.

"I don't know," he finally replied.

She waited for more. The wind blew between them, carrying flower pollen and helicopter leaves from maple trees.

"I woke up in a boat. The rock...that one back there...stopped me."

"Where's your boat? Where are your clothes?"

"My boat's gone. The river carried it off. The only clothes I have," he lifted his injured foot.

"How did you get here? How have you survived?"

"I...don't...know," he repeated. *Wait, what did she mean 'survive?'*

Her eyes darted back and forth. She trudged toward him, holding the gun by her side, finger still on the trigger. He used both his hands to cup his nakedness. She stopped five feet from where he lay. Attractive, still radiant, it was obvious she'd been in the wilderness some time. Seeing her dark eyes, he relinquished any concern about the gun. He was lost for words.

"How do I know you're not one of them?"

"'Them?'"

She looked at him with growing impatience. "Yes...them. Where have you been, man, living under a rock?"

"I don't know where I've been. That's what I'm saying. I have no memory. Who is 'them?'"

Baffled, she wanted to believe his story. Her eyes shot to his foot.

"Looks nasty."

"Feels like it too."

She knelt down and looked at it closer.

"Going to need medical attention."

"Where do I get that?"

Again, she made eye contact, as if contemplating something.

"There's a clearing up the hill where my cabin is. I can clean it up."

"You'd do that? You don't even know me."

"As long as you're not one of them, you're not my enemy."

She extended her hand to help him up. He hesitated, embarrassed about freeing up a hand and exposing himself.

"I promise I won't look," she smiled and turned her head.

He took her hand and winced as he got to his feet.

"Lean on me. Put your arm around my shoulder."

He did as told and took his weight off the injury.

"We'll take it nice and slow," she said.

They began walking toward the path.

"Thank you," he muttered between pained breaths.

The woman didn't respond; she was too busy keeping a lookout.

Carefully, they made their way across the larger rocks and began up the path. When they stepped into the shaded area, small sticks and pebbles were not kind to his bare feet.

"Not much further," she said, sensing his pain.

"What did you mean by 'them?'" he asked again.

"We'll talk in the cabin. Just keep moving."

They soon came to the small clearing. On the grass of the meadow, he was able to move more quickly. He looked around for a cabin.

"I'm just over there," she motioned to the other side of the clearing. He squinted at a bulge in the forest, tucked between two large trees. "I've camouflaged it with debris."

The more he looked at the pile of branches and brush, the more he could see the cabin beneath it.

"How long have you lived here?"

"This was my father's. He'd come up here to hunt and fish and kayak...back before everything happened."

He resisted the urge to ask what happened, but he could tell by the change in her tone that 'them' were probably responsible for it.

"So, how'd you end up here?"

"I knew I'd be safe here. Well, safer," she replied.

He nodded. She looked up at him.

"You really don't know, do you?"

"Know what?" he pleaded.

The woman looked away and shook her head. At the entrance to the cabin, he took his arm off her and leaned against the structure. She opened the door.

"Come in," she said and stepped inside.

He followed. She shut the door behind him. His eyes took a moment to adjust. There was no electricity or plumbing. The man looked at the bed, the fireplace, a makeshift kitchen with a small wooden table and chair. A wall of cabinets surrounded one small window. The brush leaning against the outside mostly covered that. The woman struck a wooden match and lit two thin candles. The interior quickly glowed amber.

Once again, the man cupped himself with his hands. She'd gotten used to his natural state, temporarily forgetting he was nude. She bent down and pulled a blue storage tote from under the bed; she popped it open and ruffled through her late father's clothes. She found a t-shirt, shorts, socks, and some heavily used underwear.

"You can have these. You're about the same size my dad was."

"Was?"

He began to dress himself. The woman didn't elaborate.

"I think it's time you tell me what's going on."

She ignored him and rummaged through one of the cabinets until she found the first-aid kit.

"Sit down," she said.

He sat on the side of the bed, his feet on the floor.

"Long-ways, please."

He swung his legs onto the small bed and reclined against a feather pillow. The woman sat at the foot of the bed, lifted his injured limb on her lap, and opened the first-aid kit. He could see a small bottle of rubbing alcohol, a few bandages, and some ointments. She unwrapped the makeshift bandage and dropped it on the wood floor, examined his foot, and grabbed the alcohol.

"This is going to sting."

She poured the odorous liquid into the gash.

The man squeezed the bedsheets in both hands and hissed. Undeterred, the woman dabbed the wound with a washcloth and administered some antibiotic ointment. She applied a cotton bandage and wrapped gauze around it several times. She patted his leg.

"All done."

"Thank you," he said, sitting back up in the bed.

"Are you hungry? Would you like a drink? I have deer meat and fish and some water from the river," she said anxiously.

She walked to the window and peered out before he could respond.

"Look," he began. "I don't know what's going on here, and I need to. It's time to talk."

"Yes," she replied, still looking outside. "It is."

There was a long silence as she continued to stare through the brush.

"What are you looking for?" he asked.

She slowly turned around.

"It'll be dark soon. That's when they come out."

"Who?"

"The ones who ended everything."

He knew the states, the countries, the oceans, the names of

all the planets. He had no clue where he fit into any of it.

"What do you mean by that?"

She walked across the small room and sat beside him. He looked into her watery eyes and, for the first time, saw through her calloused exterior.

"Everyone I know is gone," she began. "Everyone that you knew and loved is gone."

For the first time, he was grateful for his amnesia. He opened his mouth to ask what she meant by 'gone.'

"Dead," she clarified.

"How?"

"I'm not sure where they came from. I don't even know how many are left. It happened in just one night before anyone had a chance to figure out what was going on. I don't even think there were any news reports on it. I'm guessing it started here and then just swept across the globe with the dark as the planet rotated."

"What was it?"

"They're shaped like people, sort of, but you couldn't really see them at first," she explained. "They started off as dark figures just in the periphery of your vision. They screech these loud, piercing sounds. It's unbearable. That's all that night was—one horrible shriek. And then everyone was gone."

The woman started to sob, and the man instinctively put his arm around her. She leaned into his shoulder. He breathed in her natural scent.

"How did you survive?" he asked.

"I was in my apartment that night. I couldn't sleep. I

remember walking to the fridge to get something to drink when I noticed movement in the corner of the room. I thought it was a burglar at first, so I acted like I didn't see anything and stared straight ahead. I grabbed a knife from the block and spun around to see this shrieking body coming at me. I screamed and closed my eyes and just stabbed that knife forward as hard as I could. The blade went into whatever it was. It screamed louder. I ran out the front door to my car. I drove and kept driving. The horrible things I saw that night, I will never forget. I drove past everyone who needed my help, not that I could do anything. I just drove until I couldn't hear them anymore...until it was daylight. I came here. I figured I stood a chance at surviving in the woods."

"How long have you been here?"

The woman sat back up and wiped the tears from her eyes.

"A few months, maybe? I couldn't keep track in the beginning. I just hid in here and ate most of his canned food and drank all the bottled water, too afraid to go outside except to use the bathroom.

"After a couple weeks of silence, I thought I was good. I started to go down to the river and fish, even shot a deer. I started thinking about heading back down to civilization, just to see if anyone else survived. I knew there must've been more. The night before I was going to go, I heard them."

"Up here?"

"They were somewhere upriver. Their shrieks echoed down the valley."

The man saw the terror growing in her eyes.

"They're coming closer. I heard them moving around in

the valley a few nights ago. I just sat against the door with the gun. They must know I'm here because they won't leave. Maybe they smell me. Last night, I heard them in the meadow, just out there. I made myself peek through the window."

"What did you see?"

She hesitated.

"They looked like us."

The man was confused.

"They looked like humans. Not just that, I'm almost sure that they were dressed like soldiers in old uniforms."

"What?"

"That's everything. Then you show up the next day."

"With no memory to boot," he admitted.

She nodded and said, "Quite the coincidence."

He shifted his body on the bed so that he was facing her dead on.

"Look, I may not know who I am. But I know I'm not one of them," he said.

"Do *you*, though? Maybe one of them attacked me, and I fought it off. It did something to my memory. That makes sense, doesn't it?"

"Or one of them evolved into you."

He sat and thought about that for a second. It suddenly dawned on him that she knew he could be one of these things the whole time, and she still brought him to her cabin and helped him. She put her life at risk just to save him. He looked at her watery eyes and the tear streaks leading to the corners of her mouth. He felt her isolation, her despair, and the hope that he must represent.

She was no longer alone.

Before he had a chance to say anything, she put her hand on the back of his head and pulled his mouth to hers. She kissed him with all the passion she thought was lost, pushing him back into the pillow. The man didn't care who he was anymore; he just knew he was here with her and would do anything to make her forget everything she had been through, a brief reprieve. He rolled on top of her. He kissed her mouth, her cheeks, her neck as she wrapped her legs around him and let tears of joy cascade down her face. For a moment, just this moment, he made her feel normal. He was an answer to a prayer, and she loved him for it.

They made love in the cabin until they lost track of time. He cradled her in his arms, her bare skin against his warm body, something she thought she'd never experience again. The two of them held their embrace until they drifted into peaceful slumber as the sun set on the horizon.

---

"Wake up," he said, shaking her.

Her eyes shot open.

"It's night," he whispered.

She felt a rush of panic. That old fear she'd lived with was back; her pulse elevated; palms began to get clammy. There was noise outside as a horde of them moved in the darkness. The man grabbed her gun and started to get up, but she put her hand on his chest.

"Don't," she said.

"What do I do?"

"Put the gun down. Don't go to war with them."

"What?" he whispered with disbelief. "Why?"

She stared at him until he did as he was told.

"Lie back down. I don't want this to end."

Pieces of brush and branches were being ripped off the cabin. Again, the man reached for the gun, but she pushed him back into the bed. She had tears in her eyes as she climbed atop and rested her head on his chest facing the door.

The handle jiggled.

One of them looked in the window; it had the face and hat of a Vietnamese soldier. Then the shrieking started, all of them in unison like a pack of wolves that had found its prey.

She looked away just as the door was yanked open. The man tried to turn his head, but she grabbed him by the chin and held his face to hers. When he looked into her eyes, whatever was flooding in from outside didn't matter. She kissed his lips. He was among her stars, flying through her cosmos, she, his infinite universe, and nothing could harm them now.

---

Ava's eyes fluttered awake as the dream quickly swirled out of her consciousness. *Henry*, she thought, *why couldn't he remember his name in this one?* The dream was a little more unusual than the others. She normally didn't dream about monsters, though elements of war were recurring.

Ava sat up in bed. Thirty-seven-years-old now, she had spent all twenty years wondering what happened to Henry. They had spent the summer of 1971 together as carefree kids, their whole lives ahead of them. Most days they'd just floated in his jon boat on the lake trying to pick out animal shapes in the clouds. He was tan and carefree and wore nothing but those beautiful brown boat shorts.

Henry left in December 1971. She never saw him again. Many others had lost their loved ones; some got closure, but no one knew what happened to her love.

Family pictures adorned her oak dresser. After Henry left, she went to college, met her husband, had two children, and lived the American Dream. She was grateful. She did love her husband and couldn't imagine life without him or the kids.

However, it was her life—not her Dream.

Her Dream happens where dreams should: at night while she's asleep in her bed. She used to dream of Henry in the war and what could've happened. She would imagine him heroically storming the enemy to save his brothers or saying a prayer as his smoking helicopter fell into the jungle or being captured and disposed of in some unmarked grave.

She learned to stop worrying and began to imagine what wonderful adventures Henry *could* have gone on instead of the more probable, tragic end. For all she knew he could still be alive, floating down some river to meet the new love of his life.

She liked that idea.

She started seeing Henry in all types of fantastic scenarios. Henry had to climb Mt. Everest to save a stranded group.

One of the helpless hikers was a young woman who was too beautiful for Henry to ever forget. He carried her all the way down the mountain in that one.

Another time, Henry was an astronaut charged with deterring a meteor from colliding with Earth. He ended up sacrificing himself to save humanity, but he really did it for his love back home, pregnant with child.

Her favorite was when Henry rode into a western town on horseback and fell for the lovely widow of a notorious outlaw. Henry as a cowboy was not too much of a stretch for her imagination.

She didn't think about Henry most of the time.

In the meantime, she will probably forget this new Dream like many of the others. She didn't really care to analyze it. She will go on living, smiling, and when she lays her head down at night, she'll imagine a young man she used to know, and how he escaped to a new adventure, a new love, and lived happily ever after.

# VOODOO BAY

Miles squinted at the Caribbean sun through his Ray-Ban sunglasses. He leaned back in the pool chair, allowing his head to roll to his shoulder. Cassie was face-down in her chair beside him, lathered up in sunscreen, basking in the rays. *There could be worse places than Aruba to spend your honeymoon,* he thought, trying to stunt the growing feeling of restlessness. He forced himself to focus on something exterior to derail his train of thought.

There were a few other tourists floating around the pool in front of him. A young woman was softly singing something in Spanish to her toddler in floaties, sending choppy waves to a barrel-chested bald man leaning against the opposite wall. He tried to hide his scowl as a splash of chlorinated water invaded his margarita. Instrumental beach music was coming from the tiki bar by the entrance. The bartender—speeding from some illicit substance—watched his blender whizz and whirr as it pureed the slushy booze.

Scenic though it was, it all felt too familiar to him.

"Hey," Cassie said with her cheek still resting on folded arms.

"Hey," Miles smiled.

"What's wrong?"

Miles acted like he didn't know what she was talking about, even though he was secretly impressed with how well his new wife could read him.

"Nothing's wrong," he replied. "How could it be?"

She squinted through his deflection.

"You have that stare right now," she said.

"What stare?"

"The zone-out stare. You're either bored or something's on your mind."

He smiled, unable to speak otherwise.

"So?" she prodded.

He wiped the sweat off his forehead and surveyed the pool again. Out of the corner of his eye, he saw Cassie push herself up and rest on her elbows, still looking at him. He turned back to her.

"This is great," he began.

"But…"

He smiled again.

"But this feels like every other beach trip I've ever been on."

"What do you mean?"

"I mean when we decided to honeymoon in South America, I was expecting something different than the beaches and resorts back home."

"Different how?"

"I don't know. I guess I was just expecting something a little more…exotic."

Cassie laughed to herself as a lecture from one of her former college professors echoed through her head. It had only been a year since she had graduated with her master's in sociology, but that distinction currently only yielded her a temp job at a travel agency (though the discount from it was the only reason they were able to afford this trip.)

"What's funny?" he asked.

"The typical American perspective," she replied. "This is why the rest of the world rolls their eyes at us. We stumble into other countries with our fanny packs and cameras thinking that everything exists for our amusement."

Miles knew he had triggered one of her social no-nos and allowed her to finish. Cassie continued.

"The fact that just because we left the country, you expect everything to be some exotic, faraway land."

Miles took offense to her xenophobic implications.

"No, stop it," he said with a wave of his hand. "I didn't mean I was expecting some rundown, third-world country just because we left the States. I just meant that it would've been nice to experience another culture. It's gorgeous here— don't get me wrong—but if you told me that we were in Florida right now, I wouldn't know the difference."

Cassie rolled her eyes as she pushed herself all the way up and flipped to her back. She grabbed her melting daiquiri and sipped through the straw. After an audible lip smack, she returned her attention to her husband.

"So, you're seriously going to let that ruin the last few days of our honeymoon?"

Now he felt guilty. He sat up and swung his legs in her direction, giving her his undivided attention.

"Nothing's ruined," he began. "I'm just being selfish. I've already snapped out of it!"

Cassie put the straw back to her lips and sucked up the rest of the liquid until she made two loud slurping sounds. She placed the plastic cup on the stand beside her.

"Well, what are we going to do with your newfound appreciation?" she asked, buzzing from the booze.

Miles stood up and wrapped his towel around his damp swimming trunks. He extended his hand.

"Care to join me on an adventure?"

She smiled, grabbed her towel, and took his hand.

———•———

The two of them had been walking around the island shops for over an hour, and the sun was now heading toward the water. They had been in every place of interest and just reached the pier. A salty breeze blew between them. Miles looked at his watch: 4:50 PM. It wasn't until he saw the pale skin under his watchband that he realized how tanned his skin was getting.

"What do you want to do now?" Cassie said, carrying a catchall bag of souvenirs.

Miles wiped the beads of sweat from his brow.

"Are you hungry?" he asked.

"A little bit."

"Yeah, I'm getting there too," he said as he looked around for anything else that might be of interest. He noticed what he assumed to be a local tying up his small fishing boat. "Excuse me, sir?"

The man looked up from his knot. His face was dark and leathery from years of hanging around the equator. He was about six inches shorter and twenty years older than Miles, but his wiry build was impressive, nonetheless.

"Do you speak English...Papiamento?" Miles asked.

"Both," the fisherman said. "Is there something I can help you with? You lost or something?"

"It's hard to get lost on an island, isn't it?" Cassie teased with a warm smile.

The fisherman eyed her up and down and chuckled.

"You overestimate the intelligence of tourists," he said as he bent over and resumed wrapping the boat's rope around the wooden post.

"I can assure you, she doesn't," Miles teased.

An awkwardness hung in the air just as thick as the humidity.

"Well," Miles began, breaking the silence. "We saw you pull up and figured you might know a thing or two to do around here...a place to eat or a local hole in the wall. You know, somewhere a bit off the map?"

The fisherman looked up at Miles and then to Cassie and then back to Miles.

"We're just a bit tired of all the touristy stuff," Cassie elaborated. "We're looking for more of a *cultural* experience."

The fisherman finalized his knot and stood all the way up, stretching his lower back.

"Ever heard of Vudula Bay?"

"Did he just say, 'Voodoo Bay?'" Miles asked Cassie.

" *Vudula* Bay," he corrected.

They looked at each other and then both shook their heads.

"I figured as much," he said. "No one really knows about

Vudula Bay but us."

"Where is it?" Cassie inquired.

The fisherman turned and looked toward the open ocean.

"About thirty miles northeast."

Cassie remembered looking at the map of Aruba and the surrounding area in her office.

"I don't remember seeing anything on the map. There's nothing northeast of here until Antigua, and that's a lot further than 30 miles."

The fisherman smiled and nodded his head.

"You won't find Vudula on any map," he explained. "Too small."

Miles pulled out his phone.

"OK, I'll check Google Maps," he said and started pecking away at the screen. "Gotta love technology."

The fisherman took a step toward Miles and peered down at the results. Miles found Aruba and began scrolling Northeast. Cassie moved in closer to get a view as well. A little speck darted across the screen, but Miles didn't see it.

"Hold it!" Cassie exclaimed.

"Yes, I saw something too," said the fisherman, who had a pungent, fishy smell about him.

Miles used his finger to move across the digital ocean until the speck reappeared.

"Zoom in on that," Cassie instructed as Miles immediately did.

Right there in the middle of the blue map was a small, C-shaped island.

"That's Vudula," the fisherman said. He pointed to the

outer curve of the C. "That's where the village is. There's a place in a yellow building right about here…just a little bit past the docks."

"Is it just a few houses and a restaurant?" Miles wondered aloud.

"There's a bait shop and a few street vendors. The people who live there don't leave much. They make their living trading goods to the main islands and the occasional outsiders. They do have some fun stuff. I was out on the water one night and saw torches and singing. It could be what you're looking for."

"How's the beach on the bay side?" Miles asked.

The fisherman shook his head with a scowl.

"Don't even bother with the bay," he said. "It's dangerous terrain. Too hard to get down to the beach and even harder to climb back up. Stay away from there."

Cassie detected a nervousness in his tone.

"We'll stay away from there. Is there anywhere to stay on the island?" she asked.

Miles looked at her curiously, impressed that she would even consider such a spontaneous excursion.

"There are a few houses with rooms," the fisherman answered. "I've stayed there a time or two when the sea was too rough. It's not bad; it's no resort. If you want a real taste of culture though, you should check it out."

Cassie and Miles looked at each other again, sharing the same idea.

"Could you take us?" Cassie said first.

"I won't be working anymore this week."

"Right now," Miles interjected. "Could you take us right now? We'll pay well."

The fisherman pondered their request. He looked back at the boat he had already spent hours aboard that day. His fish were on ice, he had enough gas, and he could use some extra cash.

"I could drop you off, but I'm not waiting around to take you back."

"That's fine," Miles said. He turned to Cassie. "Do you want to stay the night there?"

Cassie could see in his eyes how excited he was.

"Let's do it," she said. "But how will we get back?"

"There are plenty of fishing vessels there that you could pay for a ride home," the fisherman said. "We must go now, though. OK?"

Miles turned toward Cassie.

"We don't need anything from the hotel. We'll come back tomorrow morning," he told her.

Cassie was not thrilled about abandoning her honeymoon suite—even just for one night—but she smiled and nodded her head.

"I'm game," she said.

Miles took out his wallet and withdrew a few hundreds.

"Will this cover it?"

The fisherman's eyes widened. He reached out and took the cash.

"Oh, yes. Now hop aboard, and I'll *untie* this knot."

The sun had dipped a little below the watery horizon by the time Vudula Bay appeared in the distance. Miles studied the small island as they grew closer. They were approaching from the bay side of the island. *This guy was right,* he thought. *That does look treacherous.* He put his arm around Cassie as the two of them sat on the hot cushions at the back of the boat.

"The bay is so pretty," Cassie said over the loud boat motor and wind.

Miles nodded his head. As they got closer, he noticed what looked to be a path that zig-zagged its way through the trees and cliff, all the way to the shore. *Interesting,* he thought.

About twenty minutes later, they coasted up to the small harbor. Cassie counted six other boats that were docked, all smaller fishing vessels like the one they were on. She wondered what they would even do if they couldn't find a ride. She pulled out her cell phone, and just like she thought, there was no service out here.

The boat lightly bumped into its slot and stopped.

"Welcome to Vudula Bay," the fisherman said as he grabbed ahold of a wooden post on the dock. "Watch your step."

Miles climbed out first and then reached back to help Cassie.

"Enjoy your stay," the fisherman said with a smile, the sun halfway hidden in the sea behind him.

"Thank you..." Cassie began. "I just realized we never got your name."

"Luiz," the fisherman said.

"Thank you, Captain Luiz," Miles said as he reached down to shake the man's hand. "I'm Miles, and this is Cassie."

"Miles and Cassie," Luiz repeated. "Well, Miles and Cassie, you want to follow the dock to the path just ahead. That path turns into a stretch of stony road. The village is right after that. It's beautiful; you'll love it. Remember, eat at the yellow building. Delicious."

"Thanks again," Miles said.

Luiz pushed off the dock as his boat swirled around to the open water. He turned, waved, and then accelerated back toward Aruba. They watched him shrink in the distance. Cassie looked at her husband.

"Are you ready to go eat?"

"Oh yeah," he replied. "I'm starving now."

The two of them began walking the path as instructed. Dirt quickly turned to stone and after a quarter of a mile, they arrived at the town. The first local they saw was a young dark-skinned woman who was carrying a basket of fruit across the road. She did a double-take when she saw the newbies on the island.

Miles waved and said, "Hello."

The woman forced a smile as she walked into a small cottage. Cassie looked at the row of ancient homes, marveling at the simplicity of their design and the durability they must possess to withstand years of hurricane seasons.

An elderly couple sat on a stone bench in front of a small house, watching the sunset. The man noticed the newlyweds and nudged his wife. The woman looked at the guests and smiled as they walked along the path.

"Hello," Miles said.

"Hello to you," the old man said. "What brings a lovely young couple such as yourselves to our little old island?"

"We heard there's a restaurant to die for," Miles said.

The old woman nodded her head.

"Where'd you hear that?" she asked.

"A fisherman named Luiz," Cassie replied. "We're honeymooning in Aruba and ran into him at the docks. We told him we wanted to get away from the touristy stuff, and here we are."

"I'm glad Luiz speaks so highly of my establishment," the woman said.

"You own the restaurant in the yellow building?" Miles asked.

The old man grinned, proud of his wife. The woman pointed down the road to a two-story, yellow structure about thirty yards away.

"That yellow building right there," she said. "That's mine, alright. I'm taking the evening off though. It's sort of a special night for us. A capable crew is running it right now if you want to try it out."

"That's the first place we're headed," Miles said, feeling the emptiness of his stomach. "Say, do you all know where there's a room to rent for the night? Luiz told us there are places to stay on the island."

"We should hire Luiz," the old woman laughed. "We run a—what is the expression?—a bed and breakfast."

"You don't say," Miles said as he eyeballed the tiny house behind them. "You two must be pillars of this community."

"A few of us are," the woman replied.

He looked around at the other houses and knew it would be close quarters no matter where they stayed.

"Sure," the old man said. "If you need a room, we can take care of it."

Miles and Cassie exchanged glances, coming to an agreement with just a look.

"We'd love to," Cassie said.

The old woman sprung to her feet.

"Well then, I've got some work to do," she began. "You all go eat while I freshen up the place. It'll be ready when you're finished."

"Great," Miles said. "That was easy enough."

———

After they ate the best seafood either of them had ever experienced, the two of them stepped out of the restaurant with full bellies and smiles to match. They each held a bottle of beer they took to go.

"Totally worth the commute," Cassie said and took a drink.

"Yep," Miles agreed as he stared beyond the road and docks at the tip of the sun poking out of the water. "Beautiful."

Cassie put her arm around her husband and rested her head on his shoulder. She let her gaze drift toward the rest of the town further down the main drag. There was an eclectic row of shops and vendors followed by more personal dwellings that were even more humble than the ones they had already encountered.

"Those shops look cool," she said.

Miles turned and looked at them, and one stood out instantly. It was an A-framed structure covered in dark red plaster. There was no sign or windows, only a front door with a black, circular symbol painted above it.

"Let's go check them out," he said.

They walked past a general store-type of establishment with goods that were brought over from the more populated islands. A man sat behind the counter hand-rolling cigars and didn't even notice the couple walk by. Beside that was a bait and tackle shop in which a few people were talking and smoking cigarettes. Miles nodded as they went by.

They stopped at the entrance to the red building and looked at the symbol above the door. It was a hand-painted circle, nearly two feet in diameter, with a line cutting straight across the middle. In the top hemisphere were what appeared to be little representations of people dancing in all types of ways. The bottom half was painted solid black except for two serpent-like eyes watching from the abyss.

"What do you think that means?" Cassie asked.

"No clue," Miles admitted. "But it's cool as shit."

The door opened inward, causing them both to jump. A hooded woman under five feet tall stood in the doorway. Miles briefly looked at the candle-lit store behind her, with its aisles of strange crafts and books.

"Hello," Cassie said, unable to see the top half of the woman's face under the black hood.

"Tourists?" the old woman said with a thick accent with which they were both unfamiliar.

"Yeah," Cassie admitted. "Tourists."

"From Aruba," Miles clarified as he condescendingly pointed across the ocean with his beer still in hand.

"Tourists," the woman repeated. Cassie watched the corners of her mouth curve up in a grin. "I love tourists; they're why I'm here. Won't you come in and look around?"

Miles looked back to the treasure trove of oddities inside.

"That's why *we're* here," he said.

The woman took two steps back into the dark shop and motioned for them to enter. Miles, mystified, stepped inside and tugged at Cassie's hand as she cautiously followed him in.

"Mind the door, will you?" the woman said.

Cassie realized she was speaking to her and quickly closed the door behind them, nearly dropping her beer bottle. As soon as what was left of the evening light was shut outside, the woman pulled back the dark hood to reveal her pale, wrinkled skin and bald head. Cassie felt her heart skip a beat from the shock of the woman's appearance. Her left eye was grey and dead with a deep scar cutting down through it and a droopy eyelid slanting across it. Her other eye was bright blue and wide open, darting back and forth, looking them over as if it were working double-time. She smiled, revealing purple gums with no teeth.

"Welcome to my shop," she said hoarsely, her voice

nothing more than a pained rasp. "Look at whatever you like. I'm willing to haggle on any of the prices."

"OK," Miles said as he looked away from the strange old lady and started checking out the merchandise. He tugged Cassie's hand again. "You want to come over here, honey?"

"Huh? Oh, sure," she replied.

The dark robe adorning the small woman touched the floor, and she seemed to glide as she moved toward the check-out counter. Cassie saw her from the side for the first time and noticed a bowling ball-sized belly bulging under the robe. If that woman didn't look like she was pushing ninety, Cassie would've assumed she was pregnant. She elbowed Miles and motioned for him to look. He did, made a repulsed face, and proceeded to the aisle on the opposite side of the store. Once they were safely out of ear range, Miles leaned toward his wife.

"That is the creepiest bitch I've ever seen," he whispered.

Cassie laughed but scolded him anyway.

"Oh my gosh, stop," she said with no conviction. "Did you see her belly though? What the fuck was that? What are these people eating over here?"

Her inebriation dissolved any sense of political correctness, and she was now unaware, as they stumbled through the shop, of just how they had become her version of the stereotypical American tourist.

Miles took a gulp of beer and looked back at the old woman who was now sitting on a stool behind the counter on the opposite side of the room. He noticed she was wearing a necklace with something sharp on it.

"This is as exotic as it gets," he said too loudly.

"Miles," Cassie scolded with a grin.

He finally focused his attention on the goods inside the shop. The aisle was full of hand-made crafts composed of seashells, starfish, shark teeth, and anything else one could pull from the sea. The two of them walked briskly, uninterested by the initial offerings.

They rounded a corner and began walking down the second aisle. This one was adorned with shelves of books of various sizes, shapes, and ages. Miles picked one up and looked at the cover. It was something in what he assumed was Latin. He sat his beer on the floor and thumbed through the book. It was old and probably expensive; he quickly shoved it back in its place, bending the cover just a little.

"What was that?" Cassie asked.

"I have no idea."

As they turned into aisle three, they both came to a stop. Going down both sides of the aisle were shelves filled with sculptures of reptilian sea monsters.

"Holy shit," Miles muttered.

Cassie stepped past him and looked at one after another, fascinated by the craftsmanship and detail of each piece. Miles followed, examining the artwork on his side of the aisle. Some were made from wood, some from bone, some from stone, some from glass, but it suddenly became apparent that they were all representations of the same creature. It had a snake-like torso with a fin at the end. Six elongated tentacles—each tipped with a claw—draped from both of its sides. Its scaley, serpentine neck connected to a head that made Cassie's stomach turn: it was oval-shaped and resembled something between primate and fish. Two lidless, narrow eyes (which Cassie immediately recognized from the sign out front) rested above an open mouth that was filled with rows of sharp, serrated teeth. A set of gills ran down either side of its face.

The two of them walked from creature to creature in a state of shocked wonder.

"I see you've met Vudula Bay's oldest inhabitant," the old woman spoke from her counter at the aisle's end.

"What is it?" Miles asked.

"Local legend, very local," she replied.

Miles and Cassie continued checking out one piece at a time.

"Some of us old-timers have nicknamed it Vyzyra," she explained.

"That's an interesting name," Cassie said.

The old woman grinned blackness.

"It's a demon," she said casually.

"A water demon?" Miles asked before taking a drink. "Never heard of one of those, but it does look kind of like the Loch Ness monster. Don't you think, Hun?"

"It's *nothing* like that," the old woman snapped.

The two of them looked at her simultaneously. Her scorn contorted back into a grin.

"Vyzyra doesn't poke its head out of the water for pictures," she explained. "He isn't some imaginary beast that survived the prehistoric age. No, Vyzyra or at least the legend says, isn't from our world. He's an ancient creature older than time itself." She stood up from the counter and began to slowly step toward them. "You see, once a month, when the moon is at its darkest, this devil slithers up through a crack in the ocean floor, straight out of the bowels of Hell, and... eats."

Once the woman was close enough, Miles saw that what was hanging from her necklace was the largest shark tooth he had ever seen. It was razor-sharp and curved slightly back like a hook at the end; the edges were serrated.

Cassie stared at the woman, completely held captive by her terrifying tale. Miles took the last gulp of his beer and muffled a belch.

"Do you have a lot of people here go missing?" he asked with raised eyebrows.

"Not at all."

"It seems like you would if your water demon shows up once a month for a meal."

The woman tilted her head with amusement, keeping her bulging eye fixed on Miles.

"Plus," he continued. "This thing can't exist anymore than the Loch Ness Monster, Bigfoot, or the Megalodon can, and do you want to know why?"

The woman nodded with amusement.

"The food source," he answered. "These mythological beasts are all so big that even if they could avoid discovery by sonar mapping and high-res cameras, they would need to consume so much food that they'd deplete any ecosystem they tried to live in. It's just not possible. Don't you hate when facts get in the way of a good story?"

The old woman nodded her head in silence, apparently taking what he just said into consideration. Cassie nervously took a drink just as the woman slowly turned around and crept toward her counter. Feeling bad, Cassie looked down at one of the glass creatures and picked it up.

"We will take this though," she said as the woman plopped back into her stool.

"So, people on the island actually believe this?" Miles continued.

"Miles stop," Cassie whispered.

"A few," she replied.

Cassie walked up to the counter and paid the woman for her new souvenir; Miles took his time meeting them there. The old woman carefully wrapped the figurine in a maroon cloth and placed it in a velvet satchel.

"Thank you," Cassie said apologetically.

The woman just nodded her head, leaned back against the wall, and rubbed her round belly.

Miles held up his beer as if he were offering her cheers and pulled Cassie toward the exit.

"There is one difference between Vyzyra and your other creatures," the woman said from behind them. They both turned back around. "This demon doesn't eat because it's hungry."

"Oh, yeah?" Miles replied. "He's just bored?"

The woman smiled, twirled the tooth on her necklace between her fingers, and laughed.

"It's just a legend," she said. "A way to sell my trinkets."

It was near dark by the time Cassie and Miles made it back to the couple's house with the rented room. Just as Miles was about to knock on the door, he heard the man's heavy footsteps approaching from inside. The door swung open.

"There they are," he said. "We thought you got lost. Come on in."

The two of them walked inside the small living room.

"I never got your name son," the old man said just as he turned to yell at his wife. "Myra, they're here!"

"I'm Miles, and this is Cassie," he said.

The old man gripped Miles's hand.

"Gaspar," he said just as his wife entered the room wearing a bathrobe. "That's Myra."

"Nice to meet you both," Cassie said. "This is quite the interesting island."

"Oh yeah? How so?" Gaspar asked.

Cassie withdrew the glass sculpture of Vyzyra. Gaspar and Myra exchanged a quick glance. Had Cassie and Miles not been so buzzed, they would've picked up on the concern.

"We got the rundown on the local legend," Miles informed.

"So, you met our village loon," Gaspar said.

"*Gaspar!*" Myra scolded.

"What? Every town has one, even on an island," he retorted. "I supposed Lorona down there told you all about Vyzyra appearing in the bay every month?"

"Wait... it supposedly appears in the bay?" Miles said.

"Seriously? That's a thing?"

"It's all horseshit, son," he replied, shaking his head.

Myra was staring daggers through her husband. He nervously cleared his throat.

"I'm glad you got your souvenir and got out of there. She does make interesting art," Gaspar said as his eyes were drawn to the sculpture.

"Your room is ready for you," Myra said from behind her husband. "Right this way."

"Oh, thank you," Cassie said as she and Miles followed Myra out of the living room.

"I left you all a little something in there," Gaspar said. "It being your honeymoon and all."

"OK then," Miles said.

Myra led them to a small, squared room with a decent enough bed and an open window. The sea breeze blowing in was so intoxicating that Cassie didn't notice the bottle of rum resting between the pillows. Miles walked in behind them and saw it immediately. He picked it up and inspected the label. It was obviously from a local place—authentic Caribbean rum.

"Gaspar, you're a man after my own heart!" Miles exclaimed.

"You're welcome!" Gaspar shouted back from the other room. "Crack it open. Celebrate your union!"

Myra shook her head at her husband.

"We'll leave you two alone now," she said. "Gaspar already talked to one of his friends who's willing to take you back to the main island tomorrow. Please let us know if you need anything else."

"Excellent. Thank you, Myra," Miles said.

She smiled and shut the door behind her.

Cassie fell back on the bed as Miles pulled the cork out of the glass bottle and took a swig.

"Wow! That's good stuff."

"Let me try," Cassie said, as she sat up.

Miles handed her the bottle, and she took a drink, instantly making a sour face and getting choked up.

"That is strong," she said between coughs.

"As it should be," he said as he sat on the bed beside her, gazing up at the stars through the window. "It's gorgeous out there."

She looked out and saw clusters of palm trees and the start of a steep hill. Hovering just above the trees was the barely visible outline of a new moon in the lunar phase. She turned to her husband.

"That's a new moon, right?"

"I have no idea," Miles laughed. "I doubt the moon gets any darker than that."

She waited for him to understand what she was getting at, but he just took another drink of rum. She pulled the water demon out of her pocket and made it crawl up Miles's leg.

"I come to collect what's mine when the moon is at its darkest," she said in a raspy voice.

Miles's eyes widened.

"Holy shit!" he said. "Babe, we have to go check out that bay."

"What? We can't even get down there, remember?"

"Actually, we can. There's a clear-cut path that leads right down to the water," he said and poked his head out the open window. He looked at the ocean and then to the hill right in front of him. "And you know what? All we have to do is walk up that mountain. The bay is just on the other side."

"That's crazy," she said, but Miles could tell she was mulling over the idea.

"Babe, this will be something we tell our grandkids one day. Let's do it," he said as he sat down beside her.

Cassie realized that this was the first time he had mentioned kids, let alone *grandkids*.

"What else are we going to do?" he kept on. "Stay in here for the rest of the night?"

Cassie took the bottle back from him and gulped down the biggest drink Miles had ever seen her take.

"Alright," she said. "Let's continue our adventure."

Miles took a step toward the window.

"Let's just go out this way," he said. "No need to disturb them. Who knows when we'll be back?"

———·—·———

Two hours of drunkenly hiking their way up the steep incline finally came to an end when they reached the precipice. Both of their jaws dropped when they saw the view from the top. From this high up the ocean was a motionless body of black water stretching as far as the human eye could perceive. Stars winked down from the cosmos. Were it not for the faint sounds of waves crashing into rocks hundreds of feet below them, the scene could've been a painting.

Miles, covered in a sheen of perspiration, sat down and leaned back on bent elbows, taking shallow breaths. Cassie remained standing as she held the nearly empty bottle of rum they had enjoyed on their journey.

"You know," Miles began, breathing heavily. "Even though we won't see a sea monster, we at least got to witness this."

"It's the most beautiful thing I've ever seen," Cassie said.

Miles suddenly remembered the path and began looking around for the trailhead.

"What are you looking for?" Cassie asked.

"The trail. Remember?"

"You're still wanting to go down there? Why don't we just stay up here? We'll have to walk back up if we go down."

Just then, Miles saw a three-foot-wide clearing in lush vegetation lining the interior of the bay. He hopped up and stumbled over to it. Sure enough, the rocky path was a steep descent for about seven feet, and then it began to zig-zag all the way to the shore below.

"Here it is."

Cassie walked to him and looked for herself.

"I mean, we came all this way, didn't we?" he asked.

"We're not going to see anything down there that we can't see from up here," she protested, not wanting any more exercise.

"I'm just going to go down this part to get a better view of the beach," he said as he stumbled down the steep slope, knocking rocks and debris loose behind him.

He stopped his forward momentum against a tree when he

reached the plateau.

"Are you OK?" she asked.

Miles walked to the edge of the rocky platform and looked down. From his new vantage point, the entire beach below was exposed. He sat down on a chunk of a boulder and leaned back against the dirt.

"Uh, don't worry about me," Cassie said from above. "I'll just stay up here, I guess."

Before Miles could get up to go help his wife, he noticed the flame of a torch emerge from a small cavern below that he hadn't noticed before.

"What the fuck...?" he muttered.

"Miles, are you going to help me down or what?"

He stood up and looked back at his wife.

"There's someone down there!" he said in what passed for a whisper to a drunk person.

"Huh?"

She looked down at the bay and saw the flickering of an orange flame.

"Get down here," Miles instructed.

Cassie, still carrying the rum, sat and gingerly slid down. He helped her up, and the two of them peered down at the mystery unfolding before them.

The person carrying the torch was small and covered in some sort of dark cloak. Even though his vision was starting to double on him, Miles recognized the robe and the size of the figure.

"Holy shit."

"What?"

"That's the old lady from the store. The creepy bitch."

"No way."

Just then, the figure planted the torch into the sand, faced the undulating water, and let the robe slide off her nude body.

"Eww!" Cassie said as she covered her mouth.

"What is she doing?"

The old woman turned slightly and both of them gasped at her bulging, pregnant stomach.

The bald, pale woman took slow trots, closer and closer to the water, her loose skin jiggling with each purposeful step. When she was about six feet from where the waves stopped, she carefully dropped to her knees, sat on her bottom while protecting her belly, laid flat on her back, and spread her thick, stumpy legs for the ocean.

Miles and Cassie watched, speechless.

Right where the trees met the sand, a half circle of previously hidden hooded figures stood up in unison. Each one lit their own torch and planted it in the sand to their right. One by one, going from left to right, the figures de-robed down to their exposed flesh.

"Fuck me," Miles said as he stared at the backs of eight nude, elderly people.

"I want to leave."

In unison, the group began a deep, bellowing chant: "VY-ZY-RA! VY-ZY-RA! VY-ZY-RA!"

"Miles, I'm fucking scared. Let's go," Cassie pleaded.

"VY-ZY-RA! VY-ZY-RA! VY-ZY-RA!"

The water in the bay lost its placidity as it began to rumble.

"VY-ZY-RA! VY-ZY-RA! VY-ZY-RA!"

Something massive was under the water, less than twenty feet from the shore.

"VY-ZY-RA! VY-ZY-RA! VY-ZY-RA!"

Cassie's eyes grew wide with terror as the creature in the water inched closer to the sand, slowly revealing the top of its bulbous, translucent body. In the midst of this existential crisis, Miles was still able to look at the nearly clear skin and conclude, *This is why it only comes out on the darkest night.*

The C-shaped group of people dropped to their knees in reverence as the beast drew nearer. The creature stopped, and for a moment, all was still. Miles's entire body was coursing with adrenaline.

There was a small bubbling sound from the water, and then a tentacle burst out with a misty spray. It darted up the sand to the woman's spread legs and buried itself inside of her. She gritted her teeth in a familiar mix of pain and pleasure as the slithery appendage canvassed her womb. Once it found what it was looking for, the slack tentacle jerked taut. The old woman moaned as her eyes watered.

An infant's gurgled cries echoed throughout the bay, and the tentacle slowly pulled a deformed monstrosity of translucent human flesh out of her body. The pathetic newborn abomination squirmed and cried as the massive tentacle wrapped around its neck. It was unable to breathe with only its gills.

Before it could make another sad sound, the tentacle reeled back into the dark water like fishing line. A bulbous fish/humanoid head—accurately depicted by the figures in the old woman's shop—fully raised out of the water and opened its circular mouth. It chucked the baby into its eager gullet, full of rows of serrated teeth, and the wailing thing was shredded instantaneously.

The crowd chanted again: "VY-ZY-RA! VY-ZY-RA! VY-ZY-RA!"

Miles and Cassie just held each other, unable to move... to speak... to think...

"VY-ZY-RA! VY-ZY-RA! VY-ZY-RA!"

Out of the water emerged a second tentacle, this one a darker maroon hue like the color of the old woman's shop. The snake-like thing throbbed as it found its way to the woman's opening again. It pulsated violently, filling her with the seeds necessary to incubate another offering for the next new moon. The woman screamed and gripped the sand. Even though this was a ritual she had performed for the last 70 years ever since the community and the beast had come to this diabolical arrangement, she never enjoyed this part. She felt the molten liquid running down her thighs. The tentacle, satisfied with the job, retreated into the water.

Cassie lost control of her body and let the rum bottle slip from her fingers and roll down the hill, loudly shattering and disturbing the scene below. The eight nude spectators (who the newlyweds had just realized had been masturbating the whole time) whipped around to see the source of the sound, and Miles recognized two of them as Gaspar and Myra.

The demon in the water watched it all through its narrow, reptilian eyes. Wrath filled its godly being at the thought of its subjects allowing such a disturbance to occur. With one swipe of a bladed tentacle, the beast halved all eight disciples.

Cassie shrieked with horror as she watched the tops of the bodies slide off and plop into the sand, some leaving still-standing legs that eventually toppled over. Realizing that something had gone wrong behind her, the old woman with her back in the sand tilted her head just enough to see the terrified newlyweds in the darkness above her. She smiled that toothless smile and began to laugh just as the beast emerged on land and slithered over her, pressing her deep into the sand.

Miles and Cassie didn't have to be sober to realize that the sea demon had spotted them. Before they could get to their feet, the beast released a tentacle over one hundred yards and grabbed Cassie, digging its hook into her back.

"No!" Miles screamed as his wife was suddenly jerked off the landing.

Without thinking twice, he jumped and rolled and skidded toward the beach just as the tentacle was dragging her to its open mouth, halfway filled with saltwater. Cassie saw the old woman flattened into the sand and braced herself to be dragged over the top of her. She briefly saw the tooth necklace and reacted without thinking, snatching it off her neck. Tooth in hand, she plunged the serrated point into the tentacle and desperately sawed back and forth, goring the appendage until it released her.

Miles hit the beach and stood up, disoriented and determined. The creature crawled further onto land and opened its mouth near Cassie's legs. Miles grabbed the old woman's still-burning torch and threw it like a javelin down the beast's throat. The creature shook and spasmed as it recoiled into the murky water. As it sank back from where it came, it emitted a reverberating roar that vibrated every grain of sand on the beach.

Miles grabbed Cassie by the wrist and pulled her to her feet.

"Let's go!"

The two of them ran to the path, never looking back or slowing to catch their breath. They ran left, then right, left, then right, as they ascended the steep terrain. When they reached the top, Cassie finally looked back at the carnage below. She saw the bisected bodies of the followers strewn about the crimson sand like seal carcasses washed up to shore. Her vision drifted closer to the water where the old woman had been crushed. Although it was too dark and too far away to know for sure, she swore that it was an empty hole.

"We have to keep going," Miles warned. "We have to get off this island."

Cassie snapped out of it and followed her husband.

———·——

By daybreak, they had already secured their own vessel back to Aruba (Miles wasn't taking any chances with the person Gaspar had hired to take them back). Hungover and suffering from exhaustion and dehydration, they sat on the back of the boat, fighting the urge to vomit into the ocean rushing by them. Miles rested his head on his arm and soon fell asleep.

Although Cassie was tired, her mind wouldn't let her rest. She placed her head on her husband's shoulder and stared at the rising sun until her eyes hurt, unable to think about anything other than what was in the water below them and how much those seagulls squawking in the distance sounded like a witch's cackle.

# THE WEEPING WIND

The porch swing squeaked as I rocked back and forth with the tips of my boots. A frozen wind found its way to my bones despite my multiple layers. Steam rolled over the brim of my coffee mug, and I gently blew it away. I looked out at the rolling Appalachian hills enshrined in a starless night. I take time every year to reflect, and it's been thirty since the accident. My family is safely tucked away inside. Even if they were awake, they know not to disturb me on December 6th.

I was only five years old at the time. Little girls aren't meant to see such things.

---

Maddie, my older sister, was in the backseat of the car with me. She was nine. Even in the blackness of the winter night, I could see the shiny streaks of her tears in the moonlight. She stared at the back of the empty passenger seat then let her gaze drift to the dark world passing by her window.

Something heavy thumped in the trunk as Daddy turned the steering wheel just in time to avoid driving off the sharp turn. My booster seat rocked at having not been properly secured. He made an agitated grunt and breathed rapidly. The car straightened out just in time for Daddy to whip it around another curve. Such were the roads in the mountains of Fayette County, West Virginia.

I haven't been back since.

"Don't worry, girls," Daddy said through a strained

throat. "Your mama is just fine. We'll go back for her."

I looked at Maddie for guidance, but she continued staring out the window. I wondered if she even heard Daddy.

"Where is Mommy?" I asked the back of Daddy's headrest.

Maddie shot me a look that seared my right cheek. I returned her gaze. My stomach got that cold feeling when I saw the wide-eyed look on her face. Daddy snorted deeply, clearing his sinuses like usual. He always told us he had bad allergies.

"Your mama..." Daddy began but seemed to lose his voice.

He snorted again and cleared his throat.

"Your mama stayed at the scenic overlook, baby. I told you that."

"But it's so cold, Daddy," I replied. "Does Mommy have her coat?"

Maddie looked back out the window.

"Of course, she does," Daddy answered. There was a lingering silence, until he said, "Don't worry, Belle. We'll go back for her... we'll go back for her."

I turned to my sister and asked, "Why are you sad?"

Daddy jerked the wheel to the left, and we all shifted hard to the right. Maddie bonked her forehead on the window and began to sob. Daddy just kept driving. It sounded like he was crying too. He and Mommy hadn't been sleeping much lately. I just figured he was tired and upset.

I looked out my window, confused. Shadows of trees flickered by in dark blurs. Beyond them was a deep valley with a river running at its base. I stared into the moonlit gorge. The silhouette of the surrounding hills looked like the back of a sleeping dragon; its scales replaced with leafless trees. I wondered how long it would take something to drop down the steep hillside. The river seemed a million miles away.

Daddy went too quickly around another curve and slung us to the left side of the car. He steadied as we passed another scenic overlook like the one where we had recently stopped with Mommy. *How long ago was that?* I wondered. My five-year-old mind made it seem like days, but it had only been less than twenty minutes.

---

Mommy had been in the front seat with Daddy earlier. She was smoking a cigarette with her window cracked. The smoke stunk up the car. I used to tuck my nose into my shirt when she smoked, but I was used to it now. Maddie was behind Mommy enduring the freezing outside air coming in through the window. Daddy was driving fast, and I could tell that Mommy didn't like it. She kept scowling at him when he'd hit a curve too hard.

"If you're looking for a great spot, you're not going to find it," Mommy had said. "Just pull over anywhere. I don't care. I don't feel good."

Daddy didn't say anything. As we'd pass the occasional car, the headlights would shine in, and I'd watch his tired eyes in the rearview mirror as they nervously looked back and forth at the road. Just as I was about to ask where we were going, Daddy slammed on the brakes and jerked the car to a scenic overlook spot to the left. He coasted across the rocky terrain and came to a stop a few inches shy of the metal guardrail.

I peeked around Daddy's seat to get a better view through the windshield. There was a metal pole with a strange round top that looked like it had eyes.

"What is that, Maddie?" I asked. "It looks like a robot owl."

Maddie leaned around Mommy's seat and peered through the glass.

"That's something you look through... like a telescope," she said.

"Like barnacles?"

"'Barnacles?'" she echoed. "You mean *binoculars?*"

"Yes."

"Yeah. Those are like fancy binoculars on a stick that you have to pay to use. Ain't that right, Daddy?"

"Huh?" Daddy replied. He was busy getting his and Mommy's medicine ready on his lap. "What'd you say, honey?"

"Ain't those binoculars right there? The kind you have to pay for like we saw on the pier at the beach?" Maddie asked.

"Don't say 'ain't,'" Mommy instructed as she watched what Daddy was doing.

Daddy flicked his lighter, and the car began to glow. I smelled his medicine cooking and heard the bubbles popping in the spoon. Mommy turned on one of the interior lights so that a beam shined onto Daddy's lap.

"Yeah, that's right," he said without looking up.

"I want to look through it!" I announced.

"No," Mommy said, her eyes still transfixed on Daddy's lap.

"Aww," I whined.

"You couldn't see nothing anyway," Maddie told me. "It's too dark."

I huffed and accepted defeat. Daddy's seat rocked as he shuffled around.

"Here you go," he said to Mommy.

I watched Mommy take her medicine needle from Daddy. She saw me looking and quickly turned away.

"Maddie, play I Spy with your sister," she instructed.

"Yay!" I said as I looked toward Maddie who was not thrilled with the idea.

"I spy with my little eye something that is black," Maddie said.

I looked from window to window at a world encased in darkness.

"*Everything* is black!" I said as Maddie laughed at me.

"Duh."

Mommy let out a moan and leaned back into her seat. I saw her stare up at the car's ceiling and smile as her eyelids got heavy. Daddy's hand reached across the console and took the medicine needle out of Mommy's hand.

"My turn," he said and began cooking with his spoon again.

"Play I Spy for real," I begged my sister.

"Fine," she conceded. "I spy something that is... yellow."

My eyes scanned my surroundings for any hint of the chosen color. I saw a glimmer of it in the sky through Maddie's window. After stretching my head down as far as I could to get a good look, the moon came into view.

Mommy's head fell against the window before I could shout my answer. Daddy immediately stopped trying to take his medicine and looked at her.

"Oh, shit," he said.

He sat his full medicine needle down on the console and reached over to Mommy.

"Honey! Mary, wake up. Mary!"

Daddy grabbed the back of Mommy's head with both of his hands and turned her to face him. When I finally saw Mommy's face, her eyes were all white, and a pool of drool leaked out of the corner of her mouth. My heart skipped a beat at the terrifying sight.

Daddy held Mommy's head with one hand and smacked her cheek with the other.

"Mary, wake up!" he begged, but nothing happened. "Shit!"

He let go of her, opened his car door, and exited the vehicle, leaving his door open behind him. I saw how scared Maddie was becoming. We looked at each other with mutual bewilderment. I wanted an answer, but I could tell she didn't have it.

Mommy fell out of the car when Daddy opened her door. He caught her and pulled her into the darkness. Maddie watched through her window, but I couldn't see anything. All

I heard were desperate whimpers and Daddy repeating the same thing: "Mary, wake up."

"What are they doing?" I asked, but Maddie ignored me.

She continued to stare into the dark.

"Maddie?"

She finally broke from her trance and started to roll down her window.

"What's wrong with Mommy?" she asked.

"She's just tired," Daddy said from outside. "Roll your window up right now."

Maddie only watched the scene that I could not see.

"*Maddie Louise*, roll your window up *now!*" he demanded, and Maddie immediately did as she was told.

As soon as the window shut, she fell back into her seat and started to weep.

"Did you see Mommy?" I asked.

She didn't respond.

With both front doors open, the inside of the car was now just as cold as the surrounding winter night. I began to see my breath form in front of my face with every exhale. I hadn't heard Daddy in minutes and began to worry if he was OK.

The car shook as the trunk opened behind us. Maddie and I were both startled by the sudden movement. I tried to turn around, but the booster seat limited my mobility. Maddie unbuckled herself and looked over her shoulder just as something heavy dropped into the trunk. The trunk was slammed shut, and we both jumped again.

I listened as Daddy walked around Maddie's side of the car and shut Mommy's door. He walked around the front of the car, crossing the bright headlights as he made his way to his entry. The car wobbled as he fell into his seat and shut the door behind him. He turned around and looked at the two of us. His eyes were puffy, moist, and wild.

"Listen, girls," he began. "Your mama isn't feeling good right now. She's going to stay here to cool off."

Before we could even process what he had said, the car was in reverse and we were back on the road, rounding curves at fifty miles an hour.

———·—·——

It was less than thirty minutes later that Daddy slung us against the left side of the car as we passed another scenic overlook. It must've caught Daddy's eye at the last second because he hit the brakes like he had missed his turn. He backed into the small clearing on the side of the road and turned on the interior light. I watched his hand grab his medicine needle that he hadn't got to use from the cupholder. He was quietly sobbing.

"Daddy," Maddie said.

He immediately began full-on crying. I looked at the tears in Maddie's eyes and felt like I was missing something.

"Daddy," she repeated.

"Hold on, baby doll," he replied. "I'm almost finished."

"Daddy, what's in the trunk?" she questioned with a hint of fear in her voice.

Daddy's seat shifted as his body relaxed. I knew he had just taken his medicine.

"Don't worry about that," he said, his voice trailing off.

"Daddy!" Maddie yelled causing him to jump. He looked over his shoulder at her. "What?"

"Is Mommy in the trunk?" she asked.

My belly turned to knots at the thought. I wondered why Maddie would even think such a thing. Daddy turned back around and flicked the light off. He put the car in drive and pulled onto the road.

"We're going home now, girls," he said.

I looked over at my sister, still bewildered by her question. Tears continued to cascade down her cheeks. She turned back to the window, shaking her head. Seeing my big sister this upset made me mad at Daddy. Without further consideration, I kicked the back of his seat.

"Daddy!" I yelled. "Maddie is talking to you, and you're being rude!"

"Stop it, Belle," he said with his slow, medicine voice.

I looked through the windshield just as we came to another sharp turn. Two bright lights suddenly appeared around the curve. Our car was in the large pickup truck's lane, and Daddy didn't have time to move. We collided head-on. The only thing I remember from the wreck was how fast the truck's headlights grew into giant, blinding bulbs of destruction as they came closer.

Daddy was instantly killed when the massive truck smashed the front of our car. The forceful impact combined with Maddie not wearing her seatbelt resulted in the remains of her body being found over twenty feet away from the crash site. This is all that they tell me, of course. I don't remember anything beyond the headlights. Luckily, I had already been taken to the hospital when they discovered Mommy in the trunk.

———··———

The front door opened behind me and caused me to spill what was left of my coffee on my fleece jacket. I sat up in the porch swing about to curse but saw my four-year-old daughter, Lucille, standing in the open doorway, only one eye open from having just woken up.

"Honey, what are you doing out of bed?" I asked, standing from the swing and walking toward her.

I glanced down at my watch and realized that it was after 3 AM. She rubbed the sleep out of her eyes.

"I woke up and was scared," she said.

I thought about how many times I had woken up scared when I was her age, and how many times Granny and Grampy would put me back to sleep.

The wind gently blew against my face, and the cold sensation made me realize that I had been crying. I quickly wiped away the tears before Lucille could see that I was upset.

Little girls aren't meant to see such things.

# THE NOOSE

Arizona Territory, 1876

They had been moving along at a lulled pace. The heat was that damp kind of hot that loosened the cowboy's leather boots and made the sides of the saddle so warm his thighs could feel it through denim.

Wade stroked Burt's mane as the two of them lumbered on. He knew a good horse was hard to come by. Breaking them is always the easy part. Any man worth a damn can ride and command. It's the gunshots, the coyotes, the thunderstorms that will spook even the most valiant of them. You can't prepare an animal for that. Horses flee by instinct. All you can do is be ready and hold on.

Burt had only ever been spooked once. It was the time they rode through Alabama at the site where nearly fifty men died: the Battle of Athens. By that point, the war had been done a decade, but the horse got the fear in him just the same. It was from something Wade couldn't see. It was like he could smell the dead. His reaction then was nothing compared to what was about to happen.

The horse bucked something fierce at the sight of a tree up ahead. Wade sat upright and gripped the reins, having gotten too relaxed during the ride. The massive steed reared its front legs, whinnied, and sent the cowboy ass-first to the dusty rock that passed for ground. His tailbone hit the earth, instantly deflating his lungs.

Burt continued to dance and shriek, not caring where his

heavy hooves landed. Wade did a quick roll to the left to avoid being trampled. After stirring up a dust storm, the horse stopped his frenzy and fled toward the mountains in the horizon. Wade painfully got to his feet and cupped his hands around his mouth.

"Burt! Get back here!"

The shrinking image of the horse disappeared into its own dusty path. The marooned cowboy kicked the dirt and coughed, still trying to catch his wind. A couple yards to the right and covered in dust was the black saddlebag that had fallen off with him. He hobbled over to it, each step sending a throbbing ache from his groin to his neck. He slung it over his back and looked to where Burt had fled, hoping the young buck had come to his senses but saw no movement in the open desert. He was on his own now, on a foot's pace through Arizona Territory. Not ideal for a man on the run.

———·—

He had stopped in Tucson the previous night. It was a shithole mining town just like every other shithole mining town he had blown through while headed west: saloons, whores, and assholes—all reeking of watered-down whiskey. No matter the place, he kept to himself, sitting in the darkest corners, head down with the brim of his hat covering his face.

He wasn't a wanted man or anything like that yet, but during his time fighting the Confederates, he had seen how quickly men could turn on each other. Faces—screaming, bloody faces—of every man he killed (some not even fully grown) kept sneaking into his dreams. The goal now was to hoof it to California and settle down someplace quiet, far away from people and all the damn memories, but that derailed like a locomotive when he got to Tucson.

Coming into town after a night of bad dreams left him craving the bottle even more than usual. That night it had been the old-timer who had held his thoughts hostage: the geezer Confederate, the old son-of-a-bitch who had no business wearing a soldier's uniform in the first place. Wade shot him from twenty yards out, but he kept coming even with a leaking hole in his belly. He aimed for the head the second time and tore off half his cheek, but the loon only slowed for a second. Wade had to walk right up to the old man with the wild eyes and squeeze the trigger an inch from his eye, leaving nothing inside the socket but a drippy view of gray matter. That did the trick.

He sat in the corner of the dimly lit barroom and downed shot after shot of straight rotgut, but that old bastard wouldn't leave his mind. The bartender took Wade's coin and left the bottle. He put it to his mouth and chugged. Whiskey dribbled down both cheeks, but most of it was hitting the target so he didn't stop until it was empty. Less than a minute later, he couldn't see shit.

After paying his tab, he had walked outside. Mud clung to his boots as he crossed the road and headed toward the wooden hitching post which had Burt and a white mare tethered to it. His horse livened up when he saw him approaching. The squishy steps alerted the scrawny stranger rifling through Wade's saddlebag.

"Hey, mister..." the kid began, but Wade withdrew his 1860 Colt Army revolver (quicker than he had any time during the war) and fired without thinking.

The mare next to the kid sprayed red. The bullet tore through the smiling idiot's forehead, making his eyes go cross as he dropped to his knees. He fell face-first, leaving the fist-sized crater in the back of his head exposed and looking black in the moonlight. Wade's horse just shook his long head and snorted, barely reacting to the sound: gunshots were background noise to him.

The thud of the kid's body and the way his lanky legs spasmed instantly sobered Wade. Never had he discharged his weapon so recklessly. He couldn't move, couldn't bring himself to go look at the dead youth on the other side of his horse. He didn't need another face to add to the already crowded collection of death stares that had been permanently seared into his memory from the war. For a moment, he couldn't process what he'd done or who he had done it to. It wasn't until after a crowd formed that he found out the boy was the son of the sheriff and plumb imbecile.

His stomach turned hollow when he finally looked down at the dead kid's face, the side that wasn't buried in mud. Not a strand of facial hair on him, couldn't be more than eleven, just tall for his age. Blood pulsed out of the hole in his forehead. His mouth was open, and his pink slug of a tongue flopped over his bottom lip. One of his uneven eyes was locked on Wade's, getting a good look as if he was taking his own mental picture for later.

"That's the sumbitch that done it, right there," a grizzled

voice in the crowd said, pointing in Wade's direction.

He didn't wait around for someone to suggest a lynching before hopping on Burt and hauling ass out of town. The horse didn't get a break until they had reached the Santa Rita Mountains. Once he was sure that no one was trailing them, they made camp for the night. The plan then was to get up before dawn and hoof it south until they reached the border and cross the Sonora River into Mexico. The idea of living as a wanted man in California could piss off.

———•———

With Burt high-tailed, his journey just got a hell of a lot longer. Wade whistled in one more futile attempt to call back his formerly dependable companion.

Nothing.

It dawned on him that he had no idea what had even caused the horse such a startle. He gripped his pistol's handle and looked back in the direction they were headed; the mountains they had descended were now at his back.

The flat, rocky terrain in front of him was covered with yellow sand and patches of desert grass. The sun cooked the color out of anything that managed to grow. There were trees here and there, a few just tall enough to hang a man. Nothing was out of the ordinary. No Indians, no lynch mobs, no wild animals. He waited and listened.

Still… nothing.

Just the occasional warm breeze that peppered his eyes with dust. He grunted, slung his saddlebag over his shoulder, and began to trudge. After only a few minutes, he noticed something peculiar about one of the trees a couple hundred yards ahead. He used his hand to shield the sun and squinted. The tree itself was fine, a bit bigger than most, but nothing special. It was what was *beside* the tree that irked him.

There appeared to be the silhouette of a person standing there. It wasn't moving, whatever it was, and the more Wade studied it, the more it looked like it was floating. The outlaw's hand found his pistol again and walked forward, careful never to take his eye off the stranger. With each step closer, the vision before him enlarged.

The wind lashed Wade's face with a fresh coating of dust that clung to the moisture on his eyeballs. He winced as he turned away. Rubbing his eyes did nothing but push the particles further under the lids. The more he blinked, the more pissed he got.

"Shit!"

He dropped the saddle bag and reached for his canteen. Even though he was now short on water (due to Burt leaving him stranded), some of it had to be sacrificed. He twisted the cap and poured a splash into each blinking eye. The irritation subsided, but his vision was still blurry. He used the inside of his flannel shirt to dab away the excess moisture and looked back toward the figure in the distance.

The tree now stood by itself.

"What in *the* hell?"

Wade packed the canteen as he stared in disbelief. *Was it a mirage? Couldn't be. I've seen plenty of 'em, and none looked like that.* He surveyed the area for movement. There was nothing big enough to provide cover for a man except the tree.

*He's behind the tree.*

Wade unholstered his pistol, cocked back the hammer, and strode forward at a quickened pace. Once he was within fifty yards, he paused and carefully placed his saddlebag on the ground. He resumed his approach slowly, creeping with a slight hunch in his back like a predator approaching its prey, ready to unload at the drop of a hat. It was right then that he noticed something dangling loosely from the sturdy, arm-like branch.

*A noose.*

The empty rope swayed back and forth as the breeze blew through it. He stared in disbelief. He knew what he had seen back there, and it wasn't an empty noose. An image of the floating figure flickered in his mind. The hanging body was now the dead stable boy with his bloody eyes and gaping mouth.

*No.*

Wade shook the thought from his memory before it could be processed.

*There had been someone hangin' from that rope.*

This noose hadn't been used though; its hungry mouth still hung wide open for a guilty neck.

*If it ain't been used yet, maybe I saw someone hangin' it up.*

An adrenaline fire burned through his body. Fight or flight kicked in, and, unlike Burt, Wade was all fight today. He looked at the thick tree trunk and imagined someone cowering behind it.

*But why would he be hangin' a noose? Ain't no one else here. Poor bastard must be tryin' to kill his self.*

He stopped about twenty feet shy of the tree, cleared his throat, and listened.

Still silence.

"You there," he began, "Hey, you there behind the tree. Come on out from behind there."

He waited.

There was no sound, no movement.

"I don't know what you're up to out here, but I mean ya no harm. Just passin' through."

Nothing.

Wade took two frustrated steps forward.

"I seen you from back there," he continued. "I know you seen me; else ya wouldn't be hidin'."

He raised the pistol and aimed it at the tree.

"OK then. Have it your way. I'm comin' 'round. Don't make any jerky moves and there won't be no trouble."

He began taking sideways strides to circle the tree.

"But if I see even a hint of metal, I'm unloadin' on ya."

He took a deep breath and lunged to the other side with his finger hugging the trigger.

No one was there.

He sped to the spot where he was sure someone had been hiding, now staring at the empty ground surrounding the tree.

*Can't be. There's nowhere else he coulda gone!*

He scoured the ground for footprints or bent blades of grass which would signal a presence but found no evidence.

"Son of a bitch."

He holstered his weapon and put his hands on his hips, finally entertaining the idea that it could have been a trick of the eye. As he stared at the empty spot, the shadow of someone hanging from the rope swung across the ground in front of him. His whole body tightened with shock. He whipped around and fired at the empty noose with the quickness of a proper gunslinger. The boom of the shot echoed off the nearby mountains as the bullet went God knows where.

He stared in disbelief. Sweat beaded on his forehead and trickled down the corners of his frightened eyes. That shadow was no trick of the mind. Something had moved behind him—had been swinging from the noose behind him—yet there was no one there. It was still empty and open and only moving when the wind said so. Wade was scared, and when he got scared, he got mad.

"Fuck you!" he screamed to the open desert.

He swung his gun around, *wishing* that something would move now.

"Come on, then!"

His heart was trying to break through his chest. He spun his arm back the other way, just to case his surroundings one more time. Aside from his quick, shallow breaths, everything was quiet.

*It coulda been a bird, ya damn fool.*

He thought hard about the detailed shadow that had passed across the ground in front of him—how clearly he could make out a man's figure connected to the rope's shadow.

"Nah, that wasn't no bird."

A small branch snapped in the tree. Wade dropped to his back to get a clean shot at whatever was directly above him.

BANG! BANG! BANG!

Each shot tore through the treetop in different directions. He didn't care what was up there; he wanted it dead. The pistol clicked empty on the fourth squeeze of the trigger. Except for some wounded leaves and flecks of bark trickling to the earth, there was no movement.

Wade sat wide-eyed, feeling like the butt of someone's joke. He took breath after breath, trying to hold onto some semblance of sanity.

"Hey, mister!" a child's voice said from behind the tree.

Wade's heart froze.

*No. This ain't real...*

"My daddy's on his way to find ya, mister. And when he gets ya, he's gonna kill ya."

"No!" Wade yelled as he crawled backward away from the tree. "You're dead!"

He could see a shadow on the ground beside the tree, cast down from whatever was on the other side of that trunk.

"I is dead, mister. And you's about to be too."

The muffled sounds of men's voices and trampling steeds came from the base of the mountains on the same path Wade had traveled earlier. He looked in that direction and could see specks of riders in the distance.

"Shit."

"That's right, mister. That's my daddy and his friends

comin' for ya. He's the sheriff, ya know. You're as good as dead if ya don't do somethin'."

Wade looked down at his empty gun and then over to his saddlebag fifty yards out.

"Ya don't have any ammo in your bag neither, mister. Ya shot me last night, and then ya shot the rest at the desert and the tree just now."

He dropped his gun and jumped to his feet. He thought about walking around the tree but couldn't bring himself to do it.

"Look, kid," he began. "What I did to you was an accident. I was drunker than a skunk, but that don't make it right."

The shadow on the ground beside the tree moved slightly.

"I done my fair share of killin' during the war... Lord knows I did. They was soldiers, though. You... you wasn't a soldier. You was just a dumb kid in the wrong spot at the wrong time. I mean, what the hell was you doin' there anyways? *God damnit!*"

Wade fell back to his knees, weeping into his palms. He saw the faces of the dead as soon as his eyes were shut. The last image was of the dead stableboy with his bloody eyes and hung-open mouth.

"You're all dead."

A hand touched his shoulder. It was a small hand, not weighty like a man's. Wade felt it give a comforting squeeze.

"It's OK, mister. But we gotta hurry this along."

Wade finally looked up at the dead boy standing beside him, still wearing the same dumb, blood-stained overalls. His skin had paled more since last night, making the dark veins underneath more prominent. The hole between his crossed eyes continued to bleed down the sides of his nose and around his mouth, eventually coming to a drip at his smooth chin. His breath was damp and earthy.

Ignoring every natural reaction of repulsion, Wade wrapped his arms around the boy's cold body and sobbed and snotted against his chest. The boy patted his head like a parent soothing a child.

The men on horseback drew closer. Wade could begin to make out some of what they were shouting. He heard random phrases amidst the trampling: "There he is!" "His damn horse led us right to him!" "Kill that sumbitch!" "No, he's mine, damn it!" "Hang the cocksucker!"—none of which held his attention more than this child's embrace. The boy stopped caressing his hair and guided Wade's chin up.

"Ya saved me, mister. My daddy... is a *bad* man."

The boy unstrapped his overalls and lifted his bloody shirt. His chest and stomach were covered in bruises, cuts, and burns from where his father had beat him and snubbed out cigarettes. Wade recoiled, first in disgust and then fury.

"Your daddy done this to you?"

The rotting boy nodded.

"That's not all he done," he admitted. "Him and his friends... they..."

"What'd they do?"

"Sometimes they'd wake me up and make me go in the barn and take off my clothes. They'd make me bend over on the hay bales and... and..."

"I get it, kid. You don't have to go no further," he said and put his hands on the embarrassed boy's shoulders, taking his turn to comfort. "No matter what they done to ya, it don't make what I did right. *I'm* the one that killed ya—not your daddy."

"But you set me free, mister," he said as if Wade was missing something. "I was goin' through your saddlebag tryin' to find a gun. I was gonna kill him dead that night. If I didn't ever do it, they'd just keep takin' me out to the barn. I knew they would hang me if I done it. So ya see... I was gonna die no matter what."

The men's shouts were even closer now.

Wade stood up, eyes burning with rage.

"But you're dead, and he ain't. And now here I am outta bullets, and there ain't shit I can do to finish the job."

The boy now had tears running down his face, mixing with the blood. In one second, he was in front of Wade and the next he was standing closer to the tree where Wade had dropped his gun. He picked it up and then reappeared at Wade's feet offering it back to him.

"I'm sorry I made ya waste all your bullets, mister."

Wade marveled at the way the ghostly child before him effortlessly held the heavy sidearm like it was a feather. A smile crept across his face.

"I got an idea, son."

————•—•————

By the time Sheriff Walton and his four-man posse reached

the tree, Wade was already hanging from the noose. The men halted their nervous horses and stared at the swinging corpse. His eyes were fixed and open, staring lifelessly into oblivion.

"Looks like he beat us to it, boss," Rango said from the back of the pack.

"Shit!" the sheriff screamed. "You goddamn yella' *cocksucker!*"

The sheriff's horse snorted like it just got a good whiff of danger. The other horses picked up on it and began to shuffle their legs and hoof the loose sand.

"Cut him down, Louis," the sheriff instructed the sweaty man to his right. "I'm gonna tie that sumbitch to the back of this horse and drag his ass back to Tucson. Might even put him on display outside Sally's joint."

Louis obliged and dismounted his tired animal. He drew a skinning knife from his belt and slowly approached Wade. Once the horse realized it was free, it snorted and bolted for the horizon. The other three horses spooked to the point of bucking like stallions. The men cussed and whipped and did everything they could to regain control, but one-by-one they were all thrown to the ground. The sheriff landed shoulder-first, shattering his collarbone, immobilizing half his body.

Louis, knife drawn, turned his back to Wade to see what had just happened behind him. His friends were all writhing around on the ground in pain.

"What was *that* all about fellas?"

Wade stopped playing dead and targeted the man whose back was now to him. He tapped the dead kid's invisible arms, which were wrapped around his legs, holding him up just enough so that the noose looked taut, but Wade could still breathe. The boy lifted him a few more inches so he could easily remove the noose, quietly placed him back on the ground, and then vanished, knowing full well of the carnage that was coming.

The sheriff grimaced as he looked up at Louis, prepared to unleash a verbal tirade but froze at what he saw. Louis's stomach sank when he noticed the abject terror in the sheriff's eyes.

He turned around just as Wade grabbed the wrist holding the knife and snapped it backward. He wailed in pain and dropped to his knees, cradling his arm. Wade picked up the blade, took two steps toward the crying man, and stabbed it through one side of his neck and out the other, withdrawing it just as fast. A crimson spurt covered Wade's boots, and a second one wetted the ground beside him, browning as it mixed with the sand. Louis toppled over with a gurgling thud.

The other men on the ground went for their guns. Wade dropped to one knee and yanked Louis's pistol from the holster and fired three times in less than two seconds. The squirming sheriff heard the men surrounding him each get shot in rapid succession. Blood splatters and brain matter hit him from all angles like a bunch of viscera-filled balloons had just popped. He could barely process what had just happened.

Wade stood up and assessed the wounded. Louis was dead. The skinny bastard on the far side of the pack lay still with his head nearly floating in its growing blood puddle.

Beside him was Rango, who, despite having a cracked skull, was somehow still squirming around, refusing to die. The nameless prick beside the sheriff still gurgled as well.

Wade wasted no time approaching Rango. The handle of the Bowie knife on the wounded man's belt caught Wade's eye. He kneeled on his sternum and yanked it out of the sheath, admiring its twelve-inch blade. The man tried to speak, but Wade grabbed his greasy hair and held him still while he sawed through his throat and spine.

"You... you were dead!" the sheriff screamed from the ground.

Wade chucked the severed head at the sheriff.

"He is."

The sheriff screamed and then immediately clutched his shoulder in a pained coughing fit.

"You're a bad man, sheriff," Wade said as he stood up and walked over to the other henchman still clinging to life. "But the thing is, so am I."

He dropped the Bowie knife and picked up this man's single-barrel shotgun. He placed the business-end against the bastard's temple.

"Nah," Wade decided as he twirled the weapon around like a baton until he gripped the barrel so that the wooden stock was pointing toward the sky. "You don't deserve to go out that fast."

He beat the man's face with the blunt end like he was splitting a log with an axe.

THWACK. THWACK. THWACK.

Each blow became wetter and harder to pull back out. The

sheriff could only watch in shock as Wade continued. More blood hit his face and eyes.

"I thought I was an evil man—the worst of the worst—until today," Wade said as he continued his assault. "But there's a difference between bad and evil, and I ain't you."

"You're a goddamn *child killer!*" the sheriff found the balls to say.

Wade flipped the shotgun back around and walked over to the rapist with a tin star pinned to his stained shirt. He cocked the weapon and dragged the barrel down the sheriff's body until it was aiming at his genitals. The BOOM of the shotgun echoed louder than any previous shot.

The sheriff screamed something that was somehow both guttural and high-pitched.

"You lost your right to use that," Wade said, pointing to the hollow mess where the man's crotch used to be. "Ain't nothin' but cherry pie down there now, sheriff."

With the one good arm he had left, the sheriff felt his wet wound and sobbed.

"You're a monster for what you did to your boy, but I'm done with ya."

Wade dropped the shotgun and walked away, picking up his saddlebag as he left. After only a few steps, he heard the sheriff scream from behind him—a true squeal of terror, like he had just seen a ghost—and then went silent like a noose had just tightened around his neck.

"Ya good, kid?" Wade said without looking back.

"Yes, mister," the boy replied from behind him.

"So, I reckon we're square?"

"Yessir. Where ya gonna go now? Goin' on the run?"

Wade thought about it for a moment. He looked to the horizon and finally shook his head.

"Ain't nothin' to run from no more. Suppose I'll change course and head through Tucson again, maybe make my way back east."

He waited for the kid's response, but nothing came. The boy was gone. A grin crept across his face.

"OK, kid. OK."

As he headed toward the mountains, he noticed something running across the desert in his direction. Once it came into focus, he laughed in disbelief. He put his hand on his hip as he watched his horse make its way back to him.

It didn't take Burt long to reach his recently deserted companion. Wade briefly thought about scolding the horse for being a no-good, yellow piece of crowbait, but he refrained. He patted the horse on the nose and stroked his mane.

"Good to see ya again, Burt."

The horse snorted and nodded its head.

"Don't worry. I ain't mad ya. Guess we all deserve second chances."

Wade mounted the steed. He made a clicking sound with his mouth, and Burt started trotting toward Tucson. Just before they reached the base of the mountains, he looked back one last time, knowing already what he would see because he'd seen it before. He saw the tree and the sheriff's body hanging from the noose, beautifully silhouetted against the setting sun.

# It Haunts the Mind

April 1993, Southwestern West Virginia

Three soon-to-be high school seniors sat in the idling Chevy S10. The truck's headlights pointed at a trio of poorly patched potholes on the country road ahead of them. Treefrogs and crickets were a competing symphony over the rumbling engine.

The boy and the girl sitting in the front seats looked through the passenger side window, while the lanky boy squished in the folded-down cab seat stared out his small window as he gripped the knees of his bent legs. All three of them had their eyes fixed on the missing part of the vacant house: the charred hole on the second floor where there had once been a bedroom. Now it just looked like a meteor hit it.

Locals called it "The Exorcist's House." The two-story farmhouse was just a few miles outside town. There was nothing special about it; no one the wiser would give it a second glance driving by it on Sunny Branch Way.

It was an older home, built in the early 1900s, back when homes were built to last, and it was well-kept by its previous owner, the late Merle Blatty. Locals had a name for him too. They called him "The Backwoods Exorcist" on account that he was rumored to investigate cases of the occult.

Merle was a man who kept his distance and rarely spent any significant amount of time at home. According to legend, he traveled the country, going to places he was needed, confronting horrors better left unsaid. How did he get that way? That's a longer tale for another time. Suffice it to say that he met evil, true evil, the kind that destroys families while dancing a jig, and he spent a lifetime chasing it.

Funny thing is that he met his end right back where he started: his house. The last time anyone saw Merle was at Kanawha Hardware last month. The kid running the register, a high school boy named Alan Smith, couldn't provide any details on what Merle had purchased or what frame of mind he was in. He couldn't remember ringing up the old man even when they showed him a photo of him. Furthermore, he had no clue why the police were asking him about it anyway.

———·—

When he got off work, Alan had decided to tell his girlfriend, Sarah, and her best friend, Dwight (the only openly gay kid at the high school), about the cops questioning him.

The three of them were eating ice cream on a wooden bench outside of Dairy Queen in town. It was dusk and a little cool for April, but they ate outside when they could. And always in the same formation: Alan and Sarah sat on one side of the bench while Dwight sat on the tabletop with his feet on the bench between them.

Alan put a spoonful of vanilla soft serve in his mouth, careful not to overdo it for fear of brain freeze. He looked back and forth at his two friends who were spooning bites and waiting for him to spill the beans.

"Are you going to tell us or not?" Dwight asked with a frustration like he'd been suppressing the question for hours.

"Yeah," Sarah piped in. "Why'd the cops show up at your work?"

Alan took another bite, slowly withdrawing the spoon.

Dwight stomped the bench with one foot.

"Alan!"

Alan laughed.

"OK, OK," he began. "So, you all know how there was that house fire last month where some old dude died?"

"No?" Dwight said. "That's what this was all about? And I thought it was going to be good."

"I know what you're talkin' about," Sarah said.

The two boys looked at her.

"Yeah," she continued. "My uncle lives out Sunny Branch Way. That's where it was, wasn't it?"

"Yes! That's what the cops said: Sunny Branch Way."

Dwight took another bite and said, "Where the fuck is Sunny Branch Way?"

Sarah looked at him.

"OK, so you know where River's Edge Subdivision is?"

"Yes. My old scoutmaster lives out there."

They both looked at him like this was the first time they were hearing this. Sarah scooped the last of her chocolate ice cream in one big spoonful.

"What? Are y'all shocked that I was a Boy Scout?"

"No," Alan said. "Not at all. I bet you rocked the shit outta that uniform."

Sarah spat out her ice cream and laugh-choked. She turned away and leaned to the side of the bench, heaving hysterically, spilling what was left on the grass.

Alan chuckled too.

"Fuck you both," Dwight said as he took a few aggressive bites. "If you two ever need to tie a square knot, don't even come at me with it."

Now they all three burst out laughing.

Sarah was the one to get the train back on track.

"So, what did the cops say about the house?"

Alan almost had the spoon to his mouth, but he placed it back in the plastic cup.

"They wanted to know if I remembered what he was buyin'."

"That's weird," Dwight said.

"And they also asked me what kinda mood he was in. How the heck am I supposed to remember that? I don't even remember the old man. You know how many geezer hillbillies come in that hardware store every day?"

"One for every redneck at our school," Dwight muttered in a resentful tone that Alan picked up on.

It pissed him off when the rednecks made fun of Dwight for being gay. He could only imagine how it affected him. Though ever since Dwight's growth spurt last summer and putting some meat on his bones from lacrosse, not many kids talked shit to his face anymore.

"All that and then some," Alan said. "That hardware store is like a bug zapper for rednecks. And they expect me to remember one who's not even a regular. Heck, I can barely remember the regulars. I only work three days a week after school and Saturday mornings."

"So do they think somebody killed him?" Dwight asked

with glee.

"I don't know about that, but it sure seemed like they thought somethin' was up."

"Was it city cops?" Sarah asked.

"No, Sunny Branch Way is out of city limits."

"So, it was the sheriffs?"

"I don't know. What's it matter?"

Dwight sat his empty cup on the tabletop and slid it away from him.

"Were they in plain clothes? *Please,* tell me they were in plain clothes."

Alan looked at him sideways, trying to gauge where he was going with this.

"Kinda," he finally said. "They had on suits."

"It's the FB-fucking-I" Dwight said.

Sarah laughed.

"Seriously, why would the FBI be investigating a house fire?"

"They wouldn't," Alan said as he looked at her. "Dwight is bored. And besides, only one of them was in a regular suit. The other one was wearin' one of those white priest collars. I ain't never seen one in person. Is there even a Catholic church here?"

"I think so. There are more churches than restaurants," Sarah said.

"This *town* is boring!" Dwight said. "A murder would spice things up."

"You're morbid," she said.

"A murder would be exciting," Dwight said.

Alan laughed and shook his head. He stood up and grabbed his empty ice cream cup and pushed it into the red, rounded trashcan lid. A swarm of flies flew out of the moving flap, and he recoiled.

"Eww," Sarah said. "Throw mine away for me, please."

Alan scowled but grabbed his girlfriend's cup and discarded it. Again, more flies, and this time, the flapping lid belched the stench of sour milk.

"God damn," he said and stepped away from it.

Dwight watched, still sitting on the table.

"That's an omen right there. Told ya. Murder shit. Haven't y'all seen Amityville?"

Alan looked at the last sliver of sun that had almost disappeared behind the distant hills that surrounded their city in the valley.

"Do you all know who the man was that died in that fire?" Sarah asked.

The two boys looked back at her, the comment seeming to come out of nowhere.

"The old man?" Alan said.

"Yeah. Do you know who he was? His reputation, I mean."

Both boys shook their heads.

"Like I was sayin', my uncle lives out Sunny Branch Way. He told my daddy about the few times he'd talked to the old man who lived in the farmhouse. Well, he didn't call it the farmhouse. He called it the exorcist's house."

"Oh, that's cool," Dwight interrupted.

Sarah smiled like a little kid telling a ghost story around a campfire, this campfire being the red glow of the fluorescent Dairy Queen sign buzzing above the storefront.

"Daddy said that the guy's name was Merle, I think. He lived alone because his wife and kid died. Ya'll remember Luke and Amelia and how she went missin' last year?"

"Of course," Alan said.

"And Luke's weird ass got away with something," Dwight said as he stepped off the table and into the grass. "I don't care how hot he is. He knows something. He's weird. Hot, but weird."

"Maybe he's weird because his girlfriend disappeared," Alan said.

"Luke and his dad live right down the road from my uncle on Sunny Branch Way," Sarah said.

"And?" Dwight said.

"And don't you think it's pretty weird that there's a supposed exorcist that lived on the same street as a girl our age goes missin'? And you just said you think the FBI and a *priest* were askin' you about Merle?"

"Well, maybe the priest was just a friend of Merle's workin' with the police," Alan said.

"I know that Luke did work on Merle's farm," Sarah continued. "I seen him myself when I had to ride out to my uncle's with Daddy once. He was mowin' grass."

Alan pulled out a pack of Marlboro Reds and lit one with a Bic lighter that Sarah handed him because he was always losing his own. He took a long drag and paced around the bench.

"So that weirdo, Luke, has a girlfriend who's now missing

and the guy he used to do work for is dead?" Dwight pondered. "He could be the next Ted Bundy. Holy shit, that would be so cool."

Sarah shook her head.

"I wasn't tellin' y'all that to make you think bad of Luke. It's the exorcist's house that creeps me out."

Alan took another puff of his cigarette and turned to face her.

"You don't believe in that stuff, do you?"

"No, but that doesn't mean the thought of it ain't creepy."

Dwight's eyes lit up.

"Oh my God, I know what we're doing tonight," he said.

"What?" Sarah asked.

Alan just waited for the answer.

"OK, hear me out," Dwight began. "You got your brother's ID, right?"

"You know that I do," Alan said, having already told him this when they made plans to get some liquor earlier.

"OK, so we stop by Rite Aid, get a couple of bottles, and take a drive out to Sunny Branch Way."

Sarah laughed in disbelief, but Alan was mulling over the idea. When no one else commented, she said, "Why the hell would you want to go out there?"

"Because this town is fucking boring, and we either have a killer or a haunted house just right down the road. Let's get drunk and go investigate!"

"You want to go to the exorcist's house? And what, break in?"

Before Dwight could defend his plan, Alan spoke up.

"We don't have to break in. It's abandoned. We need a place to chill anyway, right? I think it'd be cool to go out to the farm. Maybe even light a fire or something."

Sarah crossed her arms and looked at her feet.

"You said you didn't believe in that stuff anyway, right?" Alan pressed on.

She looked back up at him.

"It's easier to say right now. Pitch dark out there near a house where someone died is another story."

Alan smiled and sauntered over to her. He put his hands on her shoulders and rubbed her arms.

"Come on, baby. It'll be fun. We won't let anything bad happen."

"You got that right," Dwight seconded as he threw his trash away.

"A little booze, a little fire, a little something extra, maybe?" Alan said with a wink.

Sarah blushed and smiled.

"Fine," she finally said.

"Yes!" Dwight began and then after a moment said, "But if you two decide to spontaneously hook up near the ghost house, I'm dipping."

Alan laughed and released Sarah.

"To Rite Aid we go," he said and stepped onto the sidewalk that led to the parking lot where his white S10 was located.

Dwight draped his arm around Sarah's shoulders and squeezed her as the two of them followed Alan.

"What do you want to drink, girl? I'm thinking Smirnoff

and some juice."

"Sounds good," she said.

Alan, speaking with his back to them as he approached the truck said, "You two can share all the vodka you want. I'm getting Jack or Jim."

"Oh, so tough," Dwight teased and climbed into the tight confines of the back seat.

"Yeah, you look tough back there riding bitch," he said as he reached through his headrest and gave Dwight a little love tap on the back of his head.

Dwight tried to retaliate but was too cramped by the seats. They all laughed. Sarah got in the front seat and shut her door. Alan took one final drag and flicked his cigarette halfway across the parking lot. He got in, started the truck, shifted into first gear, and pulled onto the main drag.

In his side mirror, he noticed the cherry of the discarded cigarette glowing extra bright in the darkness.

———·—·———

After a successful score at Rite Aid, the trio now sat in the truck, staring at the house. All initial bravery and bravado were left back in town. Now, sitting in the darkness of the country night, surrounded by woods, slivers of moonlight, and makeshift cemeteries, the firm grip of rationality was softened by the screech of each incoming hoot owl. If there are no atheists in foxholes, then there sure as shit aren't any skeptics in a hellhole. Alan just could not peel his eyes away from that charred maul on the second floor. Worst of all, he couldn't shake the feeling that something was looking back at him.

"Are we getting out or not?" Dwight said from the backseat. "My ass is too tall to be folded up back here."

Alan broke from his stupor, and Sarah turned to face him.

"I guess it's now or never. This place probably won't be empty for long," she said.

"What do you mean?" Alan asked.

"Daddy said out-of-towners have been buyin' up every house that goes on the market, especially farmhouses with lots of acreage."

"Why would anyone choose to live here," Dwight grunted from the back.

"The chemical plant," Sarah said. "Daddy said it's gonna bring lots of jobs and money."

"Their loss," Dwight said. "Now can you *please* open the door?"

"Grab the booze," Alan said and exited the vehicle.

Sarah followed suit and bent her seat forward so Dwight could emerge from the back with an exaggerated stretch. He reached into the truck and picked up the brown paper bag with the two bottles of liquor and a small bottle of juice and held it like it was his newborn child.

They stood side-by-side at the start of the driveway. A warm breeze blew over them, but not one like Alan had ever felt. It felt more like a horde of floating bodies, each one exhaling dank vapors inches away from his head. He caught a hint of rotten eggs.

"Y'all feel that?" he asked.

"What?" Sarah said.

"The wind. It's just... weird. You don't smell nothin'?"

"Skunk, maybe?" she said. "Weird how? I don't feel nothin'."

"It's so damp."

"Maybe they're getting a head start on the chemical factory that's gonna give us all cancer in ten years," Dwight said.

"Seriously," Alan said, and before he could press the issue any further, the odorous breeze passed.

He wiped the remnants of phantom perspiration from his brow.

"Ahh, never mind. Let's just go get drunk."

Dwight smacked him on the back and said, "That's the spirit. Let's get fucked up and see some fucked up shit."

Alan laughed and led the way as their triangle formation ascended the lengthy gravel driveway toward the house.

The gravel under their shoes made a crunchy echo once they reached the front porch. Alan kept his eyes open and had spotted nothing out of the ordinary. Just a regular spring night in West Virginia. The only thing that was throwing him off was the temperature. Back at Dairy Queen, it had been cooler; as soon as they got to this property, it was as if a dank wave of humidity had been released by an otherworldly dam.

Dwight skipped up the porch steps. The wood creaked under his weighty build.

"What are you doin'?" Sarah asked, still standing beside Alan in the driveway.

Dwight ignored her and walked over to two old rocking

chairs pushed to the corner of the porch. He scooped one up in each hand and turned back around.

"Dwight!" Sarah said.

"What? I'm just getting us something to sit on by the fire." He stopped and looked at his friends.

"We are still making a fire, aren't we?"

Before Alan could answer, he noticed a smiling face in the window behind Dwight. It had pale skin, eyes like glowing embers, and yellow smoke twirled up from the corners of its mouth.

He froze as the face floated backward into the darkness of what looked like a kitchen.

"What is it?" Dwight asked as he turned around and looked in the window. "Eww, this is some straight-up *Little House on the Prairie* décor going on in here."

He sat both chairs back on the porch and approached the house. He put his face on the window and cupped his hands to get a better view.

"Dwight," Alan finally said. "Get away. There's somethin' in there, man."

Sarah grabbed Alan's arm.

"Don't fuck with me," she said. "I hate this idea enough as it is."

"I ain't fuckin' with you. I saw it clear as day."

Dwight, unfazed by the conversation behind him, continued to scan the interior.

"Oh, no fucking way," he said, finally spotting something that piqued his interest.

"What is it?" Sarah asked, still gripping Alan.

"There's a pile of knives on the floor."

"Knives?" Alan said.

"Yeah. Like they were all moved over to the corner. The knife block is empty."

"Well, maybe they just fell over," Sarah said, seeming unconvinced by her own hypothesis.

"Doubtful," Dwight began. "The knife block is on the opposite side of the kitchen, and it's right-side up."

Alan had had enough.

"Dwight let's get movin' now. I ain't fuckin' around."

"Wait. There's some kind of light over there," Dwight said. "It's coming from under a door. Must be a basement or something. How did I not see that before?"

"I'm getting the creeps," Sarah said and wrapped her arms around her boyfriend's waist.

"I bet the cops or firemen who came in and did the assessment or whatever forgot to turn off the basement light. No, wait..."

He stopped talking and only stared.

"What's going on?" Alan asked.

"It's..." Dwight began but spoke as if he were too in awe to form words from thoughts. "It's getting brighter. It's orange and yellow and glowing and fucking getting brighter. Holy shit, I think it's on fire!"

Suddenly, Dwight gripped the bottom of the window and jerked upward, but it wouldn't budge.

"Dude, what the fuck are you doing?" Alan shouted.

His friend's stupidity was the final straw that gave him the balls to approach the porch, but just before he placed his foot on the first step, he heard something trampling through the woods to his left. He instinctively maneuvered Sarah around his back, shielding her from whatever creature was about to burst through that tree line.

"Fuck it," Dwight said, oblivious to the beast in the forest. "I'm breaking it."

He went to pick up one of the wooden chairs, but the furious barks of a massive dog stopped him mid-blow. He sat the chair back down and leaped from the porch to his friends. Twigs snapped and leaves rustled as the ferocious bloodhound ran across the yard at the trio of teens.

"Don't run," Alan said, standing his ground.

The dog came to an abrupt stop three feet shy of barreling through the kid, clumsily sliding in the loose gravel of the driveway before steadying himself, eyes fixed on Alan. Even though the dog was growling, Alan could see no malice in his gaze. It was just a dog protecting his property.

"Easy, boy. Easy," he said as he squatted to its eye level.

The dog's growling abated.

"It's OK, buddy. I won't hurt ya."

The dog took two cautious steps forward, sniffing with that remarkable mechanism that is the snout of a bloodhound. His loose, fury skin dangled from the sides of his face. At last, his ears relaxed. Alan reached out and petted the dog's head and smiled.

"You see, guys. You just have to show them who's the alpha."

There was no response from his friends behind him.

"Guys?"

He turned around and saw that Dwight and Sarah were in the bed of the truck watching from afar.

"You go ahead and be that alpha all you want," Dwight yelled from the end of the driveway.

Sarah burst out laughing.

"Are you kidding me?"

Alan laughed and shook his head. He turned back around to the dog, whose tongue was flopping in and out as he got his first head rub in God knows how long.

"You're a good boy, ain't ya?" he said as he massaged the dog's ears.

He noticed a shiny metal tag on the dog's collar.

"Let's see who you are."

Alan held him by the collar and pinched the tag, spinning it around to see the front.

"Buck."

As soon as he said the dog's name, his ear's perked back up, and he tilted his head. Alan smiled.

"Nice to meet ya, Buck," he said as he listened to his two friends walking back up the driveway behind him.

Buck peered around at the other two humans.

"It's OK. They're with me," Alan said and stood up.

Dwight and Sarah approached on either side of him.

"Oh, he's so handsome," Sarah said as she crouched down and started rubbing his sagging face.

Buck's expression was pure bliss.

"That's a purebred bloodhound," Dwight said. "My cousin breeds them and makes a shit ton of money. He doesn't look like the greatest specimen though."

Sarah stood back up, and Alan scanned the dog's physique. He was thin, but he was by no means emaciated or starving.

"He looks pretty good for a dog that's been livin' out here on his own."

"How do you know he's been out here on his own?" Sarah asked.

"His tag has this address on it. He was the exorcist's dog."

"No way," Dwight said. "I bet you've seen some weird shit, haven't you?"

Buck just strolled over to Dwight like it was his turn to pet him, which Dwight did.

"His name's Buck," Alan said.

"Hi, Buck. I'm Dwight, and we're here to get fucked up. Alan, where'd you leave the bag?"

Alan suddenly remembered having seen the strange face in the window and the overall odd feeling he'd had since they arrived. Had he really seen something? A minute ago, he was positive, but now he wasn't so sure. In fact, he was almost positive that it had just been the moon's reflection in the glass. And that sulfurous smell... well that was probably just some rogue sewer fumes picked up in the kind of breeze that disperses decaying dandelions.

"It's sittin' against the steps right there," he said.

Dwight walked over to the bag and picked it up. He handed it to Sarah.

"Here. Carry those. We'll get the chairs," he said as he hopped back on the porch and retrieved the wooden rockers once again.

He handed one to Alan.

"There's only two," Alan said as Dwight walked past him toward the sprawling front yard.

"Yeah, but there's a big rock up here," Dwight said. "I saw it from the truck."

Alan, holding his chair, looked at Sarah. She shrugged her shoulders, and they both followed Dwight. Buck kept pace with them as they made their way across the wide-open meadow.

They walked a steady incline along a wooden fence until they reached the alabaster boulder that jutted out of the earth like a snaggletooth. It lay at just the right angle to form a makeshift bench overlooking the peaceful countryside. And, as if the stars had aligned perfectly for them, the rock was right beside a long-neglected firepit. Dwight and Alan each sat their chairs around the pit to form a small circle.

Buck walked over to the rock, sniffed it, whimpered a bit, and then lay on the grass beside it as if he'd done it a hundred times.

"I'll take those," Dwight said as he withdrew both bottles of liquor from the brown paper bag still in Sarah's hands. "You can keep the juice."

He handed the Jack Daniels to Alan and kept the Smirnoff for himself. Sarah took out the small bottle of orange juice and tossed the empty paper bag on the firepit.

"Thank ya, sir," Alan said, twisting off the lid and taking a gulp.

He tried his best to not make a face but couldn't keep his eyes from watering as the warm liquid coated his insides.

"Cheers to you too," Dwight said.

He took a drink of vodka and quickly switched bottles with Sarah so he could chase it with the orange juice. Sarah took her drink and grabbed the juice back from Dwight. They all let out a collective, "Ahh."

"Babe, you can take that chair," Alan said.

"Don't mind if I do," she said as she sat down. "Are you boys gonna build a lady a fire or what?"

"Sure will," Alan said. "I'm just gonna follow the scoutmaster's lead."

Dwight cracked a smile and shook his head.

"I'm never gonna live this down. Alright, let's go get some sticks."

---

Thirty minutes later, the three of them were sitting around a respectable campfire, as warm from the flames as they were from the alcohol. Dwight had covered the paper bag with a teepee of kindling and topped it off with a pyramid of sticks. He lit the paper bag with Sarah's lighter, and it had taken off instantly. Sarah tried to use the same lighter on her cigarette, but it didn't work. It was as if the fire had sucked every bit of life out of the disposable red Bic.

Alan thought it was weird—not just the lighter going out, but how eagerly the fire itself roared to life. It was as if it was already burning and only required the justification of them going through the ritual of lighting it before it revealed its presence. What was even weirder was that as soon as the flames engulfed the bag, Alan could've sworn he saw two fiery eyes staring back at him.

Being down a lighter but encouraged by several shots of vodka, Sarah had put the cigarette in her mouth, pulled her hair back, and bent down face-first into the flames to light it. Dwight had cheered her on and also warned her not to burn off her eyebrows. Alan had watched with a sick feeling in his stomach. It was that same sensation of dread that had overcome him when he saw the face in the window (wait, no, it wasn't a face; it was the moon, remember?).

He didn't like watching his girlfriend inhale the sinister flames into her body. (How can a fire be sinister, really?) With each successive draw on the smoke, he became more and more uneasy. But, like the other abnormalities he had witnessed since arriving at the farm on Sunny Branch Way, this feeling that something was off was buried in the depths of his subconscious.

And now, Alan could only admire Sarah's beauty through the flickering brightness as she smoked her Marlboro Light. He took a swig from his bottle and carelessly sat it beside him on the rock. He heard the glass clank and turned around to see it rolling down the backside of the bench-sized boulder, spilling its contents in its wake. The sound had woken Buck from his brief slumber.

"Shit!"

"Party foul," Dwight laughed.

Alan got to his feet and stumbled around the rock to retrieve what was left of his bottle. He picked it up, but not before noticing something small and dark that had been sitting on the far side of the rock the whole time. Once he saw that he still had a little less than half of his bottle (which was plenty to sip on the rest of the night), he redirected his attention to his new discovery.

"Did you spill it all?" Sarah asked, but Alan stood with his back to them, too interested in the abandoned tobacco pipe he had just discovered.

He picked it up and examined it from every angle. The initials "M.B." were engraved on the side.

"Holy shit," he said as he faced his friends again.

"Uh, what's that?" Dwight asked.

"Merle Blatty," Alan said, looking at Sarah. "That was the name of the guy that died here, right?"

Sarah flicked her smoke in the fire and nodded, squinting to see the object.

"What is it?" she asked.

"I think I just found an exorcist's pipe."

Buck sat up and whined as he, too, stared at what the old man had left behind.

Dwight rocked in his chair, took another shot of vodka, and chased it with orange juice.

"That's creepy... in a rad way" he began with droopy eyelids and then said, "You better keep that shit."

As Alan tilted the pipe to look into the hole where Merle would've packed it, he saw something impossible: a glowing cherry of tobacco.

"What the fuck?"

The pipe became so hot that it burnt the tips of his thumb and fingers.

"Ouch! Shit!" he said and dropped it.

No burning tobacco or smoke came out of it. It was as dead as its former owner. Before Alan could process what the hell had just happened, he noticed Buck looking across the fire and growling. He followed the dog's lead and saw Sarah's body beginning to spasm in her rocking chair. He looked at her, and his stomach felt full of cold, slithering eels.

Sarah's limbs were rigid and shaking. Her head was bent back, but Alan could see that only the whites of her eyes were exposed, and her jaw was clamped shut as if by electrocution. When Dwight finally looked at her, he leaped from his chair and ran beside Alan.

"What is wrong with her? What do we do?"

The wooden chair broke under her. She froze when she hit the ground.

Alan and Dwight could only watch, both drunk and delayed in their reactions.

"Did she just have a seizure?" Dwight said.

Sarah's body began to flop like a fish fresh out of water.

"My sister is epileptic, and I've never seen her do anything like that," Alan said.

Buck inched closer, deepening his growl, and exposing the fronts of his teeth.

"We gotta help her," Alan said and started to walk around the fire.

Before he could get to her, she stopped and lay motionless. He approached her and saw that she was staring at the night sky and had a demonic grin stretched across her face. He'd never seen a person look like that before.

"Sarah," he said.

She didn't react. He could see that she was breathing. He looked over at Dwight, who was still standing by the stone.

"What the fuck is she doing?" he whispered for some reason.

Alan shrugged his shoulders and turned back to see Sarah's wide eyes staring at him. His heart skipped a beat. The smile on her face stretched to the point of tearing her cheeks. Had he not had half a bottle of whiskey in him, he would've shit himself.

"What's the matter, Alan? Don't want to fuck me anymore?" something inside Sarah said.

The voice wasn't hers. The guttural bass of it made the hairs on the back of his neck stand up.

"What did she just say?" Dwight said with budding terror in his tone.

Buck snarled and continued to make slow progress around the fire.

"Sa... Sarah..." Alan stuttered.

"Sa... sa... suck my cock!" the thing that was Sarah bellowed with a mocking laugh that sounded so painful Alan thought her vocal cords were snapping.

A burning stick flew out of the fire and into her hand. Sarah's flesh hissed as it burned a foul odor that almost made Alan vomit. She sat up, still staring at him.

"What's wrong? You don't like me anymore?"

Alan was in shock.

"Would you love me if I did this to you?"

She opened her mouth and stuck out her tongue as she

inched the flaming stick down her throat, deeper and deeper without breaking eye contact. Alan stumbled backward, struggling to find his breath while she plunged the burning wood in and out of her mouth, watching her neck glow each time the burning tip was all the way in.

"Alan, let's get the fuck out of here!" Dwight pleaded.

The thing that was Sarah stood upright in a split-second and cocked its head toward Dwight.

"What's the matter? Jealous because you can't suck his cock?" it said and then launched the sharpened spear directly at Dwight.

Buck lunged across the fire and snatched the burning stick with his mouth, a second before it would've pierced Dwight's chest. The dog immediately dropped it and shook his head.

"Fucking *mutt*!" it hissed.

Buck took off running back toward the woods.

It picked up the vodka bottle and chucked it at the fleeing dog, but it shattered against one of the trees.

Alan and Dwight had already started sprinting for the truck. They were about twenty yards away when they heard a wailing straight from the bowels of Hell.

"Oh shit. Oh shit. Oh shit," Dwight said between breaths.

Just when Alan thought his legs and lungs were going to give out, he reached the truck. He ran around and got in the driver's side while Dwight got in on his side, slamming and locking the door behind him.

"Fucking go!" Dwight screamed, but Alan had already started the truck and put it in first gear.

He peeled out, fishtailing a bit as he was still heavily under the influence of the booze. He shifted into second, then third, fourth, and finally fifth. They were going faster than they had any business driving down this curvy backroad.

"We're going the wrong way," Dwight said. "Town is back there."

"I don't give a shit. I'm gettin' as far away as…"

He cut himself off mid-sentence when he looked in the rearview mirror and saw that pale face with burning eyes smiling at him from the bed of the truck. He screamed and slammed on the brakes.

Dwight who had just banged his head against the dashboard from the sudden stop yelled, "What the fuck are you doing?"

"Something's in the back. Look!"

They both turned around and saw nothing in the empty bed.

"What the fuck are you talking about? There's no one there!"

"I'm tellin' you. There was a face, and I've seen it before. It was in the window of that house."

Dwight was breathing heavily as he looked around his dark surroundings.

"If you're seeing shit, let me drive. I'm fine," he said.

For some reason, Alan thought back to the burning cigarette he had left in the Dairy Queen parking lot and how it reminded him of the face with the fiery eyes in the exorcist's house, seeing those same eyes in the campfire, and Sarah's reaction from breathing in the fire from that evil place. He didn't know what was real and what wasn't.

"Maybe you should drive. My head is fucked up."

"Well, let's make it fucking quick!"

The two of them exited and swapped seats in record time.

Dwight backed into the closest driveway and turned around.

"Don't go this way," Alan begged. "Please don't go this way."

"Just shut up, man. We're going home."

Alan gripped the interior of the truck as they approached the house on the left side of the road. He saw their fire on the hill by the rock dimming down. He didn't see anyone up there—that thing that had been Sarah or the dog, Buck. He looked again at the charred house as they approached it. Dwight never took his eyes off the road.

"Dwight, stop!"

He hit the brakes ten yards before the driveway to the house.

"What?"

Alan pointed through the windshield.

"It's Sarah."

"Holy shit," Dwight said as he saw the girl sitting at the edge of the driveway holding herself and sobbing.

She looked up at them, and Alan saw that her face was normal. He opened his door and stepped out of the truck.

"Alan, what are you doing?" Dwight asked, but he just shut the door.

Alan crossed the beams of the headlights and saw the blisters on his girlfriend's mouth and hands. He couldn't imagine how much pain she was in.

"Help... me," she muttered, struggling to make a sound. Whatever was wrong with her had passed. (Maybe she did just have a seizure. Maybe the booze had triggered some sort of temporary mental break.)

Alan wasted no more time and hurried over to her. She continued to weep as he gently scooped her into his arms and picked her up. Dwight rolled down his window.

"What are you doing? She just tried to fucking kill me!"

"We're taking you to the hospital. She's fine now."

He carried her around to the passenger side of the truck. Dwight pushed the door open from the inside.

"You better keep ahold of her, Alan. I ain't even playing."

Alan sat her down in the middle seat and got in beside her. She leaned on his shoulder. Dwight shifted in gear and hit the gas.

"Sarah, what's the last thing you remember?" Dwight asked.

"Dude, she can barely talk. Her fuckin' throat is burnt."

Sarah wiped tears from her eyes.

"Petting Buck," she said, gripping her throat.

"You don't remember trying to kill me?"

A fresh stream of tears poured down her cheeks.

"Stop it," Alan said and wrapped his arm around her.

"I just woke up... on the driveway."

"We have to take her to the hospital. We can call her dad from there," Alan said.

"We're going to be in so much shit. I hope you two know that."

"Least of my concerns, Dwight. She needs help."

They kept driving all the way to the end of Sunny Branch Way. Even though he had insisted on getting Sarah, he knew something wasn't right.

And then he remembered.

When that thing that had been Sarah was distracted by Buck just before they made their escape, he had picked up Merle Blatty's pipe and pocketed it. He didn't know why, but leaving it behind was anathema to him.

He looked down at the slight bulge on the right side of his jeans. As Dwight pulled onto the road to take them back into town, he slid his hand into his pocket and felt the tip of the old man's pipe and was suddenly overcome with the sensation that someone else was inside his body.

And that's when he heard an old man's voice. He didn't know how, but he knew that it was Merle's voice.

*It haunts the mind, ya know. Once you're infected, you can never escape, I'm sorry to say. You can't outrun what's already inside.*

He felt Sarah's forehead warming against his shoulder like a fire had just been lit inside her.

*They're not meant for this world. We're just cruise ships for them. A vacation from Hell, if you will. It must've gotten in through the fire. Sneaky devils.*

Her head was now so hot that it felt like an iron on his skin.

*It's too late for her, son. But you know that. It's in you and your buddy there. Just a matter of time for all of ya. I'll pray for your souls.*

Alan took a deep breath as he regained full control of

himself. Now that he could move, he put his hand on the top of Sarah's burning hot head to move her. When he pushed, the top of her scalp slid off and landed on Dwight's lap.

"What the fuck?" Dwight screamed.

Alan's eyes bulged as Sarah slowly raised her head. Her face was uneven as the flesh melted away like hot wax.

"Alan," she said and then grabbed him by the back of the head and brought his face to hers for a kiss.

He pushed her off. Strands of her skin clung to him like pizza cheese. He screamed as the grinning red demon that was inside her turned around and grabbed the steering wheel.

Dwight squeezed its smoldering forearm, but what was left of the gooey coating of skin made his grip slip off. The demon jerked the wheel to the left just as they were going around a curve in the road. The S10 went across the median and burst through the thin metal guardrail, rolling several times before being wrapped around an old oak tree.

Alan hung sideways by his seatbelt. He was numb from the neck down but could see that the truck had stopped on its side—Dwight's side—but Dwight wasn't there. He smelled gasoline and wondered if Dwight had somehow been thrown through the open window and was OK. He hoped so.

The deformed, smoldering creature trapped down by the pedals had its yellow eyes fixed on him. A small flame burst through its eyeball, and it started to laugh. In seconds, it was engulfed. Alan saw the puddle of gasoline forming on the ground through Dwight's window. He tried to think of a prayer from his childhood, but his mind was blank.

"See you in Hell," the demon sneered just before its flames

met the fuel and a fireball erupted into the night sky.

———•—•———

The full-body cast Dwight had been in since the wreck last week wasn't all that bad with the amount of morphine the doctors kept pumping into him. He remembered being in and out of consciousness during those first few days. He had mental pictures of his mom crying as she looked down at him and told him everything was going to be OK. His dad was there too, backing her up.

On the fourth day, two men had come to see him. He didn't know if his parents were in the room with them or not. He remembered them asking about what he remembered. He didn't know if it was the painkillers or what, but he thought one was a plain-clothes fed and the other was a priest. Of course, he had no idea what they were talking about. The last thing he remembered before waking up at the hospital was being at Dairy Queen with Alan and Sarah. When he said that, someone in the room—most likely a doctor or nurse—said that memory loss was typical with this kind of head trauma.

Now, still confined to the hospital bed, he stared at the fuzzy images on the box TV in the corner of the room until dusk. He watched the sun go down through the window. The evening nurse came in to help him eat or drink; he wasn't sure. They pumped some more meds into his IV drip and dimmed the lights. When they left, he followed them out with his eyes. They shut his door, and the glow of the hallway light shined from the crack under the door.

And then he remembered.

He remembered being at a house, on a porch, staring in a window. He remembered seeing a basement door with glowing lights like flickering flames underneath it. His pulse skyrocketed as the events of that night flooded his memory. Everything came back to him at once like someone had just filled his IV with nightmare fuel. His whole body became moist with perspiration.

The hospital room was getting hotter by the second. A smell like rotting eggs invaded his nose, but the confines of the cast prevented him from doing anything about it other than breathing it in. The clinical fluorescent light under the door turned to alternating hues of orange, yellow, and red. The dim light in the room shut off, leaving the flames beyond the door to illuminate the room.

It was then that he felt the pressure of a hand on the leg part of his cast. Another hand pressed down a little higher up. Something was crawling up him, but he couldn't lift his head to see.

He didn't know if he wanted to.

The hands were on his chest now. He just stared at the ceiling as tears formed in his eyes. He didn't even look when he felt two long fingers slither into his mouth and press his tongue into the back of his throat. When he gagged, he felt it flop backward and lodge in his windpipe, and just as he started to lose consciousness, a pale face with smoldering eyes appeared in his line of sight.

"What's the matter Dwight," the sexless voice cooed.

"Lost your voice?"

He would've screamed if he hadn't swallowed his tongue.

# NOTES

Sally Under the Bed: I rarely start a story or a novel with the title. The only exceptions were this one, my debut novel, *Anathema*, and another story in this collection, "It Haunts the Mind." I delivered pizzas when I was still in school, and the title, "Sally Under the Bed," just popped into my head as I was driving. I pictured some rotting woman underneath a child's bed. I wondered how she got there. She must've been summoned, but how? That's when I got the idea of the poem. I love urban legends, and this was my take on Bloody Mary or Candyman. Incorporating the Hatfield and McCoy element was just a fun way to tie my monster in with a bloody part of West Virginia history.

The Deal: This was the first short story I ever had published, and I wish I could say that I earned that publication credit based solely on merit. One of my college buddies was an assistant editor for *The Blue Mountain Review* and knew I loved to write. He asked me to send him a story and told me that he'd publish it if it was good. I thought about my own history with substance use disorder. My addiction had gotten so bad at one point that I wondered if hiring a hitman to kill me if I didn't get clean within a designated timeframe would work. Fortunately, I didn't have to really go that route to find recovery, but I recalled that thought when I sat down to write my story. What would happen if someone would actually go through with it? How could I ground the story in a way that a junkie in West Virginia could even find a hitman? This was an easy story to write and one of the few that I've written in the first person.

The Halfway House: After completing a long-term residential rehab, I transitioned back into the "real world" by moving into a sober living home and even ran the house for a few months. It was an interesting experience in holding people accountable for the good of the group. The genesis for this story was as arbitrary as me wanting to just set a horror story inside of a halfway house. I didn't know who the stranger knocking on the door was when he did it and had no idea where it was going to go as I wrote it. The grieving father who wants to eradicate addiction by killing everyone afflicted with it was where we landed. I still think "The Trojan Horse Junkie" would have been a better title though.

Thanks for Sharing: The disease of addiction does not discriminate. I don't know many people who have not been touched by it in some way. If you've never had a friend or family member struggle with it, consider yourself lucky. I wrote this story at a time when I was facilitating a weekly recovery meeting and was actively trying to get my brother to attend. When he finally showed up, he shared about his experience overdosing. The first responders had told him that his heart had temporarily stopped. He said something like, "I died right there in the parking lot." I remember being shocked by the phrasing and temporarily imagining that he had died, and I was just staring at an empty seat. When I wrote this story years ago, my brother had multiple years of recovery. It packs a heavier punch now that he has passed away.

The Paperboy: I wrote this story based on a prompt of something bad happening as a result of overhearing a conversation you weren't meant to hear. This was another attempt at writing in the first person, as an older man reflecting on a childhood experience. I had a paper route for years when I was a kid. The neighborhood I lived and worked in shared a river with a golf course like in the story. Although I never had any eerie customers like Finister Shell, the real horrors I experienced were the times my friends would peddle away on their bikes to go play while I had to work.

Hunting Season: My extended family is big and continues to grow, but Thanksgiving remains a holiday when we all gather. The problem is trying to fit everyone into one house. One solution we had was to rent a lodge in the woods of West Virginia. The description of the lodge in this story and the bustling atmosphere was exactly what I experienced. Right before dinner, two of the teenage nephews went on a walk through the woods. This wasn't a problem until we realized that it was deer hunting season and probably not the best time for a stroll through the forest. Luckily, the kids made it back unharmed, but it easily could have gone bad.

Grandma Ruth: This was another prompt story, but a much broader one: What is your greatest fear, and what happens when you face it? The character I created was terrified by the titular character. I had a blast writing this one as I got to inhabit the mind of a sinister grannie doing all sorts of nasty things to her loved ones. No one wants to imagine a sweet, elderly grandmother doing anything other than spoiling her grandchildren. Flipping that image on its head resulted in what I consider to be my darkest and most disturbing story yet.

Percepto!: A couple of years ago, I saw an open call for an anthology about classic horror monsters that are in the public domain. This anthology turned into a record-breaking Kickstarter campaign, which I was happy to support as a backer. It also inspired me to write one of my most bizarre and unique stories. I figured everyone was going to try and write about vampires or werewolves or Frankenstein's monster, so I scrolled down the list of accepted monsters and stopped when I read *The Tingler*. I didn't even know what *The Tingler* was, and I consider myself to be a solid horror film buff! I had seen most of Vincent Price's films and was familiar with William Castle's gimmick in the theaters regarding *The Tingler*, but I didn't know what the movie was actually about. I dropped everything and watched it and wrote a meta version of *The Tingler* mixed with a pinch of *Inglourious Basterds*. It didn't get accepted into *Classic Monsters Unleashed*, but it found a home in another stellar anthology.

The Bitter End: I had this phrase in my head and wanted to work a story around it: "pawn shop chainsaw massacre." The problem was I couldn't think of a compelling character to insert in that scenario. Years ago, I spent some time working for a nonprofit homeless resource center and got to meet some colorful characters. I also got to hear some heartbreaking stories and see the humanity behind the stereotypical "bum begging for change." I realized that many Americans were living just a paycheck away from being homeless. And so, my flawed protagonist, Gene, the laid-off alcoholic who lost his family and never got back on his feet, was born. My next task was to get Gene into the pawn shop. After writing pages of Gene's daily life, I reverted back to the ultimate motivator: money.

The Devil's Road: True crime podcasts were really picking up when I wrote this one. I wanted to have a character who was obsessed with solving a cold case and using a podcast to document his journey. The story changed from that once I started writing (as they always do), and I ended up with a young college couple going home for the boy to meet the girl's parents. I ended up making the boy in the relationship have a personal stake in tracking down the killer and using this as justification for manipulating his way into his suspect's life. It wasn't until after the story was published that I learned that there have been several fictional serial killers who do a countdown with bodies. And here I was thinking I was so clever.

Two Decades Down and I Only Love You at Night: My mom asked me to write a love story for her birthday. I took it as a personal challenge because I'd never written anything lighthearted or centered around romance. Well, I have no problem admitting that I failed that challenge even though the piece did get published. The resulting story *is* centered around a lifelong love, but I couldn't help putting my own weird little spin on it. And just so you know, it's super awkward to write a sex scene in a story for your mom; however, it was crucial to the narrative, and I'll die on a hill defending narrative authenticity.

Voodoo Bay: I wrote this story for an open call about beach horror. I didn't outline or have any idea where it was going, but I knew I needed two slightly obnoxious American tourists wanting something more "exotic" than the typical beach honeymoon. As I wrote, I stayed with the couple as they made their way around, talking with locals and eventually hearing about an island off the grid. Once I had that set-up, I channeled a bit of H.P. Lovecraft's Dagon mythos and had some fun writing about my nasty little cult and their sea monster.

The Weeping Wind: If I could choose one of my non-horror stories for more people to read, it would be this one. It's not an enjoyable read, and it might upset readers who have either been exposed to parents in the grips of addiction or were the addicted parents themselves, but that's kind of the point. I felt that the reader needed to see these shocking scenes from the perspective of a child almost old enough to know what's going on. It's *Requiem for a Dream* driving down a West

Virginia back road.

The Noose: Like many others in this collection, this story was in response to an open call; this time, it was for a horror Western anthology. The first draft read like I was trying too hard to write a Western. Luckily, I have great beta readers who don't hesitate to hit me with the truth. In my discouragement, I started to reread Cormac McCarthy's, *No Country for Old Men*. I made it four pages in and was reinvigorated. I opened my document, stripped back the try-hard language, and focused on the character and narrative. At about the halfway point, I felt like I was writing a decent story, but I wasn't thrilled with it. It wasn't until I had the ghost of the sheriff's kid reveal that he was being abused and grateful that Wade had killed him, that I knew I'd found a twist worthy of elevating it to a story of redemption. Plus, writing the violent climax is still the most fun I've had writing a scene.

It Haunts the Mind: My second novel, *The Exorcist's House*, exceeded my wildest expectations regarding sales and reviews. So many readers demanded more stories set in that universe, and this is my response to that. I knew I wanted to have this tale take place after the prologue of *The Exorcist's House*, but before the first chapter, in that brief period after Merle dies in a house fire and the Hill family purchases his house. A vacant farmhouse with a spooky local history would be too much for a trio of teens to pass up as a spur-of-the-moment party spot. I knew I had to bring back Buck, the fan-favorite bloodhound, but other than that, I didn't know what would happen when the kids got to the house. I was pleased with what resulted, but again, a beta reader made it better by saying that my original ending was too abrupt. I went back and drastically altered the climax. I'm pleased with the resulting story and what doors it opens for future installments.

# THE END?

**Not if you want to dive into more of Crystal Lake Publishing's Tales from the Darkest Depths!**

Check out our amazing website and online store or download our latest catalog here: https://geni.us/CLPCatalog

We always have great new projects and content on the website to dive into, as well as a newsletter, behind the scenes options, social media platforms, our own dark fiction shared-world series and our very own webstore. Our webstore even has categories specifically for KU books, non-fiction, anthologies, and of course more novels and novellas.

# Author biography

Nick Roberts is a native West Virginian and a graduate of Marshall University where he earned his doctorate in Leadership Studies. As an active member of the Horror Writers Association, his short works have been published in various literary magazines and anthologies. His novel, *Anathema*, won Debut Novel of the Year at the 2020-2021 Horror Authors Guild Awards. His best-selling novel, *The Exorcist's House*, was released in 2022 by Crystal Lake Publishing. He currently resides in South Carolina with his wife and three children and is an advocate for people struggling with substance use disorders.

Readers...

Thank you for reading *It Haunts the Mind*. We hope you enjoyed this collection.
If you have a moment, please review *It Haunts the Mind* at the store where you bought it.

Help other readers by telling them why you enjoyed this book. No need to write an in-depth discussion. Even a single sentence will be greatly appreciated. Reviews go a long way to helping a book sell, and is great for an author's career. It'll also help us to continue publishing quality books.

Thank you again for taking the time to journey with Crystal Lake Publishing.

You will find links to all our social media platforms on our Linktree page: https://linktr.ee/CrystalLakePublishing.

# MISSION STATEMENT

Since its founding in August 2012, Crystal Lake Publishing has quickly become one of the world's leading publishers of Dark Fiction and Horror books in print, eBook, and audio formats.

While we strive to present only the highest quality fiction and entertainment, we also endeavour to support authors along their writing journey. We offer our time and experience in non-fiction projects, as well as author mentoring and services, at competitive prices.

With several Bram Stoker Award wins and many other wins and nominations (including the HWA's Specialty Press Award), Crystal Lake Publishing puts integrity, honor, and respect at the forefront of our publishing operations.

We strive for each book and outreach program we spearhead to not only entertain and touch or comment on issues that affect our readers, but also to strengthen and support the Dark Fiction field and its authors.

Not only do we find and publish authors we believe are destined for greatness, but we strive to work with men and woman who endeavour to be decent human beings who care more for others than themselves, while still being hard working, driven, and passionate artists and storytellers.

Crystal Lake Publishing is and will always be a beacon of what passion and dedication, combined with overwhelming teamwork and respect, can accomplish. We endeavour to know each and every one of our readers, while building personal relationships with our authors, reviewers, bloggers, podcasters, bookstores, and libraries.

We will be as trustworthy, forthright, and transparent as any business can be, while also keeping most of the headaches away from our authors, since it's our job to solve the problems so they can stay in a creative mind. Which of course also means paying our authors.

We do not just publish books, we present to you worlds within your world, doors within your mind, from talented authors who sacrifice so much for a moment of your time.

There are some amazing small presses out there, and through collaboration and open forums we will continue to support other presses in the goal of helping authors and showing the world what quality small presses are capable of accomplishing. No one wins when a small press goes down, so we will always be there to support hardworking, legitimate presses and their authors. We don't see Crystal Lake as the best press out there, but we will always strive to be the best, strive to be the most interactive and grateful, and even blessed press around. No matter what happens over time, we will also take our mission very seriously while appreciating where we are and enjoying the journey.

What do we offer our authors that they can't do for themselves through self-publishing?

We are big supporters of self-publishing (especially hybrid publishing), if done with care, patience, and planning. However, not every author has the time or inclination to do market research, advertise, and set up book launch strategies. Although a lot of authors are successful in doing it all, strong small presses will always be there for the authors who just want to do what they do best: write.

What we offer is experience, industry knowledge, contacts and trust built up over years. And due to our strong brand and trusting fanbase, every Crystal Lake Publishing book comes with weight of respect. In time our fans begin to trust our judgment and will try a new author purely based on our support of said author.

With each launch we strive to fine-tune our approach, learn from our mistakes, and increase our reach. We continue to assure our authors that we're here for them and that we'll carry the weight of the launch and dealing with third parties while they focus on their strengths—be it writing, interviews, blogs, signings, etc.

We also offer several mentoring packages to authors that include knowledge and skills they can use in both traditional and self-publishing endeavours.

We look forward to launching many new careers.

This is what we believe in. What we stand for. This will be our legacy.

Welcome to Crystal Lake Publishing—Tales from the Darkest Depths.

# THANK YOU FOR PURCHASING THIS BOOK

Made in the USA
Columbia, SC
21 July 2024